W9-BGU-913

"For sheer pageantry and character development, both major and minor, Akers far outshines any other writer writing this type of story, and the tales of Dray Prescot are a feast for the fan of adventure tales."
—*The Jackson (Tenn.) Sun*

"During the seventeen years that I have been reading science fiction I do not believe that I have ever come across a more entertaining, fast moving series than that of Dray Prescot of Antares. I've read the John Carter of Mars series, the Gorean series, the Lensman series, and Philip José Farmer's series . . . all of these made good reading but I believe Akers has done the finest job to date. He has created an almost believable culture and all that goes with it."
—*A reader*

"While Akers does not have the headlong pace of Burroughs, he seems to be building a more detailed world. Although Kregen has many aspects of Barsoom, it is more reminiscent of John Norman's Gor."
—*Erbania*

"Here is escapism at its best and most wondrous."
—*Montreal Star*

"Between the flying islands stretched a bridge of vines."

ARMADA
OF
ANTARES

By
ALAN BURT AKERS

Illustrated by
Michael Whelan

DAW BOOKS, INC.

DONALD A. WOLLHEIM, PUBLISHER

1301 Avenue of the Americas
New York, N. Y.   10019

Published by
THE NEW AMERICAN LIBRARY
OF CANADA LIMITED

Copyright ©, 1976, by DAW Books, Inc.

All Rights Reserved.

Cover art by Michael Whelan.

The Saga Of Dray Prescot

The Delian Cycle

I. TRANSIT TO SCORPIO
II. THE SUNS OF SCORPIO
III. WARRIOR OF SCORPIO
IV. SWORDSHIPS OF SCORPIO
V. PRINCE OF SCORPIO

The Havilfar Cycle

I. MANHOUNDS OF ANTARES
II. ARENA OF ANTARES
III. FLIERS OF ANTARES
IV. BLADESMEN OF ANTARES
V. AVENGER OF ANTARES
VI. ARMADA OF ANTARES

First Printing, April 1976

1 2 3 4 5 6 7 8 9

PRINTED IN CANADA
COVER PRINTED IN U.S.A.

TABLE OF CONTENTS

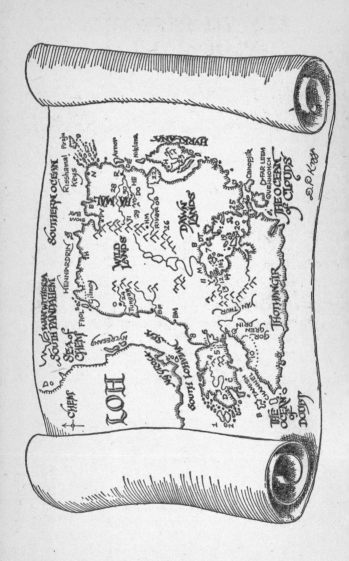

KEY TO PRESCOT'S
MAP OF HAVILFAR

D	Djanguraj	1	Hyr Khor
H	Huringa	2	Uttar Djombey
HM	Heavenly Mines	3	River of Wraiths
DT	Dap-Tentyrasmot	4	Mountains of Mirth
P	Pellow	5	The Yawfi Suth
R	Ruathytu	6	The Wendwath
Y	Yaman		(all of Djanduin)
O	Ordsmot	7	Lesser Sharangil
BM	Ba-Marish		Archipelago
BF	Ba-Fela	8	Sava
E	Eomlad	9	Herrelldrin
N	Nulvosmot	10	Tamish
DO	Dovad	11	Cnarveyl
HE	Hemlad	12	Migladrin
DE	Denrette	13	River Magan
B	Brodensmot	14	Tyriadrin
S	Smerdislad	15	Methydria
C	Cafresmot	16	Canopdrin
		17	Neagrom
		18	Rapa island
		19	Sorah
		20	The Shrouded Sea
		21	Gulf of Wracks
		22	Ifilion
		23	River of Leaping Fishes
		24	Orange River
		25	Xilicia
		26	Clef Pesquadrin
		27	Hyrzibar's Finger
		28	River Havilthytus
		29	Black Mountains
		30	River Mak
		31	Mountains of the West

LIST OF
ILLUSTRATIONS

A Note on Dray Prescot

Dray Prescot is a man above medium height, with straight brown hair and brown eyes that are level and dominating. His shoulders are immensely wide and there is about him an abrasive honesty and a fearless courage. He moves like a great hunting cat, quiet and deadly. Born in 1775 and educated in the inhumanly harsh conditions of the late eighteenth century English navy, he presents a picture of himself that, the more we learn of him, grows no less enigmatic.

Through the machinations of the Savanti nal Aphrasöe —mortal but superhuman men dedicated to the aid of humanity—and of the Star Lords, the Everoinye, he has been taken to Kregen under the Suns of Scorpio many times. On that savage and beautiful, marvellous and terrible world he rose to become Zorcander of the Clansmen of Segesthes, and Lord of Strombor in Zenicce, and a member of the mystic and martial Order of Krozairs of Zy.

Against all odds Prescot won his highest desire and in that immortal battle at The Dragon's Bones claimed his Delia, Delia of Delphond, Delia of the Blue Mountains. And Delia claimed him in the face of her father, the dread Emperor of Vallia. Amid the rolling thunder of the acclamations of "Hai Jikai!" Prescot became Prince Majister of Vallia, and wed his Delia, the Princess Majestrix. One of their favorite homes is in Valkanium, capital city of the island of Valka of which Prescot is Strom.

Prescot is plunged headlong into fresh adventures on Kregen in the continent of Havilfar. Outwitting the Manhounds of Antares, ghastly parodies of humans used as hunting dogs, and fighting as a hyr-kaidur in the arena of the Jikhorkdun in Huringa in Hyrklana, he becomes King of Djanduin, idolized by his incredibly ferocious four-armed Djangs. But Hamal, the greatest power in Havil-

9

far, ruled by Queen Thyllis, is bent on conquest; Prescot acting as a spy under cover of the alias of Hamun ham Farthytu, has discovered half the secrets of the airboats that give Hamal so much of her power. Now Prescot must bend every effort into thwarting the egomaniacal plans of Queen Thyllis and her iron Empire of Hamal with whatever weapons he can find. . . .

This volume, *Armada of Antares*, sees the conclusion of the second cycle in the saga of Dray Prescot, the "Havilfar Cycle." With the next book, tentatively titled *The Tides of Kregen*, we are launched onto the third cycle of Prescot's adventures under the Suns of Scorpio which, because of the locale and the mystic order of which Prescot is so valued a member, I have called the "Krozair Cycle."

ALAN BURT AKERS

Chapter One

Swordplay in a garden

"Drak!" said the Princess Majestrix of Vallia, walking unhurriedly across the grass to the pool's edge. "If you insist on climbing the tree I shall be cross." She put one bare toe into the water and shook her head, looking so gorgeously lovely that I marveled anew at her beauty. "Of course, Drak, if you fall in I shall be more than cross. You are wearing your best clothes."

"I'm not wearing my best clothes," said Lela, higher in the tree. She looked down at her brother, giggled, and threw a leafy twig at him. "Silly boy! All dressed up to see his soldiers."

"I will climb up," said Drak, with the solemn ferociousness of extreme youth. "And pull your hair."

Delia's smile vanished. Her face took on a most purposeful look as she stared up into the missal tree which overhung this small private pool in a walled garden of Esser Rarioch. The garden rioted with flowers, their colors and scents filling the air with brilliant beauty and sweet perfumes. And, over all, the high blue sky of Kregen smiled down, fluffed with cloud. From that sky shone the twin suns, the Suns of Scorpio, Zim and Genodras, the red and the green, streaming down their glorious mingled opaz radiance.

Well, I was home. Home in my island Stromnate of Valka, off the coast of Vallia, and my Delia had very quickly led me to understand that bringing up twins, a boy demon and a girl demoness, was a far cry from racing off into

11

adventure with my red cloak flaring and the glitter of a rapier in my eyes.

I looked up at young Drak, whose vigorous body swung from the tree branch as he hauled himself up with a determination of which I approved despite his mother's stern admonishments about his best clothes. "Drak," I said, speaking in my relaxed at-home voice. "Drak, my lad. If you fall into the water you will not please your mother. If you fall at all you will not please me. And, anyway, if you fall into the water you will hardly be ready to present the standards to your regiment."

"I will *not* fall, Father."

"Humph," I said. But he was right. The little devil could climb like a grundal, one of those rock-apes of the inner sea.

No doubt some deep realization that his mother meant what she said penetrated at last, making him heed her rather than his desire to scare his sister. For I had noticed that for all the bloodthirsty threats young Drak made against Lela, he did not carry them out—or not many of them and only very briefly. I had, like any parent, a deep concern and apprehension over the relationship of my children and, thank Zair, I saw they loved each other. Now he began to shinny down the tree, with a careless, casual abandonment that masked his exquisite care over his bright buff clothes and the red and white sash.

I smiled.

Delia, I saw, contained a tremble at the corner of her mouth, that mouth which in its soft ripe redness held the whole universe of beauty, and she half turned away so that her twins should not see how easily they could move her. She wore a brief white tunic, flowing free, and I would have stepped forward and taken her in my arms.

The little wicket gate in the angle of the old red brick wall, drowned in white and purple flowers, opened with a smash. A Valkan archer stumbled through. He wore the usual Vallian buff, bedecked with the brave red and white Valkan favor. His bow was broken in two, dangling by the string. He had lost his wide-brimmed hat and his fair hair tumbled about his face. He opened his mouth and tried to speak, one hand groping before him, the fingers outspread. Speaking was difficult, for a thick spear had passed between his ribs, and I did not think he had long to live. But, before he died, this guard tried to cry out his warning.

12

The comfortable little family scene had been ripped apart.

"Largan!" cried Delia, and her hand went not to her mouth but groped emptily at her side. She was not wearing a belt and there was no long slender dagger scabbarded there.

"Go up into the tree, Drak!"

I spoke quickly. I must have used something of that old command voice, for Drak jumped and instantly began to climb again.

"Do not worry about your clothes, Drak! Climb up high, with Lela. Hide in the leaves! Climb quickly, my son."

"We will buy you new clothes if you tear them, Drak!" Delia spoke firmly, but I heard the choked sob in her voice.

"And you, too, wife," I said. "Get inside and—"

"There is no time, Dray."

They walked into the cool scented garden, arrogant, confident, vicious. There were four of them. They came like executioners into a schoolroom.

I put my hand to my waist. I wore a white shirt and buff Vallian breeches and black boots. I did not wear a sword. I cursed then, deep in my throat. Here. Here! In my own walled garden of Esser Rarioch overlooking my capital city Valkanium and the Bay! This was incredible. It was obscene.

The four carried rapiers in their right hands, and left-hand daggers, and they walked forward without haste. They were men who knew their work. They had been hired to do this. They were men accustomed to the quick and efficient dispatch of their business.

Each of the assassins wore a steel domino-mask beneath the wide Vallian hat. Their clothes were unremarkable: good solid Vallian buff. They spread out a little as they advanced. I wondered how much they knew of me, how much they had been told.

Delia began to shout. She did not scream. She shouted, a high ringing call that should bring attendants, guards, and friends running.

The first assassin's mouth widened beneath the mask.

"You are too late, lady," he said. His voice sounded perfectly normal. To me, he said: "You are the Strom of Valka?"

"It is clear you do not know me," I said. "Else a mere

13

four of you, with rapiers and daggers, only, would never have taken the gold."

He laughed.

"Brave words, from a man about to die."

He was clever in his trade. Even as he spoke he sprang. He thought he would catch me completely unprepared.

The rapier lunged for my midriff. I leaned to my left and I swayed; I thrust my leg forward and struck him a cruel blow between wind and water. As his face turned green and his eyes popped I took the rapier away, jumped his collapsing body, and circled number two, spitting him through the guts. I saw number three's dagger spin and glitter and extend into a streaking silver blaze as he hurled it at me. The old Krozair disciplines brought the rapier up; the dagger chingled against the blade and flew to splash into the pool.

Number four yelled in a shocked voice: "The man is a devil!"

Number three tried to meet my attack, but fell away with his face slashed open. I knocked him down, and I said to this number four, who backed away, the rapier circling: "Yes, you poor onker. I am a very devil!"

He tried to run and I thrust him through his kidneys. There is no chivalry in me when a man tries to slay my Delia. None whatsoever.

Number one was holding himself and trying to get enough breath to gasp, making a most distressing groaning and hissing. I hit him on the head, enough to put him to sleep, and then the little garden filled with servants and guards.

I shouted so that at once everyone fell silent.

"Take this offal away. Chain up the one who lives. I shall question him later. See to poor Largan."

Delia was halfway up the tree. I tilted my head back and called up: "Take your time, my Delia."

"Yes, Dray. But the little devils will have seen all, through the leaves—"

"Yes." This was true. "They live on Kregen. The quicker they understand what that means, the better." But I felt a soreness at my heart. Innocence of youth should be continued for as long as possible, in an ideal world. Kregen, under the Suns of Scorpio, is not ideal, even if there is much in that beautiful and terrible world I prefer to my own Earth, four hundred light-years away.

Delia glanced down, about to say something, but called up to the children instead.

I knew I had spoken thoughtlessly, even after all the time I had lived on Kregen under Antares. How do you explain to your wife that you were never born on the world she was born on, that you came from a distant speck among the stars of heaven?

Like any weakling I had been putting off and putting off the time when I must explain to Delia. I had been brought from Earth to Kregen many times through the agency of the Scorpion, through that mysterious blue radiance that encompassed everything and which transported me from one world to another. The Star Lords, those unknown, aloof, supernal beings manipulated me from time to time, to carry out their wishes. Certainly I had been able to manufacture a crazy kind of strength that had given me some opposition to them; but I was always conscious that their purposes, dark and unknowable at that time, demanded more from me than I was prepared to give. As for the Savanti, those mortal but superhuman men and women of Aphrasöe, the Swinging City, their purposes were altogether more direct of purpose, for they wished to make the world of Kregen a fit place for men and women to live, in friendship and peace, with dignity and honor.

The four corpses and the unconscious would-be assassin had been removed. As stikitches these four must have been high in their trade. They had successfully penetrated the high fortress of Esser Rarioch overlooking Valkanium, and managed to make their evil way right to the target. It had been their misfortune that their potential victim had been a ruffian called Dray Prescot.

No stikitche would go around wearing a special kind of fancy dress proclaiming him an assassin, of course, for his days would be smartly numbered if he was so foolish. I bent and picked up one of the steel dominoes. There was blood clotting around the milled edges. This came from the fellow who, before he died, must have pondered the lack of half a face. The metal was still warm. It was merely an artifact, a lump of metal, fashioned into a mask with two eye-pieces, a swell for the nose, with straps to secure it in place. I had worn a similar steel domino during that fracas in Smerdislad.*

---

*See *Avenger of Antares*, Dray Prescot # 10.

At once impatient urgings closed on me. I threw the mask to the grass. Today a newly raised regiment of archers was to be given new standards. The important thing to remember here was that in Valka, an island Stromnate which prided itself on its own Valkan archers, armed with the compound reflex bow, this new regiment had been raised and armed with the great Lohvian longbow. The men had practiced religiously with this great bow and I had received tremendous help and encouragement from that master bowman. Seg Segutorio, the Kov of Falinur.

He had said in his feckless way: "To make a longbowman you must start training with his grandfather!"

To which I had replied. "But these Valkans of mine, Seg, are used to drawing the bow. They only have to draw that extra notch, to snug the string under their ear, and to feel the extra power across their shoulders. They will grow into it far quicker than you would credit."

And he had said, "I'll train 'em for you, Dray. Aye, by the Veiled Froyvil! I'll run 'em in little circles until they can shoot out the chunkrah's eye!"

He had been as good as his word. But then, I never expect anything less from Seg Segutorio, a good companion and a friend.

So, with the honor of Hyr-Jiktar going to my son Drak, the regiment would receive the new standards today.

I bellowed up: "Come on, Drak! You must learn never to keep honest soldiers waiting on parade. Least of all bowmen, who are a rough lot at best."

"I am coming down, Father."

And down he came. He did not come down as he had expected.

Delia let out a little ladylike shriek. Lela let rip an enormous laugh from so dainty a little maid. For Drak went down headlong from his high branch, a fluttering, yelling bundle that hit the water with an almighty splash.

We stood on the poolside as he swam across and climbed out, lily pads hanging around his ears.

"Drak!" said his mother.

Lela giggled.

Drak tried to get at his sister to push her into the water; but I took him up into my arms, all wet as he was, and carried him off for one of the fastest dryings and changings of clothes he had ever endured.

The urgency in me was not just to have the standards presented to the longbow regiment. Thoughts of Smerdis-

16

lad, where I had overheard much that still puzzled me, thoughts of the airboats that my country of Vallia must acquire for the coming struggle with the overweening Empire of Hamal—these were the imperatives urging me on.

Quite simply Hamal, the greatest power on the continent of Havilfar, which lay south of us below the equator, was bent on a road of conquest; abandoning her attempts to fight on three fronts simultaneously, she had concentrated her strength for the thrust north against Pandahem. Pandahem was the island to the north of Havilfar and to the south of us in Vallia. Vallia and Pandahem were old-time adversaries on the oceans of Kregen. If all the countries of Pandahem went down in ruin there was nothing to stop the ambitions of Hamal from turning against us in Vallia. And Hamal possessed fleets of superb flying ships, airboats which they manufactured, which we did not. I had discovered some of the secrets of the airboats and I wished to put through a big program of building. The Emperor of Vallia, Delia's father, had promised to make up his mind. The parade this afternoon would provide a good opportunity to force him to give his consent, I had thought, for he was flying in to see his daughter and his son-in-law and, no doubt, to find out what I had been up to in Havilfar.

"Who were those men, Father?"

"They were foolish fellows, Drak, paying a visit without telling us first they were arriving."

"But you hit them—you hit them hard."

By the lice-infested scaled hair of Makki-Grodno! How did you tell a little boy that men had come to slay his father, and his father had slain them instead? In cold words? Drak had seen. Maybe he thought this was a game in which one thumped a playmate over the head and fell down, shouting out that he was dead, and the next minute jumped up ready for further mischief.

I said, "Sometimes you have to do that, and you will find out when to do it and when not to do it. I promise you, Drak, you will know. For now, you must always listen to your mother and do as she says—"

"I know, I know! But, Father, why do you have to go away? Dray's father doesn't."

"And if you don't hurry up Dray's father will not be pleased." That was true. Like myself, Seg Segutorio, the father of young Dray, intensely disliked keeping bowmen waiting on parade.

So, spruced up, young Drak was hauled off to do his part in the presentation of the standards to the First Regiment of Valkan Longbowmen.

We met this same Seg Segutorio riding up at breakneck speed as we wound down the narrow path from Esser Rarioch. The fortress pile reared stark above our heads, dominating Valkanium with its ordered streets of neat houses, the parks, the boulevards, the shops, the docks, all spread out below. The industrial sections were over on the other side. Seg reined his zorca in, so that the animal scattered sparks from his four dainty steel-shod hooves. Seg looked extremely upset.

"Dray! Delia! By the Veiled Froyvil, my old dom! I heard—I thought—"

"We do not yet know who it was. But one did not die."

"I give thanks to Erthyr the Bow you are unharmed."

The streaming mingled light of the twin suns cast those familiar and dear double shadows as we trotted on, going down from the high fortress and out onto the paved kyro with colonnaded shops all around. People there were, honest Koters and Koteras of Valka, who set up a shout as their Strom appeared. I waved a hand to them, knowing some of them by sight, able to recall the lusty days when together we had fought the slavers and the aragorn for this rich and beautiful island Stromnate of Valka. Seg and my other friends, Inch in particular, had learned to accept the puzzling aspects of my life, and I had made a half-promise to tell them all one day. We trotted on, a brave cavalcade, out through the new walls and so over the ditches and onto the wide and dusty plain called Vorgar's Drinnik. This Mars Field now held a splendid array of bowmen, lined up in impeccable and yet not rigid ranks. Despite all our attempts at knocking some kind of discipline into these rough and hairy fighters of Valka they set up a hullabalooing cheer as their Strom rode out onto the field.

A knot of zorcamen waited at the saluting base, and many orderlies stood ready. The new standards, cased, stood planted by the piled drums. Colors and panoply blazed everywhere. A trumpet blew and flags and banners unfurled from staffs set in ranks along the edge of Vorgar's Drinnik.

Among that small group of waiting zorcamen I saw Lykon Crimahan staring at me beneath the brim of his

18

helmet. I did not much care for the expression on his face. This Crimahan was the Kov of Forli—often called the Blessed Forli—and he had been one of that company with whom I had supped when first presenting myself as the Strom of Valka to his Majister the Emperor of Vallia. During the time of troubles Lykon Crimahan had been fortuitously absent on his estates of Forli, which lay on one of the eastern tributaries of Vallia's marvelous central water, She of Fecundity. His allegiances might lie with the powerful Racter party, with the panvals, with any other of the many smaller political and territorial parties. I did not know. He had managed to retain both his head and his estates. Now he stared at me with a bright and merry look of evil that made my back go up and made me sit straighter in the saddle.

"Lahal, Prince Majister."

"Lahal, Kov Lykon."

Others of the group made their greetings, and Lykon Crimahan sidled his zorca closer. The zorca, with that close-coupled muscled body and those four spindly tall legs of wind-blown fleetness, is a superb animal; I did not much care for the tightness of rein, the curb, the whole way this Crimahan had harnessed his animal—a superb specimen, full of fire and spirit.

"The Emperor is delayed," said this Lykon Crimahan. His whole demeanor showed the zest he took from conveying this news to me, Dray Prescot, the upstart barbarian clansman who had dared to woo and win the Emperor's daughter. This Kov Lykon's face grew a thin fuzz of dark beard beneath his jaws, and his mouth rat-trapped shut when he stopped speaking. He was gaunt with prominent cheekbones and eyes as malicious as those of any pagan idol of Balintol. He kicked his zorca and instantly kicked again as the animal objected.

"Quiet, you rast of a beast!" he said. Then, to me, and as though the words were a mere continuation of his thoughts: "The Emperor will arrive late, after the ceremony."

About to blast and curse, I halted as Kov Lykon went on, speaking smoothly, with the expressive pleasure he might feel as he drove his rapier into the guts of an opponent.

"There has been much discussion in the Presidio about your plans to build a great fleet of fliers. Your information from Havilfar has been laid before our wisest men. They express doubts—"

"Doubts! By Vox! There is no time for doubts."

"Nevertheless, Prince, the Emperor is not convinced. There will be no program to build an air fleet."

Give the rast his due. He probably believed what he was doing was for the good of his country. But his country was my country now. And I knew a damn sight more than he did. I could say that in all humility, knowing it to be true.

"Vallia *must* have an air fleet!"

"You may shout and bluster all you will, Prince, but it will avail you nothing. The Presidio is firm on this decision. You must resign yourself."

He could not leave well alone.

"After all, Prince, a clansman from the wastes of Segesthes is hardly in a position to understand the high politics of a great empire like Vallia."

I did not hit him.

Chapter Two

We argue in Esser Rarioch

I had risked my life—for what that was worth—to steal the secrets of the fliers from Havilfar and send them to Vallia. I had expected the Emperor and the Presidio which guided him to leap at the opportunity to construct fliers that would not break down, vollers we must have to counter the threat from Hamal.

And now, calmly, maliciously, evilly, they refused the opportunity. They sat in their pride and arrogance and said I had wasted my time and efforts, that this was no concern of mine, that they ran the country, not me.

Well, that last was true, Zair knows.

This was a matter of far greater importance than that four stupid stikitches had tried to assassinate me.

I caught up my zorca's reins and even then, through my rage, I refrained from jamming my heels in hard. The zorca was Snowy, a priceless animal, a mount with whom I had a great relationship. At my urging he trotted away from Lykon Crimahan, turning his hind quarters on him, and with this fitting gesture I trotted over to Seg.

I spoke loudly. Many men in the ranks heard me. The news would circulate, scuttlebutt that would explain what was happening.

"The Emperor has been delayed, Kov," I said in a penetrating bellow. "And, by Vox, I won't have these lads hanging around waiting! And they have a right to have the Emperor on parade when they receive their standards. So if you'll have their Jiktar dismiss them and tell him to order them a double ration of wine tonight, I will be much obliged."

Seg understood some of my ways. He responded in fine style.

"At once, my Prince!" he bellowed and swung away, riding with a light rein, shouting the orders to the regiment's Jiktar, its commanding officer.

There followed a most unpleasant few murs with young Drak, highly incensed that he had been all dressed up and promised much—for nothing.

"When your grandfather arrives, Drak, you will present the standards. It is important for the regiment. Do you see that, lad?"

"If you say so, Father."

About to say: "It's not if I say so!" I held my tongue as Delia trotted her zorca across and leaned down to speak to this young limb of Satan. Well, I'd had dealings with young limbs of Satan before—notably Pando, a real rapscallion who was now the Kov of Bormark, and Oby who had once dreamed of becoming a kaidur, and even the son of Rees the Numim, young Roban to whom I had given a dagger in time of trouble. If I cared to think that far back I could recall to mind some regular roarers who had been powder monkeys with me and had run on bleeding feet across the scarred decks to bring the leather buckets of cartridges as the great guns thundered. But the most confoundedly odd thing about it all now was that this particular young limb of Satan, whose lower lip stuck out so threateningly, was my own limb—making me the Satan

21

of the piece. I admit I am one of the biggest rogues in two worlds, but I wouldn't father that on young Drak.

"We shall have squish pie for tea," I said very firmly. "And if Inch was here he would eat some, because he cannot resist squish pie. Then, my lad—you tell me—what would happen then?"

Drak turned his face up from the cub-zorca he rode, a delightful little animal which could carry the child even though not fully grown itself. Drak's face betrayed conflicting emotions, then his trembling lips parted and he laughed.

"Why, Father, Inch would stand on his head!"

"Aye, lad!" I said, feeling relieved. "And I need at least six cups of tea, not one less will suffice."

So we trotted back to the promise of that rich Kregan tea which is priceless above all wines of two worlds.

If you, listening to these tapes spinning through the heads of your machine, now reflect that the Dray Prescot of whom you hear is a very different person from the Dray Prescot of his earlier days on Kregen—you are absolutely right. And yet if, say, that Dray Prescot who had so intemperately refused to bow his knee to the Princess Natema had lived through the scene on the parade ground on Vorgar's Drinnik, would not Kov Lykon be lying on that dusty ground with a mouthful of smashed teeth? And, that being so, what of my fine and fancy plans for Valka and Vallia?

Four armed men had tried to slay me. Well, there was nothing new in that. I did not think Kov Lykon had sent them. He might have, of course. But if I had acted as that old lusty, headstrong and foolish Dray Prescot would have, I'm absolutely sure that more than four stikitches would be assigned my death.

That was an eventuality I would have to face one day. But I had no intention of allowing my Delia to face any unnecessary danger. Nor would I allow danger to touch my twins if it was humanly possible. Now, of course, I recognize that I'm speaking like a bumbling, impractical parent, anxious to keep the world away from his family. As I have said, those children of mine led me as many a merry dance as ever I led when I was that old headstrong, willful Dray Prescot—as indeed I still am, to my shame, when the need arises.

There was no need to take vove to catch a ponsho.

So, filled with the self-satisfaction of the piously righ-

22

teous, I walked into the Great Hall of Esser Rarioch with the carved beams and the banners and the weapons along the walls and, like any idiot stuffed up with pride, I was to fall long and heavily, headfirst, into disastrous troubles. Wild alarms and frantic action lay before me, and I sat at my ease with my friends, sipping fragrant Kregan tea all unknowing!

But, first, there were important secrets to be unveiled.

Naghan the Gnat, that crafty armorer, thin and wiry and full of sly humor, drank his tea down and said: "I have chained him up so that he does not even feel the kiss of the iron. Oh yes, my Prince. He will be in good shape."

A bit of a savage, the good Naghan the Gnat. He and I had shared a few scarlet moments in the arena of Hyrklana. Now with his invaluable assistance we fashioned weapons for the men of Valka in the coming struggle with Hamal.

Balass the Hawk, fierce and predatory, laughed. "By Kaidun, my Prince! I think he will sing so that all the shishis in Xanachang will yearn for him and his song."

"You are a bloodthirsty devil, Balass," I said.

"Aye! If a stikitche tries to kill me I serve him as I serve a stupid coy in the arena."

This Balass the Hawk had improved the burs in Valka by trying to organize a Jikhorkdun and had been most put out when I had, very firmly, told him to desist. He might practice his skill, and teach Oby and the others, but the weapons must be of wood, and it must be practice only. The itch to step out of the red's corner and stand once again on the silver sand, clad in the armor of the kaidur, and face his fate as thousands upon thousands roared from the stands of the amphitheater—yes, that passion had got into the blood of Balass the Hawk.

He was a black-skinned man from Xuntal, with fierce predatory features and brilliant eyes, and he was a fine fighter, a kaidur.

The friendship we had been unable to allow full rein in the Jikhorkdun had grown since our escape. Now Balass was in command of the training of recruits to the army. Oh, yes. I was in the business of forming an army. I will speak of this later, at the proper time. Now, as we sat drinking Kregan tea, our conversation revolved around the fate to be meted out to the captured stikitche.

The matter was important.

Seg sat very quietly, occasionally taking a piece of

squish pie and, no doubt, thinking of Inch. He knew my mind better than the others. Even the Elders of Valka who ran the island for me in my many absences could not penetrate past the facade I put on for them.

Now Encar of the Fields shook his head and said, "What you do to this man will not affect the crops for next season."

"But," said Tom ti Vulheim, very intense, leaning forward on the table so that his tea spilled, "but what we do to him may have a very great effect on the life of our Strom!"

The others nodded, agreeing, hardly noticing that Tom had called me by the old title. I was the Strom of Valka first to these men of the island, Prince Majister of Vallia a long second after.

So we sat and drank tea and argued the pros and cons of torturing a man for information. Hard, fierce, intense talk. The assassin's life meant nothing. What he could tell us of who had sent him was the vital information. No one drank wine. Only pigs drink wine at all hours of the day. Our heads remained clear. I did not wish to hurt the man. He had been hired to do a certain thing and he had failed. That assassins are particularly loathsome forms of life is true. But the fellow was suffering how, hanging in his chains, waiting for what he must know would follow.

I said, "I think we can find out what we wish to know without touching him."

Some nodded, comprehending; others scowled and their fingers gripped up. They would take the hot iron and the pincers to the fellow, to make him talk.

I marked them all.

Vangar ti Valkanium, the captain of my personal airboat, poured milk ready for a fresh cup. "He will sing without a hair of his head being touched, if the Prince says so. For myself, I believe all this talk of the sanctity of human life. But when the life of the Prince is involved—"

"Not so, good Vangar!" I did not speak sharply, but they all looked at me, held in their actions, motionless. "No man can pretend to a position which allows him to deny the rights of another human. That is not my way. It is not the way of Opaz. What a man has is what a man fights for; nothing in this world is given free."

They laughed. "You may say that again, Prince!" said Naghan the Gnat, cunning in the ways of fashioning metal.

Delia walked in, having seen to the twins, and we all stood up, as was proper.

She sat at the table at my side, for we observed no high protocol here and the table was shoved into a paneled corner of the high hall, with the stained glass windows above opened to allow the full glory of the suns to shine on the opposite wall. Truly, I think that the Great Hall in Esser Rarioch is a wondrous place!

A heaping pile of sandwiches lay on a silver platter. They were covered by a pure white linen cloth. No one had touched this particular platter of sandwiches, although all the others had been plundered. The famous Kregan bread had been cut into extraordinarily thin slices, and that superb Kregan butter spread by a hand with the skill to spread evenly and not too thinly, not too thickly. The sandwiches contained crisp slices of banber, a kind of succulent cucumber. Delia lifted the cloth as I poured for her and took one of the banber sandwiches.

I did not look at her as she ate, for the sight of those lips . . . Well, I went back to what we were talking about, trying to carry on my policy—which I thought was approved of by the Savanti—of civilizing the barbaric men of Kregen.

The others were arguing the pros and cons and I half turned and looked past Delia to where that superbly muscled, superbly built, superb man sat, unspeaking, a glowering look on his handsome face.

"Well, Turko!" I rallied him. "What do you say on this matter?"

Turko the Shield put down his cup. He looked directly at me. Those hands so gently holding the cup, a fine piece of porcelain from Rensmot in Vallia, could tear a man to pieces, could hurl him cunningly with a mere twitch of the wrists, in the dreaded disciplines of the Khamorros.

"What do I say on this, my Prince?" Turko was over his astonishment about the maniac Dray Prescot and his place in the scheme of things; but he always hesitated when he called me Prince, an echo of that mockery laughing behind his eyes. "I would say do as any sensible man would do. We Khamorros can make a man tell us all we wish to know without using clumsy instruments, blunt or sharp."

Turko would still not use a weapon apart from his own body; the shield he habitually carried for me in battle hung on the high walls of the hall, dust motes dancing in the suns' beams before its massive bulk.

Truly the Savanti in their civilizing task, faced ingrained attitudes on Kregen.

But I had to try.

The Savanti had thrown me out of Paradise because I had failed them. I would do exactly the same thing over again, too! And this time I'd do it a damn sight more quickly! I stole a glance at my Delia, and she turned, caught my eye, and smiled. For Delia, Delia of the Blue Mountains, Delia of Delphond, I'd be thrown out of every paradise in those four hundred light-years between the worlds of Earth and Kregen!

Still and all, the Savanti had set themselves the task of bringing order, civilization, and dignity to Kregen, and I saw it as a worthwhile task to which to set my hands. One day soon, I had promised myself, I'd go off to Hamal with the intention of finding the Todalpheme, those wise men and mathematicians, and ask them what they knew of Aphrasöe, the city of the Savanti, the Swinging City.

The Empire of Hamal had to be beaten in war first, or at least halted in the tide of conquest, some *modus vivendi* arrived at, before I could consider my own selfish ends.

So I said, "My friends, torture is not the answer. It may give us the information we seek. But think what it will do to us who practice it—"

"It'll keep us alive," said Balass the Hawk.

"Certainly. But, Balass, and all of you, the brands you use on your victim must surely brand you yourselves."

Some of them could see, most could not. They were all good-hearted fellows, prime companions, chosen comrades to have around me in battle or roister. But it is truly said that Kregen is a hard world.

I had gone through torments enough in the past to know that from bitter personal experience.

A rumbling bellow from the far end of the table made us all look that way, and some of us smile, and all of us listen as Naghan Kholin Donamair burst out: "By Zodjuin of the Silver Stux! All this is emptiness, fit for Obdjangs! Take the cramph by the throat and choke it out of him!" N. Kholin Donamair had clearly been holding himself back from the conversation, for now, glaring around, his four fists clenched, he recollected himself and finished: "That is what I would do, my King."

I do not forget that I am king of Djanduin.

My Djangs are the most fearsome warriors in Havilfar, with their four perfectly matched arms and their proud heads and defiant step. With weapons no Khamorro can stand against them. There is a great deal more to tell of the relationships there, in southwestern Havilfar, far away down south below the swell of the equator; but for now here was the typical Dwadjang philosophy exemplified. The four-armed Dwadjangs are unexcelled fighting–men; but they are a trifle thick at affairs above a Chuktar's rank. The gerbil-faced and extraordinarily clever Obdjangs handle affairs of state and strategy in Djanduin.

I am king of Djanduin. I said: "Well spoken, Naghan. But the fellow is a professional stikitche. He will have steeled himself to being choked, even by a Djang."

"These affairs seem simple to me," said the Djang, and he reached his left lower arm for a vosk sandwich as his left upper brought the teacup to his lips. Both of his right hands fondled the little gyp sitting at the side of his chair, gobbling crumbs.

No one said to Naghan Donamair: "You stick to your flutduins and what you know, Naghan!"

The comment might have been apt; it would have been cruel, unnecessary, and boorish, and these are things I will not tolerate in my Great Hall of Esser Rarioch. This is known by my friends who sup with me there.

As for the flutduins, those marvelous saddle flyers from Djanduin, after their initial reticence the good folk of Valka were now agog with the idea of flying through the thin air astride the back of a giant bird. I was actively arranging for more flyers to be brought all the long way to Valka, and the recruiting Deldars were forming enormous lists of bright young Valkan lads who wished to join the aerial cavalry.

Seg, his black hair and blue eyes as always very reassuring to me now that I knew his feckless and yet deeply moving ways, laughed and said, "If Thelda were here instead of caring for young Dray and the twins back in Falinur, I think she would understand, Dray."

"I am sure she would." I am loyal to my friends.

So we talked on through that glorious afternoon tea, arguing whether or not a man should be tormented. The mingled lights of the suns glowed on the high walls. We laughed a lot and banged the old lenken table. Tilly, the glorious little golden-furred Fristle fifi, quite accidentally knocked her tea over the white robe of Elena, the matronly wife of Erdgar the Shipwright. Erdgar was away supervising the building of certain unusually shaped ships at this time. Elena made no great fuss, Tilly was filled with contrition, and a fresh cup was poured. While no one laughed, we all felt the spirit of the occasion. Truly, those days of sunshine in Esser Rarioch provide rich memories in a crusty old shellback like me.

Delia suggested we go out to the high terrace where the mushk glowed yellow in the suns' light and the bees droned most contentedly among the perfumed flowers.

So it was that among my friends, on that high terrace with the radiant lights of Antares reflecting back in refulgent gleams from spire and pinnacle and tower, with Valkanium spread out below in a chiaroscuro of brilliance, bowered in greenery and flowers and mellow with the splash of fountains, I turned and held up my hand and said: "We will not torture this miserable stikitche. If he does not tell us who employed him we shall hand him over to the Emperor's justice."

"And is that all, my Prince?" That was Balass.

"Aye, that is all." I screwed up my eyes. "Do you relish the idea of the mercy of an emperor, if you had tried to slay his daughter?"

The others nodded, no doubt thinking their thoughts. I knew I had bungled. But, about to correct that slip, I was arrested by the sight of a voller skimming perilously low over the rooftops toward us.

Seg said, "Another attempt, do you think?"

"It could be. Roust out Jiktar Exand."

Seg nodded and ran back off the terrace. Exand, an old battle campanion, had been appointed Jiktar of the fortress guard. Seg returned far too soon. With him stomped Jiktar Exand, furious, beet-red of face, almost stuttering in his anger.

"Strom!" he burst out, enraged with himself. "The miserable cramph of a stikitche is dead! Assassinated while he hung in his chains! Strom, the fault is mine!"

So there was an end to all our academic arguments.

Chapter Three

Evold Scavander reads from Drozhimo the Lame

The voller, a swift and brightly painted craft, swirled up from that mad dash over the rooftops. It was headed for a landing platform three stories below the level of this high terrace.

Tom ti Vulheim let out a shout. "That is no stikitche, Strom! That is Lish! He always flies as though his tail is on fire."

"The fault is mine, my Strom," repeated Jiktar Exand. He crashed his right fist against his breastplate, rather as a housewife takes a rolling pin to a cheap steak. "The guards were in the act of changing when two were struck down; two others were lucky to escape with their lives, although wounded. The prisoner's body was slashed to pieces."

"Hum," I said. Then: "Do not blame yourself, Exand. The fault is more truly mine. We did not realize that we were up against highly professional stikitches. Ordinary swods of the guard could scarcely comprehend the villainous expertise of these hireling murderers."

"The Strom takes upon himself the fault of his people," shouted Exand. These tough old warrior birds all seem to shout in normal conversation about their business. "I understand the need. But, Strom, I failed you!"

This Jiktar Exand—broad, heavily boned, thickly muscled, with a gut that extended the massive arch of his chest —was of that breed of men who serve, it seems, in the armies of all countries of two worlds. His square face bristled under the helmet. The brave red and white slashed his sleeves. He wore the usual rapier and main-gauche, and

29

"The airboat spun end over end, tumbling from the bright
air."

his tall black boots gleamed with the loving polish adminis-tered by his batman.

I sighed. He wouldn't forgive himself, even if I did.

About to reason with him, I was arrested by a shocked gasp, a shout of horror, from the people on the terrace. I swirled around.

The airboat was falling. Like a tossed chip of wood it spun end over end, tumbling from the bright air. Everyone held rigid in a stasis of horrified anger as the voller struck a domed roof, bounced, turned over into a spire, re-bounded, and so smashed into kindling and vanished into the slot of the street far below.

We had all seen the tiny dot of the pilot, arms and legs pinwheeling, pitch out and plunge to his death.

"Lish!" said Tom. He gripped his hands together.

Lish Sjame had been a battle comrade of ours when we cleansed Valka of the slavers and the aragorn. Now that laughing man with the lean, intense face and the in-tellectual grasp of a problem, that man who had sung many a fine song with us, emptied many a filled flagon, was gone.

We stood looking down. And mingled with our sorrow ran an ugly murderous thread of anger: anger against the builders of airboats that failed; anger against the manufactories of Hamal which sold us vollers that mur-dered our friends.

"If ever we needed the secrets of the vollers, now is the time to show all men that truth!" said Seg.

"Aye!" I said. Then, in my old way I burst out: "Sink me! I'll take that damned Presidio, one by one, and shake them by the scruff of the necks! Vallia *must* build her own vollers!"

We went down the long flights of stone stairs to the dungeons. Oh, yes, if you feel surprise that there should be dungeons you must have forgotten that the high fortress of Esser Rarioch had been built in the old times, in the days when dungeons featured as essential adjuncts to the gra-cious living of Stroms, and Kovs, and high nobles. Also, I think you may judge Valka better now if I tell you that the only occupant of this complex series of dungeons in the rock had been this same stikitche.

He hung in his chains, hacked to pieces.

Which made me ponder.

The two dead guards had been carried away. The wounded two had been treated. Bound up in clean yellow bandages, acupuncture needles cunningly inserted to take away their pain, they awaited the Strom's verdict of their crime. For, make no mistake about it, they had sinned. Their dereliction of duty could very possibly cause severe problems for the future.

The two swods braced themselves up the moment I appeared. They stood to attention as best they could, so that my first words were: "Stand at ease, you couple of famblys." I looked at them, cast a single glance at the hunk of bloodied meat hanging in the chains, and said, "You, Larghos. Tell me."

"Yes, my Strom." He swallowed. A youngster, newly appointed to the fortress guard, he was now clearly appalled at what had happened and what he had been part of. "We were changing guard. I saw Nath and Pergon set upon and I attacked the nearest of the men and he whickered his blade and—"

"Steady, lad." His lorica had been unbuckled so the doctor could more easily get at the thrust that had gone cleanly through above the top segment, above the collarbone. These stikitches are fine swordsmen. "Now, who did you attack?"

"The assassins, my Strom."

"Yes. Yes. Tell me what they looked like."

"Dressed in black, Strom. All in black. With steel faces."

And that, I knew, was as fair a description as I would get.

His comrade, Yaldy, was in worse case, the rapier having thrust through his cheek, scraping the bone. It had missed his eye, the target; but for the acupuncture needles Yaldy would have been in great pain. He leaned on his glaive as he spoke. I pondered the wisdom of the glaive, that wicked bayonet-blade splined into a five-foot ash shaft, and yet the Valkans normally have no fear of a rapier man with the glaive in their hands.

"No more to add, my Strom!" bellowed this Yaldy. His parade ground shout whispered out weakly. I nodded. There was nothing more to learn here except, perhaps . . .

I spoke with a forceful presence of urgency and importance.

"Did either of you hear the stikitches say a word? Anything?"

They shook their heads, and then Larghos checked, his head going up.

"Well?"

"The assassins did not say a word. I do not know how many of them there were. But this one here—" He gestured vaguely to the hunk of meat hanging in the chains. "This one cried out as they went up to him."

"Ah!"

"He shouted in mortal terror. He shouted, 'I did not say a word!' Then he swore by a name I do now know. He said: 'As Lem is my witness, Traga, as Lem—' Then they cut him."

Although it seemed to me Kregen exploded around my head, I felt it expedient to keep the shock from my face and voice.

Lem!

That evil cult of Lem the Silver Leem had found its vile way to my own home of Valka. Well, I made a most solemn vow that I would never allow that evil superstition of Lem the Silver Leem to sully Valka. I would uproot the whole foul practice, root and branch. By Zair! This was a matter of supreme importance, far outweighing the mere stikitches' attacks.

Now I asked, "Traga? Does that mean anything to anyone?"

They all shook their heads. The name was not common, but there had been a Traga in Valka, that Traga ti Vandayha, the city of silversmiths. I thought this was merely coincidence, nothing more. The Traga we knew had perished when the aragon's fortress above Findle's Crossing had burned.

"Jiktar Exand."

"Strom!"

"Fetch me a man from the city who swears by Diproo the Nimble-Fingered."

"Aye, my Strom." He knew exactly what I meant.

His red and white banded sleeve, made from first quality humespack, bashed across his breastplate as he clanged off, his booted feet loud on the unyielding stones of the dungeon floor.

With a few further words to the guards, for they were brave young men and had been woefully overmatched in their encounter with the stikitches, I led the way back into the upper terraces of Esser Rarioch.

The remains of Lish Sjame had been brought in and I saw to it that he was given a decent funeral, with all the proper rites accompanying the burial, as was proper. His wife had long since died, victim of one of the diseases that, notwithstanding the skill of Kregen's doctors, still carry off far too many of her people. The remains of the airboat were taken up to that long and lofty room with the tall windows I had set aside as a laboratory. Here I had been carrying out experiments, with the help of the man who was, I fancied, the wisest wise man of Valka.

"Ha! My Prince!" he cried as I came in, and then he sneezed. He was smothered in fine dust, and he kept sneezing. I kept upwind of him.

"You seem to be immersed in your work, San," I said.

I called Evold Scavander, the wise man, San. As you know, San is the respectful title given to a dominie or sage, and how well San Evold Scavander earned this mark of respect.

But, for all that, sneezing, he had to say: "Nothing, my Prince. Not a movement, not a sign. And the bags grow less with every trial."

A spluttery, bewhiskered, round-faced man, with crab-apple cheeks and snapping brown eyes, he wore an old stained smock and a pair of decrepit foofray satin slippers. I always had the feeling that, with his contempt for the Wizards of Loh, he missed something of their dark power. But he refused to adorn his clothes with archaic symbols or wear the tall conical hat, and he used his long sensitive fingers to good purpose in the many schemes to improve Vallia and Valka I put forward. His temper was of the same order as a leem's.

On a scarred bench lay a number of silver boxes. I felt my heart go thump at the sight. These were boxes we had made up here, in Valka, in imitation of those silver boxes made in Havilfar that powered and lifted fliers. I had uncovered many of the secrets of the various minerals that went into the vaol boxes, at some discomfort to myself, as you know. With a mix of five minerals of certain kinds of voller would fly and might be pushed by the wind, with the effect of gripping the sub-etheric forces of the structure of the universe, of sliding against these forces as the wind pushed. With a mix of nine minerals a voller would fly independently of the wind.

As for the paol boxes, those boxes that for so long I had thought contained only air, there lay the heartbreak.

"Dirt and air!" I said, somewhat heavily, I fear.

"Aye, Prince! The minerals would seem to operate well enough, and I have that lazy scamp Ornol out searching for them in the Heart Heights. I feel confident they will be found." His brown eyes snapped at me. "If they are not Ornol will get a striping, by Vox!"

"Yes, but, San, what of the paol boxes? What of cayferm?"

He crowed his triumph.

I stared at him, willing it to be true, willing that he had discovered what that mysterious immaterial substance truly was, if substance it was at all.

He reached down a monstrous old hyr-lif, massively bound with brass bands and with a brass lock. He produced a key from under his clothes, a key of brass hanging on a brass chain. With this and much creaking and groaning, he turned the lock and opened the book. I swear I expected a black cloud of bats to fly forth. He blew away dust and sneezed again.

"Here, Prince, in *The Secret Lore of San Drozhimo the Lame* is to be found the only reference I have run across to cayferm."

He turned the pages, ancient and stained and yet supple still in that perfect atmosphere of Valka. A little spider crept out and ran across the lines of black writing, and Evold Scavander leaned down and gently blew to help the spider on its way.

I was fully aware of the gravity of the moment. Dirt and air! How they had mocked me in my struggles in distant Havilfar! But I had come through in the end to an understanding of the names and the compositions of the minerals. We might not find all of them in Valka; we must find them all in Vallia! And cayferm! That mysterious substance, cayferm that was supposed to be steam, when all of Kregen knew steam as kish; could old San Scavander have found the secret in this musty book?

He found a page very nearly at the end. I breathed more easily when I saw the page was untorn. How often at the end of a book a torn page has destroyed all hope . . .

He cleared his throat, sneezed a mighty sneeze, and peered close.

"Listen, my Prince, to the words of a sage dead these thousand seasons and more!"

"I listen."

"Then this is what Drozhimo the Lame has to say." He read in a loud wheezing voice, and I felt the shadows come closer in that high ceilinged room with the tall windows and all the splendor of the Suns of Scorpio flooding in.

" 'The Freeing of an Ib from a Mortal Body Undiluted.' "

35

He looked up. "The spirits of the dead do not always leave the body the moment men are killed. Sometimes a man retains his ib, to his own mortification in the blessed light of the Twins."

"Aye. Read on."

" 'Take the body and wash in the water taken from a maiden's first bath after the marriage night. Place the body undried in a brazen coffin above a fire heated seven times, and with bellows pumped by a dwarf. A dwarf with red hair ensures complete success; if a red-haired dwarf is not to be found then a black-haired dwarf will suffice, or a brown-haired dwarf; but then the fire must be pumped over twice. Into the coffin over the body pour the water used in the bathing. To this add the same weight of squishes. The fruits may be used entire, but they must be scrupulously clean. Add in double-handfuls so that the spirit may boil from them into the water and the cayferm enter the submerged body and so remove from it the ib. When all has boiled away the body may be taken up and given due burial; it is wise to place a tuffa wand at the head and feet until the first night of Notor Zan passes.' "

He looked up, resting one hand on the open hyr-lif. His eyes wrinkled up, regarding me. I was aware of a flick-flick plant snaking out a six-foot tendril, taking a fly on the wing, and popping it into one of its orange cone-shaped flowers. The shadow of the plant in its pot on the window-sill, the sound of laughter from outside, high and shrill, meant nothing; the sight and sounds were as distant as the planet of my birth.

"Cayferm," I said.

"Aye, Prince. I think after treatment like that any body would be willing to go down into burial, aye, and be glad to."

"Yes, that would be the way of it. But, Evold, it must be! Don't you see? Steam! If you boil water you must get steam!"

"Steam," he said. We used the Kregish word, the most common word for steam, *kish*. "I can find no other mention of cayferm in all my library."

"You have done well."

"I remembered one horrific time in the Heavenly Mines where I had sweated, as number eight two eight one, to dig and tunnel for minerals. And how a little Och stylor, writing in his notebook, had jumped with alarm, deep in a tunnel through a seam, and called to the Rapa guard to prod the slaves out fast. We had not gone back to the seam. And now I recalled that over the smell of the cheap oil lamp I had sniffed the scent of squishes. I had thought of Inch, and then the little Och had near-pan-icked.*

Now I thought I knew why.

"Steam made up with boiled squishes," I said. "Cay-ferm."

Evold sneezed. "Maybe, maybe. But we must test it first. We can only talk now, we must—"

"Yes!" I bellowed. "Everyone must gather squishes! Every perishing soul, by Vox!"

Evold Scavander nodded, the excitement getting to him.

"Although . . ." I said. And I felt a chill. "Although this cannot be so. It is against nature."

"Many things are against nature, my Prince. Every time you put on a hat to go out into the rain, it is against na-ture."

"I grant that. But I mean that boiling will produce a purity; the steam cannot possibly contain any part of the squishes! This is a matter of common knowledge."

He put a yellowish finger alongside his nose, which had a large brown lump on the larboard side.

"Maybe nature winks, my Prince. For a man to fly through the air using boxes filled with dirt and air— surely that is so against nature as to make all the rest simple."

"Oh, the vollers work. There is no doubt of that. Aye," I added viciously, "and they crash, also."

We looked at the pathetic pile of wreckage. Lish's vol-ler had come down hard at the end. The two silver boxes had been taken from the smashed jumble of sturm-wood and bronze orbits. They lay on the table, separated from those we had made ourselves.

They were also well separated from each other. I walked across and gently pushed one of the boxes toward the other, along the lenken tabletop. I could feel nothing at first. And then like a thrilling of rubbed amber, like a million warrior ants of the hostile territories marching over my skin, I felt the tremble, the vibration. When the two boxes came within that certain special distance from each other they both, together, sprang into the air. Up

---

*See *Fliers of Antares*, Dray Prescot # 8.

they went, glittering in the light of Antares. We stared upward, knowing what would happen.

The boxes flew up together until wind pressure divided them. They curved out and away and so, separated, plummeted back to the floor. One hit so heavily that the corner split. I cursed.

Evold Scavander scuttled for the box, lifted it, and stuck it under that lumpy nose of his. His mad old eyes snapped with intelligence, with baffled intelligence.

"Ha, my Prince! Squishes! When I was a small boy, cleaning the retorts and collecting the frogs' legs and sweeping the floor, aye, and being well beaten by the old San, I remember a piece of squish pie as a direct gift from Oolie Opaz himself."

I sniffed. Squish, without a doubt.

"It has gone, drifted into the air and gone."

"True. But we will do as you command, and boil many squishes. The whole fortress will be perfumed with squishes."

"But," I said, fretful, seeing that first quick flash of hope utterly ruined, "if we boil squishes and put the steam in a silver box, why, then, the steam will condense and we will merely have a box of water."

San Evold shook his head. What I said was true. But he had no other suggestion.

"Let me first try, my Prince. Afterward, if it does not work, we must think again."

"You see about the squishes and the boiling. Inform me and I shall come at the right time. Meanwhile, there are the other minerals to be found."

"Ornol will be back by nightfall, my Prince."

So, with a few cheerfully intended words which sounded dismal even to me, I took myself off. Seg met me in the long hall of the images where, in ivory and chemzite and bronze and marble, the ancient ones of Valka stared endlessly out upon the blue sky of Kregen. His face was reassuring and refreshing to me, but he said, "Dray! The Emperor has arrived and is in a foul temper!"

Chapter Four

Standards for a regiment and answers for an Emperor

"We are not well pleased with you, son-in-law."

The Emperor looked just the same as when I had last seen him, big and powerful, standing with booted feet thrust firmly on the ground, his back erect, his hands on his hips. He wore a fine Vallian tunic-coat and breeches, and his hat glowed with feathers. He wore a rapier and left-hand dagger, and a cloth-of-gold cape glittered finely, slung from his left shoulder. But the creases at the inner corners of his eyes had grown more deeply etched, and his face showed a pallor that I saw, with a pang, distressed his daughter Delia.

Across this end of Vorgar's Drinnik the First Regiment of Valkan Longbowmen stood in their long lines, braced, ready, waiting. They made a fine show. I admit I would far rather deal with them and their like than the gilded popinjays who surrounded the Emperor and his suite, the Pallans and the courtiers, the nobles and the high Koters. I made no direct challenge to the Emperor's annoyance. He had been feeling his way back to greater power than he had enjoyed for many a long season, and all because I had saved his neck, I and my comrades there in the immortal fight in The Dragon's Bones.

So I placidly said, "It is right that the first regiment of this kind formed in Vallia should be honored by their Emperor's presence at the presentation of the standards."

"As to that, Dray Prescot, I agree. But I talk of weightier matters."

The zorcas moved gently in the lessening heat of the late afternoon. Soon Zim and Genodras would be gone.

Then we could go up into the Great Hall of Esser Rarioch to see what kind of banquet my people could prepare for the Emperor.

"You do not question my meaning?"

"I know you have surrounded yourself with men who are not worthy of you."

He felt some shock; but I also remembered that this man was the Emperor, the most powerful man in all Vallia, which made him the most powerful man for many dwaburs around in this northern hemisphere of Kregen. He could order me executed. He had already given that order once, and he had not been obeyed. If he tried to tell his men to take off my head now, they would find an abrupt and unyielding wall of Valkan steel—not protecting me but threatening them.

"You persuaded me to send a great host of men and fliers into Havilfar, son-in-law. A great battle was fought. But what has come of that? Where is the profit? You promised to bring me back vollers, Dray Prescot. Where are they?"

"You do not speak as I hear the Presidio speaks."

The flush in his face deepened. This was an old story: powerful as he was, the governing body held certain authorities that could check him. I knew I had slackened many of those strings—and all men understood the Emperor had been even more firmly seated on the throne—but the Presidio still counted in council. Also, I had to admit I had been rewarded. I was Prince Majister and Kov of this and Strom of that and Zair knew what else in the mazing glitter of titles and lands of Vallia. All this meant nothing. I think he understood me just a little better now and realized that titles meant as little to me as they did to him. Land, canals, corn, cattle, minerals—these were power. He would have added slaves to the list earlier, but he understood the views that Delia and I held on slaves. He did not grasp that being a Krozair of Zy was far more important to me than all the titles he could bestow.

"There are those in the Presidio who have set their faces against this talk of Vallian fliers."

"I have talked briefly with Kov Lykon. The man is a fool."

"Not so, Dray Prescot. He is clever and cunning and wields certain powers. You would do well to be wary of him."

My surprise was genuine. Was this puissant Emperor nurturing a spark of feeling for the hairy barbarian who had come bashing his way in to become son-in-law? Then I saw Delia trotting out with young Drak, and Lela on an exquisite pure white pony, and the moment dissolved. Delia greeted her father with warmth, although, as I say, she too saw the betraying tiredness in his eyes. I was pleased —I admit, by Zair, I was very pleased—that he seemed genuinely attached to his two grandchildren. He stood, blocky, square, the golden cape glinting in the suns, and he talked with Drak and Lela for a while. I let my bowmen stand and wait for that, for I believed they would understand. Delia met my eye and smiled. It was not too difficult to find a smile for her in return.

The Emperor looked up quickly.

"What is this of men in the garden—men you hit?"

"Later," I said. "It has been dealt with. The bowmen await their standards and I warrant their throats are drier than the Ocher Limits."

He took the reference well enough. He was hardly likely to forget it.

He mounted up, his zorca stiff with imperial trappings, his massive, handsome face still flushed and dark as we rode out to present the standards.

I will not weary you with a full description, although you must guess the moment was important not only to me but to Valka and Vallia, and therefore to all this part of Kregen, these continents and islands called Paz. The parade was an emotional and moving occasion, filled with meaning; as the standards were presented I saw the ensigns stiffen up with fierce and dedicated pride in the symbols of Valka their regiment would carry into battle.

There lives in Valka a small bird with white wings and back, and a rosy breast. We call it the valkavol. That small bird, normally eating fruits and nuts, will turn into a fighting fury when attacked by the gawky, clumsy brown birds called threngs when the threngs try to steal eggs from the high nests. These are the names we give these birds in Valka, at least, and it is this small bright bird, the valkavol, which crowns the standards of my regiments. This cheeky, loyal, intelligent bird with its peaceful, herbivorous way of life is well liked by farmers, for the valkavol eats those unpleasant gall-like fruits of the deep forests. So far it has not decided to come down to the orchards to sample gregarians, squishes, malsidges, and the many other kinds of luscious fruits we grow. It does eat palines, but no true believer would grudge another living soul the delights of palines. This peaceful bird, a bundle of incredible ferocity if its nest is threatened, was perched atop each standard pole. Oh, the carvings were of wood, but they were gilded so they gleamed and flashed bravely, and the claws were finely sculpted from balass. They presented a fair and heartening sight, slanting into the rays of the twin suns.

The colors beneath each valkavol flared with symbol and number, for I had authorized an individual standard for each pastang and, as was proper, two standards for the regiment as a whole. There was reason in this open-handed distribution of standards. Each pastang numbered only fifty men, when in most of the regiments of Hamal the pastang numbered eighty. There were ten pastangs to this regiment, whereas the regiments of Havilfar were normally composed of six pastangs.

Treating the first pastang like the first cohort of a legion, I had given the company its full complement of eighty, so that the regiment numbered five hundred and thirty, plus ancillaries. All this was done with an eye to the future.

And, though I say it myself, who with Seg had wrought the work, they looked grand!

Yes, there was reason for this panoply and this structure, as you shall hear.

Young Drak conducted himself well. He sat astride his cub-zorca stiffly and, young as he was, he was already on his own. He carried the affair off superbly, at which I felt all the fond, fatuous, foolish pride of a parent. If I didn't know my Delia better I'd have thought a tear glistened in the corner of her eye.

The banners flared in the suns, the zorcas behaved with perfect composure—always a good omen—and the men formed and marched in perfect alignment. The bands played cheerful rousing music, *The Song of Tyr Nath, The Heart Heights of Valka, Paktun's Promenade*, and a national Vallian song of some consequence to my family and to Valka, *Drak na Vallia*. This marching song is called by the swods in the ranks *Old Drak Himself*.

Seg did not fuss as the men took rank to shoot the exhibition three shafts apiece. He looked at the flags fluttering from their staffs, and Jiktar Targhan ti Vulheim—a battle comrade, one of the old freedom fighters selected by Seg with the advice of Tom ti Vulheim—trotted his zorca over for a last-minute word. All the bows leaped into the correct position, all the bows spanned as one. The Jitkar's rapier slashed down and his bellow made Lela's pony jump. All the shafts loosed simultaneously.

Next to me Seg grunted. "By the Veiled Froyvil! I swear a good twenty out of a hundred missed the mark!"

To Seg that was so miserable an example of shooting as to be beneath contempt. So I said gently, "They will improve."

"If they do not those rasts of Hamalese will riddle 'em with their confounded crossbows."

With bands playing and colors flying, the regiment marched back. The crowds who had come out to watch broke up and drifted back to the city. This night there would be many gallons of wine drunk and many boasts made and songs sung, aye, and a few broken heads to show for it in the morning. We are a rough old lot, in Valka, and we take our pleasures when they come.

"So my grandson is Hyr-Jiktar of this new regiment, Dray Prescot?"

"He is, Emperor. And I tell you that in the days to come you will have to accustom yourself to using soldiers of Vallia, formed into regiments, rather than merely sending for mercenaries and paying them to fight for you."

"We are a nation of the sea. Our galleons—"

"Of course! I grant the galleons are the finest vessels afloat—vessels of Paz, that is—but you face new threats now, Emperor."

He wanted to pursue the conversation, but I did not wish to talk about those shanks from over the curve of the world, those fishmen with their fast-sailing craft who would, I felt sure, one day pose so great a danger we must all band together to resist them. At the moment Hamal was the great threat.

We rode back and I saw Delia with Lela in tow talking to Turko the Shield. He had not brought that massive shield; it still hung in my hall. Drak rode at the head of his regiment, a small and lonely figure, but proud, proud!

I had not asked for him to be born, but I had been very happy with his and his sister's birth. Now he must face the never-ending threats of life, and I could only help and guide. So we rode back through my capital city of Valkanium to the high fortress of Esser Rarioch. A Hyr-Jiktar is a purely honorary position, of course. Drak

43

would not be leading this regiment into action for a good many seasons yet. I felt a pang. I would far prefer he never had to involve himself in the mad red obscenity of war at all.

Tharu ti Valkanium, the leader of the high assembly of my island Stromnate of Valka, arrived as we were about to go in stately procession into the Great Hall for the feasting. Tharu, as always grim with purpose, his leonine head with its shock of brown Valkan hair proudly lifted, greeted me and then said, "I made all haste, Strom. But the flier failed us—"

"You bring no news in that, Tharu."

"Aye! I heard the terrible news of Lish. He was a good man. I vow there will not be a man of Valka who will not go willingly, aye, and gladly, when we deal with these cramphs of Hamalese."

Tharu ran Valka for me, with the high assembly of Elders. I trusted him implicitly. He was reconciled to my absences. With Tom ti Vulheim, who had accepted the rank of Chuktar with his reckless laugh and a pledge to see that the men of Valka fought in the ways I directed, Tharu in his grim, thorough way kept Valka as an island paradise. Now he joined us as the feasting and drinking began. Well, I have spent many and many a roistering night in my high hall of Esser Rarioch, and Zair willing, will spend many more before I die. On this evening, as the moons of Kregen floated over the horizon to cast down their mingled pink and golden radiance, I felt restless. My plans were going very well where they touched Valka; they had gone disastrously astray over this business of the vollers we must build.

Presently, with a song from Erithor of Valkanium, that preeminent skald, finishing on the last defiant notes of *The Lament for Valinur Fallen,* the Emperor motioned to me in a sign that meant he wished to retire.

Valinur Fallen did not suit my mood. The lament begins with: "Glaive-bearing marched they in storm-light and thunder." It finishes on a high note of apotheosis, of the ending of days, and the defiant expectancy that Valinur's sons and daughters will refresh the land. The last few words are: "The zhantil will rest in the dusty earth under; but the heart in the human breast never."

I hasten to add that this is a mere literal representation of the words; all the beauty of the original is lost in this clumsiness of my expression. The Valkans practice a finely

44

tuned form of kenning, and one must listen carefully and tease out the meanings from the golden words, the ringing phrases. I did not wish to dwell on death, on the destruction of a country, and of the resurrection and revenge through the children. That was the way of Kregen, of course, but the mood left me hollow and chill, thinking of Drak and Lela, and I welcomed the opportunity to go with a few of my closest people and more of the Emperor's retinue into the Chavonth Chamber. This room, comfortably furnished, was held for talks that, while not of the stiff and formal kind held in the audience chamber, were not yet so informal that they could be held in my inner and private rooms. The floor was covered by a single enormous carpet embroidered with chavonths engaged in many of the scenes of the hunt; the walls were hung with tapestries where more chavonths snarled and showed their claws. The carpet, the tapestries, the curtains, all were of Hlinnian weave, good and solid and vastly expensive.

The closeness of the room, although it was large, and the sound-deadening effects of the draperies, meant that only one with keen hearing might pick up the racket bouncing from the Great Hall. They'd started on *The Bowmen of Loh* down there, and Seg licked his lips, picking up a fresh goblet of Gremivoh.

A very great deal of power, wealth, and majesty was packed into the Chavonth Chamber that night. I knew most of those there, and many of them you have already met in these tapes. There were others who were to figure in my story at a later date, but I will confine myself to talking only about those who affected me in the immediate dealings with which we were engaged.

The chief of these, of course, was Lykon Crimahan, the Kov of Forli.

"Let me fill your glass with this excellent Gremivoh, Kov," I said, very friendly. We wanted no servants with flapping ears when we talked high state business. And I wanted to let this damned Kov think I was something less than he expected. Here I believe something of my double-dealings in Havilfar came to me and, despite the lessons I had learned there, I admit I took a nastly little pleasure from the thought of fooling this Kov Lykon.

Now Gremivoh is a wine of Vallia much favored in the Vallian Air Service.

This Lykon, despite my manner, took the point.

45

"I would prefer a more subtle Pastale," he said, very—smooth.

I took that point, also. For Pastale—and I admit it is a reasonable vintage—is the export monopoly of the House of Operhalen, whose colors are blue, green, and ivory. And the Operhalens, a noble house of the enclave city of Zenicce, were at that time allied with the Ponthieu and against my own noble house of Strombor. The ruler of Operhalen was a little frog-like man with a stoop and a leer, and a reputation for inspecting his own consignments of Pastale too lovingly and too frequently.

This damned Lykon Crimahan would know I was Lord of Strombor and that the Operhalens would like to see me dead, so he asked for a glass of their Opaz-forsaken wine.

I smiled.

"Certainly, Kov. As it happens, I was able to board and take a ship of the Operhalens. Their wine is yours, freely given as it came to me, free."

Seg laughed and then turned away, drinking.

Tharu did not laugh, but his fierce old whiskers bristled up a little more.

The Emperor spoke and everyone stopped talking.

"We are here to discuss serious matters," he began. "I have said I am not happy with you, Dray Prescot, you whom I made Prince Majister. I would like an accounting of what you have done with the treasures we have poured out for you."

The damned old scoundrel! He'd lent me a parcel of fliers, which he had got back, and some of his Crimson Bowmen of Loh, almost all of whom he had got back. As for hard cash, that had been conspicuous by its absence.

I said, "You found your journey here pleasant, Emperor?"

He didn't like me calling him by title, and he knew I knew it.

"Yes, it was comfortable. The voller you presented me is a fine craft."

"It should be. It was taken by the Kov of Falinur and his friends from Hyrklana, and is a first-class voller."

"That is as may be. Where are the fliers you promised me? There was much fine talk, I remember," and here he waxed most sarcastic, "of bringing to us the secrets and the methods of the contraptions inside fliers. We should build our own, you promised me. Well, Dray Prescot? Where are these secrets?"

Mind you, the old devil had the right of it, for all that he overdramatized his part. I had signally failed to gain all I had dreamed of. But I did know a very great deal now.

"The wise men are still laboring to reproduce the silver boxes. For reasons I will not go into now, the full secrets did not come my way."

That was the signal for the dowager Kovneva Natyzha to thrust up her lower lip and let go one of her famous barking laughs, like the blow of an ax striking a tree.

"I warrant you do not wish to go into the reasons, Prince! I warrant you enjoyed yourself in Hamal."

I stared at her with a cool expression on my face, I hope, my eyebrows raised. This old biddy, this Vallia-renowned Natyzha Famphreon, the dowager Kovneva of Falkerdrin, was a noble woman with whom I had always tried not to cross swords. Her face held that nut-brown, cracker-barrel, experienced look of iron authority exercised over many seasons. Her mouth curved down at the corners, and grooves alongside her chin extended the arc. Her chin thrust forward so that her lower lip was habitually upthrust, giving her a scornful, arrogant look of power. She was well past her one hundred and fortieth year, I knew, and her face showed something of that, although on Kregen people change little from their coming of age to the time when they are battened down for the last journey to the Ice Floes of Sicce. But her body! She had pampered that body of hers, so that it remained firm and pliant, soft and supple. She was known to say that a man couldn't care less about a pretty face, but no man could stomach an ugly body. She was generally right about it, too, if many of the men surrounding the Emperor at this time counted.

She wore a bright red gingerish wig, which gave her a comical appearance as well as a great and horrific presence. In addition, her eyebrows, a fierce and wiry black, jagged upward like black wings over her dark eyes.

"You have heard of the Heavenly Mines?" I asked.

"Some stories," she said offhandedly. "Answer the Emperor. Where are the fliers and their secrets?"

"Yes," chipped in her son, the Kov of Falkerdrin. "Answer the Emperor." He was a product of bad breeding: chinless, weak-eyed, pimply faced. That was not his fault, of course, but the fault of near-incestuous parents greedily grasping each other in lust that did not consider the consequences. The result had made him a straw in the hands of his mother, who ran him and his official position as Pallan of the Armory.

Delia put a hand to her breast. She knew me. She half rose, and, on a breath, said, "You would not go back to the Heavenly Mines?"

"No one but a fool who wished to commit suicide in the most painful of ways would go back there."

The unspoken thought lay between us. She knew just how much of a fool, a true onker, I am in these matters.

The door opened and San Evold Scavander put his head in, his brown eyes mad and snapping, glee written all over his crusty old face.

"My Prince!" he tried to bellow, sneezed, and wiped his nose, gurgling with laughter. "My Prince! The cayferm is true cayferm! A residue is left—I do not know how. The boiling has been a success! Come, my Prince, and let us test the gift of Oolie Opaz."

I rose. "Then let us go to the laboratory," I said, not without a sneaky feeling of satisfaction. "And see if Opaz shines upon Vallia."

Chapter Five

Cayferm?

The vaol boxes and the paol boxes lay nearby.

I said, "Majister, if you would push this box toward this other box . . ."

He did so.

We all clustered around the scarred lenken table in Scavander's chemical-smelling room, where the wreckage of Lish's airboat, the silver boxes, and the supplies of minerals Ornol had brought were piled. Two new boxes awaited the imperial blessing.

A brass vessel still bubbled on a dying fire, and the sweet scent of squishes hung in the air. Samphron-oil lamps had been lighted, but through the high windows She of the Veils smiled in from the night sky of Kregen.

The Emperor, most tentatively, pushed one box toward the other.

They reached that particular distance from each other and they both sprang into the air!

We all let out our breaths. I was enchanted. Delia hugged me and everyone was one beaming smile.

The boxes rose straight up. They struck the ceiling among the cobwebs, parted, and so fell down again with a great clatter. Everyone laughed. I say everyone—even in my mood of great euphoria I noticed that Lykon and the dowager Kovneva Natyzha did not laugh, did not even smile.

"And this can be repeated?" asked the Emperor.

"Oh, yes, Majister," piped up Scavander. He wiped a hand across his forehead. "Indeed, it is a mere matter of—" And here he launched into a description which made me frown. It was recondite and extraordinarily complex, filled with arcane words, and made little sense even to me, who ought in the nature of things to have known what he was talking about. I felt the whisper of unease. The Emperor waved all that aside brusquely.

"Suffice it that my son-in-law has succeeded in his task. I will have sums set aside for the building of fliers. Indeed, if all we hear out of Hamal is half true, we shall have need of them."

"I do not believe it, Majister," spoke Kov Lykon. "I am not at all persuaded that Hamal means us mischief. Their quarrel is with the countries of Pandahem. And we of Vallia should welcome anyone who can ruin the Pandahem."

The growl of assent saddened me. Vallia and Pandahem were rivals on the outer oceans of Kregen. That rivalry seemed stupid, wasteful, and altogether ugly to me. I had friends in Bormack, a Kovnate of Tomboram, a kingdom in Pandahem.

"You may stake out a ponsho for a leem," I said, somewhat heavily. "That does not prevent the leem from eating you after he has finished the ponsho."

Seg at my elbow quaffed off his Gremivoh. I knew

what he was thinking: by the time the leem was halfway through crunching up the ponsho Seg's superb longbow would have feathered the devil of a leem like a pincushion. But they all took my meaning. I was finding the importance of talking at an oblique angle to the direct statement, in dealing with these people around the Emperor. As a one-time first lieutenant of a seventy-four on the oceans of Earth I had been used to belting out my orders and seeing that the hands jumped to it, or there'd be a few red-checked shirts at the gratings. Now, as I had discovered, the soft approach often worked better at this level of statecraft. Not that either Lykon Crimahan or Natyzha Famphreon much cared for the soft approach; they employed it in the same fashion I did.

These two eyed the Emperor. They no doubt fancied themselves laboring under the enormous disadvantage of not being related to the Emperor or his daughter, whereas I was the old devil's son-in-law. Little did they know of the true situation at that time if they thought my marriage to his daughter had softened him to me! He tolerated me —was indeed more than a little afraid of me, as I well knew—yet the affection he could give was stunted and could only flower where his grandchildren were involved.

There was a great deal of further conversation, in which I caught the anger against me more clearly than ever. The fact that I was a barbarian clansman from the Great Plains of Segesthes, as well as being Lord of Strombor, was held against me with as much venom as my marriage to the Emperor's daughter and my schemes to create friendship with Pandahem. Crimahan and the dowager Kovneva argued vehemently against squandering money on my crazy fliers. Since Hamal had begun her war against Pandahem they had refused to sell us vollers. Hyrklana was even selling vollers to Hamal. Queen Fahia of Hyrklana, that fat and evil lady, had trouble with her flier factories, and I knew there were men in Hyrklana who burned her manufactories and sought to topple her from the throne. Yet Hamal insisted she sell to them. No, we had to go on as I had planned. The only nit in the fleece was this puzzling attitude of San Evold. What in the name of Zair was he up to?

The answer came like a thunderbolt when I got him alone in the laboratory after all the others went back to the Chavonth Chamber to carry on the drinking and the discussions.

"My Prince! I am desolate!"

I saw—or thought I saw.

"You fixed it, Evold! The squish steam was not true cayferm so you used another silver box—a genuine one from Hamal!"

He shook his head, holding out his hands, palm up, and then he sneezed. Spluttering, he said, "Not so, Prince, not so."

"Well, spit it out, Evold!"

"When the steam condensed I began to wonder if the water could have anything to do with the secret at all. What was left in the box apart from water? Air!"

"Ordinary air, from this damned laboratory of yours."

He beckoned me over to an apparatus on a low lenken table.

Ornol, his assistant, hobbled in. Ornol had fallen into a Valkan canal and before they'd fished him out he'd drunk some of the canal water. He had not died, but he'd never be able to walk properly again. His left leg in some mysterious reaction to the poison in the canal water, had shrunk and become almost useless. Now Ornol, a cheerful fellow with a shock of lank yellow hair that was pulled back from his forehead and streamed down over his shoulders, limped forward and set up the amphora, boxes, and tubing.

"See, Prince! With this tube I draw off what was left in the box after the steam condensed. . . ."

I knew of this strange non-substance called vacuum, but I hesitated to mention it. I had an idea that the box would collapse, for it was of exceedingly thin metal, tinned, as I have said. I grunted and Evold went on, excited by his work.

"The next time I collected the steam in this amphora, inverted it, and drew off what was there through this pipe. It must, my Prince, be the true cayferm!"

In that he was wrong, but we were both engrossed now and so I sniffed. There was the scent of ripe squishes. He had been unable to get to me through all the ceremony and knowing the urgency of the work had gone ahead alone. I did not fault him in this. Instead I said, "So it does work!"

"Aye, my Prince. And yet there is a strange discrepancy in the action. It does not operate as the others do."

I heard a shout from the long hall of the images.

"Dray! The Emperor is waiting."

If I did not care for my skin, Seg Segutorio, the Kov of Falinur, most certainly did.

"Two murs, Seg, and I am with you." Then, to Evold: "Explain!"

"I have placed the new boxes in their correct positions in the orbits taken from a flier." These circles of sturmwood, their bearings of balass and bronze, revolved intricately and so carried the silver boxes into different aspects with each other. By these movements the upward and forward directions of the flier were controlled, as the backward and downward.

"Hurry!"

"Their reactions are different. There is no directional control. . . ."

I kept my face impassive. "You mean these boxes—*our* boxes—will only rise in the air? You cannot make them move forward?"

He nodded, and his lumpy nose glowed in the samphron-oil lamps' gleam. "That is so, my Prince."

"By the disgusting, worm-eaten kidneys of Makki-Grodno!" I was furious. All the work, all the pain, all the indignity—only to be rewarded with half the answer at the end!

"Very well. Have supplies made up. I will talk with Erdgar the Shipwright. We must change the plans again."

"But, my Prince—"

"*Dray!*"

"Do it, Evold!"

"Yes, my Prince."

I went out, my long white robe swirling, feeling thoroughly annoyed.

All my pretty schemes were falling in ruins around my head. There were a few farsighted men of Vallia who could see what the future portended, could understand that the insane ambitions of Queen Thyllis of Hamal would not be slaked when all of Pandahem lay under the sway of her iron legions. But for every such one there were a hundred, no, a thousand, who could not see. These proud men of Vallia put store in their great galleons, in the mercenaries their gold could buy. These men would never see—let alone acknowledge—that Vallia might be threatened by any other country or empire.

Now would not be the time to tell the Emperor the true situation. I would not tell him I could build fliers that would rise in the air but would not fly forward or backward!

Later, when I had him alone with Delia, then would be the time to broach the subject. Such were the powers of nepotism already swaying me. I have said earlier that nepotism in theory is loathsome, but in practice it often works. Without it and its concurrent corrupt practices of selection and advancement Nelson would never have risen to command at Trafalgar. That it had kept me as a mere lieutenant was the reverse of the coin.

The drinking and argument were well underway when I returned to the Chavonth Chamber, but my heart was not in them.

And now I must tell you of an occurrence which at the time struck me as singular, and the answer to which was not vouchsafed me for many a long season. I will keep the account brief. Suffice it to say that it began with Jiktar Exand informing me that he had unearthed a certain man who swore by Diproo the Nimble-Fingered.

Those of you who remember Nath the Thief from Zenicce, who had assisted my wonderful clansmen in the rain, and ever since swaggered a little as he remembered those golden days, will recall that Diproo the Nimble-Fingered was that saint or deity revered by the fraternity of thieves. Where there is portable property not chained down there will be thieves, I think, until the spirit in men is changed.

Here one must draw a distinction between those of the fraternity who pocket portable property and those who reive away a whole community and those who, like Korf Aighos of the Blue Mountains, look upon legitimate loot as their property anyway. So, excusing myself and telling Delia this was to do with the stikitches and to inform her father as discreetly as possible why I absented myself from his august presence, I went down with Jiktar Exand.

Seg Segutorio, the Kov of Falinur, accompanied me.

He, too, had not welcomed Erithor's rendering of *The Lament for Valinur Fallen*, although conceding the greatness of the song and its content, and notwithstanding that his Kovnate of Falinur lies in Vallia, whereas Valinur is a ruggedly beautiful area of northern Valka south of the stretch of ocean containing the Penal Islands. As well, further north, rises the island of Jynaratha where once I had been taken up in a blue radiance by the Scorpion, taken away from all this grandeur and pomp and power and brought to a proper understanding of my role on Kregen. And, too, north of Jynaratha lies the island of Zamra, of which I am Kov.

Trouble over slaves plagued me in Zamra; but that it a story for another time.

Expecting perhaps another Nath or Naghan, I went down with Exand to see the thief. He was a fat and oily fellow, all smiling and hand-washing, a far cry from the lean and hungry villain I had expected. He was no Nath or Naghan, either, being a soberly named Kornan, and very willing and lubricious with it.

What he had to say may be summed up as: Yes, there had been strangers in the city, frequenting the taverns and dopa dens, hard, edgy men, with faces scarred and seamed from experiences most men might shudder away from. In the taverns they had asked questions, mainly of the guards of the fortress. Some had given them dusty answers, carelessly, others had drunk enough to tell more than they should. Here Jiktar Exand swelled. His face turned that purplish plum color and I fancied later this Kornan would remember a few names and faces for Exand. Well, that was his province. I admit I felt an unease at the simplicity with which the guards of Valka had beel culled. The tavern at which these strangers had put up was named the Admiral Constanto and I halted Exand with a word as he prepared to storm off.

"Hold, Exand. There is more to tell yet."

"Aye, Prince," he said, with that sullen fury boiling away in him. I felt that since I had escaped with my life I could therefore scrape some comfort from the improvements in fortress discipline that would follow. My men of Valka are the very devil in a fight; this intrigue among simple swods came as altogether fresh. I did not blame Exand. But I would blame him if the same thing occurred again. This he knew.

"Old Naghan the Hook tried to dip one of these men," said Kornan. He belched and afterward covered his mouth with his hand, being in polite society. "They cut off his hand."

"I was not informed of this."

"No. The reasons would be obvious, Prince. Naghan the Hook prefers to take his chances with one flapper."

There were no names to be had. No, Kornan had never heard of any Traga. No, these men did not wear black, only decent Vallian buff. The thieves steered well clear of them, and the sequence of events was all too obvious. Seg said, "I will go down to this Admiral Constanto tavern and ferret them out."

"Aye," I said. "And tread carefully."

He went off, taking with him a party of guards clad in civilian clothes, a mere party of roisterers out for a night's airing. Kornan the Thief swallowed and licked his lips. "May I ask what—?" he began.

"No, Kornan," said I, very friendly and cheerful. "It is best for your state of health you do not ask."

His lubriciousness congealed a little, but he nodded and mumbled that he knew nothing, by Diproo the Nimble-Fingered. As soon as he spoke, he cursed himself.

And then, as we stood there by the lower guard gate, with the frowning walls of Esser Rarioch rising above and the watch fires burning, with all the stars of Kregen spread above and She of the Veils swimming in her golden haze, Kov Lykon descended the narrow stone steps to us. He walked with the dainty and yet heavy tread of authority picking its way. With him he had two Chail Sheom, poor girls scantily clad and in silver chains, after the debased fashion of Hamal or Hyrklana or any of those nations which feel a woman in chains gives pleasure to a man. I had spoken to the Emperor about this; he had merely replied that this had been a custom in the long ago and there were no laws of Vallia proscribing the custom.

With Lykon Crimahan and the two girls came down also a young Numim, very thick of arm and leg, very bull-like of neck, with the small round head of the fighter, dressed in leather clothes of supple cut. A rapier and dagger swung at his sides from golden chains. His nose was broken and set quite well, except that it lent his whole hard lion-face an aura of savageness much in keeping with his attitude of overweening pride.

"What goes on here, you cramphs?" demanded the Kov before he came fully into the torchlight, obviously before he had seen that I stood there, also.

"A mere matter of routine, Kov," said Jiktar Exand.

"A mere matter, eh? You all look confounded glum."

"Some business over a wench," said the thick-necked muscular young Numim, switching his rapier up. "The foul rasts waste their time instead of guarding us. I'd have them flogged jikaider, every last mother's son of them!"

This was Ortyg Handon, a young Jen* of Crimahan's retinue. We all knew what he was: a professional bully, a man kept to provide sport for the Kov, a man who delighted in thrashing other men who lacked his strength and his skill at arms. I had to tolerate him in my home for the sake of his Kov, who was high in the councils of my father-in-law.

Balass the Hawk, a hyr-kaidur, had marked this Handon and mentioned him to me with a few belittling words. I had had to say most sternly to Balass: "Do not cross swords with him, Balass! I don't want a corpse spouting blood over my carpets of Walfarg weave."

So Balass had kept out of his way, and I had given the word to my chamberlain, old Panshi, to pass along to Kov Lykon's chamberlain that the professional swaggerer, Ortyg Handon, must behave himself or else he would be guested in the dungeons for his visit here. I meant it, too.

I was about to step forward and make myself known when I saw a shadow cast in the pool of torchlight above the last step leading up from the great Kyro of the Tridents. A black, deformed shadow leaped the steps, and then a young man appeared, walking forward into the lights. I looked at him and felt a strange—a weird!—sensation in my throat. I had never seen him before. I knew this to be so and it was true. I did not know this young man.

But something about him—the way he held his head, the way his open, ruddy, handsome features broke into a genuine smile as he advanced, all the clean limber strength of him—caught at me. I was in shadow and I remained there, staring at the young man, feeling this uncanny sensation and not liking it one little bit.

"Lahal!" called the stranger in greeting. He wore a beard, which I thought heavy for him, and mustaches which jutted arrogantly above his upper lip. He wore a rapier and a dagger, and his clothes were clean although poor and patched, the decent Vallian buff. He wore sandals, not boots.

The effect of what I call his open and handsome features, as I have recounted it, was purely subjective. For he

---

*Jen: the usual word for *lord* in Vallia.

wore the usual Vallian hat with the wide brim and the two slots over the eyes. There were no feathers in the hat.

"Lahal," said Jiktar Exand, no doubt experiencing relief at this excuse not to talk further to the bully and rapier-rattler Handon.

"I have business in the fortress," said this young man.

"Your name?"

"I am called Zando—"

Before he could speak further Kov Lykon burst in with anger trembling his voice.

"We are talking about your dereliction of duty, Jiktar! Tell this scum to clear off before he is treated as his sort deserves."

Still I did not intervene. There are uses for lengths of rope if allowed to lie around.

"But my business is pressing," persisted Zando. His face, as I have indicated, lay mostly in the shadows of his hat and the beard concealed the rest; yet I clearly received the impression of a genuine smile. "I must speak with the Prince Majister."

"Ho!" said Exand. But he knew me and knew I would speak with anyone, given the correct procedures. "I think we have had enough of strangers seeking to speak to the Prince this day. Your business?" The last lashed out like a risslaca tongue.

"That I am not at liberty to reveal to any living soul but the Prince. But I can give you messages for him that will—"

"Enough!" Kov Lykon swaggered forward. His day had not been the best, for the Emperor had heeded my words on the Hamalian question and Lykon Crimahan still smarted. "Schtump, you cramph! Schtump before I have you flogged."

This young man Zando put his left hand to the pommel of his rapier. His back went up. Clearly he did not relish being thus addressed with *schtump*, which is a crude way of telling a fellow to take himself off, a word meaning hurry.

"I do not have the pleasure of your acquaintance," he said. "But I assure you, sir, I do not take pleasure in being addressed in quite that way."

Lykon gave a half-snarl and swung to his toady Handon.

"Unsheathe that blade of yours, Ortyg, and teach the cramph manners!"

"With the greatest of pleasures, Kov." Ortyg Handon stepped forward, sleek and feline like a leem, and drew his rapier and dagger with that slow languid grace of the professional Bladesman thirsting to draw blood.

Even as Ortyg Handon stepped forward, clearly about to take the utmost pleasure in killing this young man, the rapier and main-gauche appeared in a twinkling in the fists of Zando. I saw that draw, and I sucked in my breath.

"I cannot allow brawling here," protested Jiktar Exand.

Kov Lykon said, "Keep a still tongue in your head, rast. I shall deal with you later."

Kornan the Thief withdrew into the shadows, so near he almost touched me; his hoarse breathing rasped with his terror. If Exand wondered why I did not step forward, he knew enough about me to know I would never allow him to suffer unjustly at the hands of this popinjay from Vallia.

Young Zando spoke softly. "I do not wish the blood of any man upon my blades. Put your sword up, Koter, and let me be about my business."

"I shall cut you up first, you who call yourself Zando, and then I shall spit you through like a side of vosk!"

"I wish you all to witness that this is upon this man's head." Zando spoke firmly. Then, to Jiktar Exand, he said a few words that made the whole of Kregen spin about me, in a whirl of disbelief and impossibility:

"I would take it as an honor if you, Jiktar, would inform the Prince Majister that one called Zando wishes to speak to him. Say to the Prince, this Dray Prescot, say to him that I am a messenger from a Krozair brother who needs his assistance at this moment. Remember that, Jiktar, a Krozair of Zy."

Chapter Six

The mysterious Krozair

I, Dray Prescot, Lord of Strombor and Krozair of Zy—
I stood there like a loon. About to step forward, I saw
the quick and deadly glitter of the rapiers and the daggers as they crossed and clashed. If I stepped forward
now, I knew only too well what would happen. This
young Zando would put up his blades and that kleesh
of a Handon would spit him as he stood.

So I stood, with all the wild surmises hurtling about my
head. What an onker I am! I should never have allowed
this to go so far. Fully prepared to stop it at that moment,
I had been halted, stone cold halted, in my tracks by those
few quietly spoken words.

Only a few people of the most close relationship with
me—Delia and Seg, Inch, Turko, and Korf Aighos,
too, and some others who knew more than most about me
here in the island empire of Vallia—knew that I was a
Krozair of Zy. They did not fully comprehend what being a Krozair brother meant. Long and long had I yearned
to return to the inner sea, the Eye of the World, far away
on the western side of the continent of Turismond. But
quite apart from the long months of sailing, quite apart
from the awesome mountain ranges of the Stratemsk and
that hideous crack to the very bowels of the planet exud-
ing its noxious vapors, the Klackadrin, there had been no
time in my desperate adventurings for any return to be
possible.

So how could a stranger come walking out of the night
and talk about the Krozairs?

It could not be.

But he had said the words. And now he was hotly en-

59

gaged with a noted Bravo fighter, a Bladesman who would laugh as he skewered home his final thrust.

This Zando was not a Krozair. He had not used the words in speaking of those mystic and martial orders which would identify him as a Krozair and, if he wished, the order of which he was a brother and, further, if he so willed, the rank in that order he held. I was a mere Krozair; I was Pur Dray, not a Bold or any other of the adepts, yet to me, as you know, being a Krozair of Zy is the most important fact of my life on Kregen—apart from my Delia, my Delia of Delphond, my Delia of the Blue Mountains. I could only hold my passions and watch to see how quickly young Zando would dispose of this Handon.

He was not a Krozair, those superb fighting men who use the Krozair longsword with such uncanny skill. His rapier work was smooth and businesslike, economical, with many touches about the art that reminded of my own style. I watched and, like any fighting man, I became absorbed with the art and the skill as the blades screeched and rang, touched and parted. The torches flared down and the stars shone, and She of the Veils was joined by the Maiden with the Many Smiles, so that a bright and fuzzy, pinkish golden moonslight glowed down and gave all the light needed for the death of a man.

The fight was quick and deadly, very close. Handon began with cocksure swagger, confident that he had the measure of this youngster, for all his heavy beard. But soon Handon grew to understand that he faced a swordsman. The blades flung back the golden moonslight in drops of purest gold, and then those drops turned to drops of blood as Zando delicately sliced through Handon's guard and pierced his right wrist. The two daggers clashed and fell away, and Handon staggered back, cursing foully.

I stepped forward.

"Let this be a finish," I said. "Jiktar Exand, take the Diproo Nimble-Fingered man away and see him rewarded by ten talens. I shall ask him again, later, so let him keep his eyes and ears open." I turned to Handon. "You. Go up and have your wound attended to." I half turned to glance at Kov Lykon. "I think you overreach yourself, Kov. I command here. Go back to the Emperor and ponder well what you nearly accomplished."

"I go, Prince, and I shall ponder well."

Well, it was just about all he could say without having me knock him down on the instant.

Now I could speak to this Zando.

But he was staring at me with a look of sickly surprise on his face. I looked into his eyes, liquidly gleaming below the wide brim of his hat, and I thought I saw fear lurking there. Fear? I thought I must have misread him. He was pallidly white now above the beard, below the shadow.

"Dray Prescot!" he said. He breathed the words as though he did not believe them.

I took his arm. He shuddered at the touch. I led him up the stairs along the wall of Esser Rarioch and through a small postern then, by flang-infested stairways—for this was a private way to which only a few of my intimates had the key—we went up into a small study. There I flopped him down into a chair and poured him wine. I poured him the best Jholaix. He sipped, but he was over his panic and he looked up at me over the brim.

"You spoke of Krozairs," I said. "Krozairs of Zy. Tell me, Zando, what is a Krozair? What is a Krozair to you!"

"I bear a message from a Krozair brother. He is in some desperate straights. It is necessary, for the sake of your vows, that you supply him with arms, with money, with a voller."

I nodded. "All that I shall do, of course. But tell me of this Krozair brother—"

"I may not do that, Prince." He got the title out with a slight hesitation, as though playing a part. "It is an interdiction laid upon me. The Krozair said you would give me all I asked for, without questions."

"That is so," I said. I felt certain that this could be no confidence trick on a gargantuan scale. No stranger could possibly know of the connection I had with the Krozairs. He could scarcely know of them, although that was a possibility.

"So you will not tell me?"

He was over that fraught reaction, I thought, to the fight. "I may not do that, Dray."

I looked up quickly.

"That is—Dray Prescot, Prince Majister."

"Hum," I said. "Very well. You wish the supplies to-night?"

"As soon as is humanly possible."

I rang for Panshi and he slippered in, smiling, bringing

with him a fresh bottle of Jholaix. I said, "Panshi, give
this young man Zando all he requires. Do not stint." I
glanced over as Zando finished his glass at a gulp. He was
one relieved mysterious visitor. "As to vollers, you ask a
great deal. We have a need for every voller we can lay
out hands on."

We used the word *voller*, which is more generally heard
in Havilfar, although coming more into use in Vallia.

"I understand that. I may only ask of your goodness."

"Hum," I said again. I detested the procrastinating
word, but it served a purpose. I said to Panshi: "Have
Hikdar Vangar ti Valkanium turn out a first-quality flier.
The best we have. When he shouts that the order is impossible tell him I know he will shout and object, but that
the order is so."

Panshi bowed, put the bottle down, and went out. A
quiet, patient, knowing man, Panshi my chamberlain could
organize a twenty-course banquet in the fiercest typhoon
of the outer oceans, and bring on a theater production
to follow.

Zando laughed. He threw back his head and laughed.
"You ask all the right questions and behave exactly as I
knew you would. By Zair, Dray Prescot! I praise Opaz the
day I met you—"

"You swear by Zair," I said somewhat sharply. "And
you do well to thank Opaz for what I give you. You will
leave something of my treasury to me?"

"A thousand talens, I think, will suffice."

I took some pleasure in not allowing any expression to
cross my ugly old face, and so pique him, I thought, by
my lack of response. He merely chuckled.

"And Dray Prescot, your iron self-control is also pleas-
ing to me."

I knew he was mocking me, like so many of my friends,
and so I said, still in that sharp voice, "When you are
ready to take off let me know and—"

"I shall, with your permission, take the money and the
supplies and the voller and depart as soon as I may." He
stood up. "If you would have someone show me the
way . . . ?"

He was a cool customer, all right. I had him seen to
and then, on an impulse, I stretched out my hand to shake
his, in the wrist-gripping way favored over most of Vallia.
He hesitated. When at last he clasped hands I felt his arm

62

trembling. Then he said, "Rembereee, Dray Prescot. May Zair have you in his keeping."

"Rembereee, Zando. And tell your mysterious friend, this Krozair brother, that Krozair vows are to be kept." I then added a few words I did not think Zando would understand, words I knew would bring a grim smile of pleasure to the face of the Krozair. Then Zando was gone.

As I say, this whole little episode had been strange in the extreme and also a little unsettling. I went back to the Chavonth Chamber prepared to be unpleasant to Kov Lykon; the man had had the sense to take himself off to bed.

Chapter Seven

"I believe you are some kind of King of Djanduin."

The twin suns shone down magnificently as I walked out into that secret walled garden with Delia radiant and lovely at my side. There is much to tell of this period in Valka when I labored to prepare the Empire of Vallia to measure her strength against the Empire of Hamal; but I must press on, and indicate with only a few brush strokes the main outlines of the work. This garden was not the one in which we had been surprised by the stikitches. This garden, hung with flowers, shrubs, and trees, glowing, colorful, and odoriferous with perfume, with a pool in which Drak and Lela might push each other, was entirely surrounded by a high stone wall, creeper-covered on the inside but stark and bare on the outer. The door from the fortress of Esser Rarioch was of stout lenk, iron-barred and banded, and the keys were kept always with Delia or myself.

On the grass of this sunshine-filled day in which an

argenter of Pandahem was brought into the harbor as prize, I walked with Delia, talking of our plans. On that grass, starred with tiny yellow chremis flowers that Delia had not the heart to order mown, Drak and Lela played and romped with Kardo and Shara, the twin baby man-hounds.

Melow the Supple paced by our side. She was dressed now in a way befitting a devoted mother, with good Val-ka buff relieved by bright colors—for she was genuinely fond of all bright things after her life as a Manhound of Faol—and her yellow hair had been neatly coiffed and delicately scented. How strange to see a fearsome, fright-ful, unnatural manhound thus walking with us and even laughing at the antics of our children. Delia, with all that womanly virtue and that glorious compassion which made her delightful mockery so precious a facet of her char-acter, had welcomed Melow and her babies with coos of delight. Of course, the two baby jiklos, being manhounds and adapted to run on all fours, with snarling mouths filled with jagged teeth, developed very quickly. Drak would pummel and roll over and over fighting with Kardo, and the snarls, roars, and yells often brought a quick pang of apprehension; but through all their mutual scuf-flings it became clearer every day that my son Drak and the son of Melow the Supple, jikla, were growing into a close comradeship of love and affection. And the same was true of Lela and Shara, for together they did all the things little girls do—which for the most part are mys-teries to grim fighting men like me.

So, on this day, I kissed my Delia and ruffled Drak's hair and kissed Lela, and swung down the long ways to the habor.

Here the argenter rode at anchor, surrounded by guard boats as the prisoners and the booty were brought ashore. The argenter had been wounded in the action, her sides caved in by a massive rock flung from a catapult, and she needed attention. Broad, slow, and comfortable are the argenters of Pandahem. I had given my captains of Valka strict orders not to attack an argenter from Bor-mack, for that was the Kovnate of my friends Tilda and Pando. But this argenter came from Jholaix—glory be!—and was crammed with the finest wines imaginable.

Seg had had to return to his Kovnate of Falinur, and I admit I missed that feckless practical man immensely. So

I flung myself into the prepartions needful, and one such preparation was the acquisiton of information.

The captain of the argenter, a certain Captain Rordhan, a genial enough fellow with the bluff seafaring ways of Kregen making him a good drinking comrade, and yet, to our mutual folly, an enemy of Vallia, was happy to tell us all he knew. He had been on his way to the Chulik Islands loaded with the finest wine to pay for the hire of Chulik mercenaries. Well, the Emperor had sent off a convoy loaded with manufactured goods of Vallia and with a great treasure, to effect exactly the same thing. The price of mercenaries would rise on Kregen, that was for sure.

The argenter in the usual way had for topmen those agile long-limbed men of the Hoboling Islands, and I said to the captain of the maintop: "Well, dom, and are the pirates still at their trade, up along the Islands?"

"Yes, master, they are." He looked disgruntled.

"And have you heard of a certain Viridia the Render?"

"Indeed I have, master. She took a fine argenter on which my brother was captain of the foretop . . . sent him back naked with a demand for a sackful of dhems for the rest of the crew."

I stopped myself from laughing. It was good to know that Viridia still lived, even if she was still about her rending trade with all the old panache. They had been cut-and-thrust days, when I had sailed with Viridia the Render!

So I gave orders to treat the Pandahem kindly, and we went back up to Esser Rarioch. The Emperor and his closest advisers awaited us, and soon Captain Rordhan was telling us of the frightful gloom that had spread over all of Pandahem which had not already fallen to the iron legions of Hamal.

"The bloody Menahem," he said, shaking his head. We had given him a goblet of his own cargo, and he drank feelingly. "They assisted the Pandrite-forsaken devils of Hamal. The ships flew through the sky and the iron men marched. Tomboram is beset—"

I asked the inevitable question, but he shook his head.

"You may know all I know, Prince. There is little news out of Tomboram. As to Bormark, which I know a little, Pandrite alone knows what has happened to their Kov."

The upshot of this was that I worked my way a little closer to a scheme I wished to carry out at once. The building of ships in the yards of Valka and Vallia and all the other Kovnates and provinces of the Vallian Empire went ahead. I had told the Emperor of the difficulty, but had softened the blow by taking him up in the first vessel we had finished.

Later I will have to tell you of the exact construction of these new vessels, so that you may understand what we intended. For now I will content myself by saying that the Emperor was convinced that we must fight the Hamalians with whatever weapons the wisdom of Opaz placed in our hands.

"The news from Pandahem makes me believe you, Dray. This Captain Rordhan is a shaken man. The doom he sees ahead stinks in him."

"And it is now clear the Hamalians will leap from Pandahem once they have conquered the whole island. We are next."

Kov Lykon attempted to pooh-pooh the idea; but even he could not shake the beliefs we now saw to be true.

"No, Kov," said the Emperor in his authoritarian voice, so that men listened most carefully. "You have lost your cause, so plead no more, or else, perhaps, men will say you have been bribed by the Hamalians to strip us of our defenses."

I looked narrowly at Lykon Crimahan at this, but he dissembled well, and blustered and protested his innocence.

But I pondered the thought. It made sense.

Later, closeted alone with the Emperor in the samphron-oil lamps' gleam, we spoke long into the night. I told him of the plan I thought might give us a breathing space.

"What it boils down to, Majister, is that we must afford assistance to Tomboram. Even to Jholaix. When they go down there is nothing between us and the Hamalians."

"There is the sea, Dray! That has been our defense and our highway to fortune for generations."

"I have seen Hamalese skyships. They burned a great galleon of Vallia. They will burn all if we do not stop them short of Vallia herself."

He was a deeply worried man. Being emperor is fine when things go well, but things seldom go well, least of all on Kregen.

"Very well. You must draw up a list of the forces you

think proper. I will give you what I can. The newly hired Chuliks will not arrive in time. But we have a few thousand Pachaks, and they are redoubtable fighting men."

We talked more and then I said, "And the Crimson Bowmen of Loh?"

At this he hummed and hawed. The Crimson Bowmen of Loh were his own personal bodyguard, superb archers, mercenaries, a corps which had been completely reorganized by Seg and Dag Dagutorio after the shambles of the attempted coup by the third party and the battle at The Dragon's Bones. He propped a fist under his chin and gazed at me, holding the goblet of Jholaix in his other hand, so that it spilled a little on my carpet. I waited.

Presently he answered, "I gave you three thousand of my Crimson Bowmen when you fought for the Miglas against the Canops. I have yet to see any great reward for that."

We argued. I was taking as many men from Valka as I felt safe. I would not strip my island Stromnate of its fighting power, but here a strange and true phenomenon showed itself: any country which has gone through a recent war, in particular a civil war, produces skilled soldiers in great profusion. I probably had in Valka, which is not a particularly large island, as many first-class trained soldiers as in the rest of Vallia, which formerly relied on mercenaries for its land forces.

In the end we compromised and he let me have a thousand.

Only for their longbows would I prize them. I said, "Our foot soldiers cannot go up with true confidence against the Hamalians, with their shields and thraxters and their discipline."

He was surprised. "You thrashed the Canops on the field of the Crimson Missals."

"Archery did that. And we were lucky—make no mistake. The Hamalians will be in large numbers and they will have the benefit of a superb Air Service. They will have saddle flyers, also."

"There are these flutduins you had sent from Djanduin." He glanced up at me and, in the nasty way he more than half meant, peevishly said, "I believe you are some kind of king of Djanduin."

"As to the flutduins," I said, keeping my old mahogany features straight. "They are perhaps the best saddle flyers in all Havilfar. But we have less than a hundred couples.

The Hamalians will fill the sky with fluttrells and mirvols, aye, and some of the damned young fools will be flying zhyans."

"I know nothing of all these flying creatures—"

"But your army will!"

Well, from this you will see the obstinacy with which we both argued. In the end I scraped together a little army of some fifteen thousand. Small enough, when I recalled the regiments of Hamal, but it was a start. With this army then, and a welcome reinforcement from Djanduin—of which I *was* ruler!—we would sail for Pandahem and stand shoulder to shoulder with Pando, the Kov of Bormark, and deny those cramphs of Hamalians the springboard to Vallia their evil Queen Thyllis sought in her conquest of all Pandahem.

Before we left I decided that a little object lesson might not be lost upon the doughty warriors of Valka. As you know, the fighting men of Turismond and Segesthes, as of Pandahem and Vallia, consider the shield a coward's artifice, something behind which to hide in the heat of battle instead of striding out, rapier or clanxer or glaive flashing.

I said to Balass the Hawk as we paused in our strenuous leaping around in the tiny sandy arena we had erected for practice purposes: "Now, Balass. You saw how Ortyg Handon disposed of that poor onker Larghos the Unrequited yesterday?"

He nodded. "I watched with great interest, by Kaidun!"

Yesterday Ortyg Handon, still smarting from his handling by the mysterious Zando, had forced a quarrel on Larghos; that young man, well-named as the Unrequited, had responded to the challenge. Handon's wrist wound had mended under treatment. He had made a spectacle of Larghos, killing him with unnecessary messiness. Once the challenge had been given and accepted there lay no other recourse under the codes of honor and chivalry of Kregen save it be settled in blood. The Emperor might have stopped it, had he willed. But Larghos had been determined to rush upon death or honor.

So I asked Balass the Hawk, "Can you take him—with sword and shield?"

He nodded. He did not boast. Not in a matter of seriousness.

So it was arranged and two days later, out on the field

of Vorgar's Drinnik with the assembled fighters of Valka watching, the quarrel that had suddenly flared between Handon and Balass was to be settled. I admit I felt some disquiet. A rapier- and dagger-man, versus a sword-and-shield man. I knew *I* ought to win if I handled either set of equipment, but that meant nothing. Balass was a hyrkaidur. Handon was a Bravo fighter, a Bladesman. The contest held far more than the old question in its outcome, for if Balass failed my scheme would be ruined.

I remembered Vomanus, calling merrily as he fought against armored men, "They don't like it through their eyes!"

To make everything equal apart from the weapons, the two combatants wore no armor. Clad in breechclouts, they squared up to each other. Balass was used to fighting as a secutor. He carried the shield with which he had run out into the Jikhorkdun of Huringa, the capital of Hyrklana, when I had fought the boloth and my Delia had been chained with silver chains to the central stake to make a spectacle for the crowds. He hefted his thraxter, which was not the same weapon, being a specimen specially forged by Naghan the Gnat, of superb temper. The straight sword, despite its cunning and balance, looked heavy and clumsy beside Handon's slender rapier. But the main-gauche against a shield? Well, it all depends on the men using the weapons, when the Deldars are ranked.

I do not think it necessary for me to say that Balass wore a red breechclout. After all, we had fought for the ruby drang. Handon wore a white loincloth. I trusted it would show up the blood spots brightly.

Against the white of his loincloth Handon's golden Numim fur glowed and gleamed in the light of the suns. Balass' shining black skin and his red breechclout afforded to me, also, a touch of the contrasts I so much admire.

Balass, like me, was apim. Handon was Numim. This made no difference. Had there been a Rapa, say, or a Bleg, a Kataki, or a Chulik in this confrontation, my impulses would very easily, I am ashamed to admit, have leaned in the other direction.

Everything was done with propriety and the Emperor and his suite attended, for this had been turned into a gala festival. Kov Lykon was there, taking enormous bets on his man. I told Panshi to take what we could get on Balass. How this reminded me of the days of blades-manship in Ruathytu, capital of Hamal!

The Emperor nodded and Jiktar Exand, acting as mar-shal, dropped the scarlet scarf. Instantly Handon leaped with that ferocious feral snarl of the Numim, his golden mane blazing.

The unequal contest was beloved by the connoisseurs of the arena in Huringa in Hyrklana, and we had many times seen secutor pitted against rapier and dagger. I do not think Handon had.

Balass the Hawk was a wily old bird. He backtracked and his shield rang with the scraping thrusts and blows of the rapier. The rapier is your true cutting weapon as well as a thruster. So is the thraxter. Balass foined his man away. The main-gauche caught the thraxter, but then the curved shield smashed out like a battering ram and knocked the Numim a clear six feet away. Handon did not fall. But he snarled deep in his throat and took a fresh grip on his weapons. He came in again, weaving, feinting, aiming to thrust his longsword past that infuriating shield.

I could spare only half my interest on the fight. I must watch the faces of my fighting men of Valka. How their faces betrayed each moment of the fight! Of course, they were all for Balass. Wasn't he a blade comrade of their Strom? And wasn't this Handon a lackey of the popinjay Kov Lykon? Well, then! So they cheered and roared, and I watched them, trusting they were taking in the skills of the superb shieldman exhibited before them.

The fight might have gone on a long time, but Handon thought he had the mastery of the sword-and-shield com-bination. He feinted away, swirled his rapier overhand so that Balass' shield angled up to deflect and then—quick! oh, so quick! for the rapier is faster than the thraxter—the slender needle of steel whipped in like that risslaca tongue, whipped in to pierce high over the shield rim. Ba-lass took three quick steps backward and the rapier ripped free, dark blood staining three inches of its point.

"First blood!" called Jiktar Exand in a surly voice.

"To the death!" bawled Kov Lykon.

It seemed my comrade Balass would most certainly be slain before my eyes in the next few murs.

Chapter
Eight

*News of Pando
and Tilda*

Kov Lykon laughed in high glee. He jerked the silver chains binding his two Chail Cheom.

"There, my pretties! See the great Numim. And shall I set him on you tonight, to our mutual pleasure?"

They rattled their chains and emitted high false shrieks of pleasure, feigning love and affection for the man. I turned away. Chaining women up and threatening them are sports for things from under flat stones.

Many men say women enjoy this treatment and, of course, there is truth in this. But how do you judge the honesty of a girl's reactions? How do you know for sure that a girl means it when she says she pines to be chained and wishes only to be humiliated by her master, that she wishes only to be a slave? How can you tell? And, if in the end, you believe her and understand she thinks this is what she ought to do—she may even derive genuine pleasure from the humiliation, a supposed role between man and woman—then, perhaps, you ought to consider just how sick in the head she is.

So Kov Lykon maltreated his girls and laughed, and Handon bore in for the final killing thrust.

Balass still kept his shield up. His thraxter moved in that short deadly arc, a blurred upthrusting of steel, and Handon staggered back, screeching, his rapier and dagger falling from nerveless fingers, spraying his guts out from his ripped-apart stomach.

I relaxed. It had been a near thing, but Balass the Hawk was a true kaidur; he had fought in the arena and he knew what the taste of blood was all about.

Lykon looked abruptly defeated. The girls at the ends

of the chains were very quiet, anticipating unpleasant evenings for a long time ahead.

I walked across.

"Your boastful Numim is dead, Kov. I would like to buy these girls from you."

He looked at me, hot-eyed, but there was a haggardness about him. I think he was as well aware as any one of my freedom-fighters there, now creating an enormous hulla-baloo of triumph, that I myself had not fought because too much was known about the fighting habits of Dray Prescot, Lord of Strombor. Had I won no man would believe that it was because the shield is a powerful in-strument in battle. They would have put the victory down to my own prowess at arms. Now Balass had proved my point.

"Sell them?" Kov Lykon recollected himself. I did not know just how much he had bet. "Sell my little pretties?"

The two girls were looking at me as though I was either mad or of divine origin. That settled it in my mind. They were no voluntary slaves; they did not enjoy being chained up, humiliated, and expected to shrill, squeak, and feign enjoyment each time the master playfully tortured them with words or whip.

"You owe me the wagers, Kov. You owe me much money, for your Numim failed you. I will cancel the debt for the girls."

So that was how we arranged it, and I struck the chains off. Tilly, my gorgeous golden-furred Fristle fifi took them off to wash the sores, bathe them, and dress them in fine sensil and so decide their future as free women.

The very next day the army sailed for Pandahem.

Before I left I told Balass, most sternly, "He got over your shield, Balass! Careless. Although, I will admit, he was very good."

"Aye, Dray," said Balass. "He was good. *Was*."

I laughed. "And now you will train the coys—that is, these brave young fighting men of mine—train them to stand in line and use sword and shield, train them to stand against the iron men of Hamal."

"Such will be my pleasure. But I can only train them to fight. For tactics and drill—all these things—you will need a drill master."

"Yes. You train them to fight with shield and sword, or see how the glaive fits in. Tom ti Vulheim will pro-

72

vide the drill masters, and for the new drills we shall need . . . well, I'll have to think on that."

The truth was that I had already thought of this problem and had already reached a solution. I feel sure you will guess easily where I intended to obtain my drill masters in this new-fangled—to my blade comrades of Valka —mode of fighting.

Naghan Kholin Donamair was absolutely furious. His four fists beat the air. His eyes protruded. He was one enraged Djang.

"But, King! My flutduins are ready, the young Valkans trained—well, trained enough to give an account of themselves, by Zodjuin of the Silver Stux! And the chicks are hatching well, so the next generation is assured."

I shook my head. "I do not punish you by asking you to stay here, Naghan. Your task is great. We must build up a corps of flyers here in Valka. The flutduins are vital."

"But, my King! You go off to war and I do not go with you?"

"By Holy Djan himself! I ask this of you as a favor, for I know the agony you suffer. But if Hamal wins, if Vallia goes under, won't those cramphs of Hamal turn south through the Dawn Lands? How long will it be before they come knocking on the Mountains of Mirth? And do you think they will be sucked in as the Gorgrens were? Well, by Zodjuin of the Stormclouds, what do you think, Naghan Donamair?"

It just wasn't fair of me. I know that. These wonderful four-armed Djangs of mine have no heads for statecraft, strategy, and the intricacies of diplomacy. Give them a sword and a shield, a bow and a quiver of arrows, a joat or a flutduin, and they are the bravest fighters one could ask for. So I bamboozled poor Naghan, but I was right. His place was here, in Valka, training my aerial cavalry.

Saying goodbye to Delia came with the shock of abrupt agony.

She had said she was coming with me and had started rummaging out her leathers and the brave scarlet breechclout and sash. But I knew her condition would prevent her from joining me, as, of course, she knew herself. But, still, being Delia, she argued.

"And suppose the little fellow's born in the middle of a

73

battlefield, under a flap of canvas, with headless corpses all around?"

She laughed at me. She mocked me. "Oh, Dray, Dray! And don't you think that's just about the most fitting place a son of yours could be born?"

I was furious. "Delia! Anyone would think I liked wars and bloody battles—"

She was serious at once, those wonderful brown eyes warm and tender. "I know, dear heart. But your life has been hard, one of fighting—yes, all for very good reasons! And I think that long before Kregen is a fit world in which to bring up children, as you have so often told me, then he must learn to cope and fight as quickly as may be."

"But suppose he's a girl?"

"Suppose he's twins again?"

I sighed. "Well, Delia, my girl, you are not coming with me, and that is final. You'd best get Thelda for I know she loves you, even if she means well, poor soul." Here I did Seg's wife Thelda an injustice, and both Delia and I knew I only prattled on about yesterday. "And Inch, too. Time that long streak was married, anyway."

"I shall stay here, in Esser Rarioch."

I hummed and hawed, but I suppose she was right. Valka was now a real home to her, and she had many friends here.

"And Doctor Nath the Needle."

"Do not fret, dear heart!"

"Excellent advice that it is impossible to take!"

There was no question of my not going. Delia was the daughter of an Emperor and she would have looked at me rather strangely if I had said I was not going because she was to have a baby—or, as she lived on Kregen, the strong possibility of two babies.

"Turko the Shield will bear his great shield over you, so promise me you'll stay there, and not rush out like you always do!"

In giving her the promise I recollected that I might rush out anyway, forgetting in the heat of the moment. And she, the witch, understood that, too, for she said: "Well, I will not take your promise and lock it in my golden chest with a golden lock. But, Dray Prescot!" When she spoke like that it paid me to take heed. "Take care of yourself and come back with everything still attached to that body of yours! Do you hear?"

I kissed her most tenderly and said goodbye to the

twins, and everyone else. There were so many *remberees*
I was two long burs about it. Then I went down to the
galleon and so, at last, we set sail for Pandahem.

A number of high nobles and Pallans made a last-
minute attempt to halt the expedition. Led by Kov Lykon
and the dowager Kovneva Natyzha, they put forward
powerful arguments, the chief of which worried me. His
ran like this: "If we send a force to Pandahem to fight the
Hamalians, and they are not at war with us, won't this
enrage them, be tantamount to a declaration of war on
our part, and won't they then really determine to overthrow us?"

I had thought about this, and decided that the obvious
answer, "A Zorca shod today is a herd saved tomorrow,"
while being true, was not ample enough. We had to make
an attempt to stop the Hamalians at any risk—and I knew
the risk did not exist for it had already taken place.

One of the Emperor's council of the Presidio, a lean
tall man with a scarred face who talked little, one Nath
Ulverswan, the Kov of the Singing Forests, spoke and out
of surprise obtained all ears. "You do ill, Majister, in
allowing this headstrong son-in-law of yours to drag
honest Vallians to their deaths over the sea. We are a sea
people and we rely on our galleons. Buy mercenaries to
fight, in the old way." Then he ceased and sat down.
The Singing Forests extended for many kools just south
of the Mountains of the North in Vallia, and this Kov
Nath Ulverswan was a man rich among rich men.

I stood up and said, "Much of what Kov Nath says is
true. But times have changed. In any case, the expedition
will seem to be composed entirely of mercenaries. We will
not wear Vallian clothes or colors. We fight for pay, on
behalf of the Kov of Bormark. There should be no re-
percussions."

I had sought for this scheme and used it desperately.
But it was accepted, for the Emperor still wielded power
to push through this kind of measure against the opposition of his enemies in the Presidio.

So it was with much regret that I left my flag, that
yellow cross on a scarlet field, that battle flag fighting men
call "Old Superb," in the high hall of the fortress of Esser
Rarioch.

Instead we carried Pando's colors, the blue field
charged with the blazing golden form of the wild zhantil.

The same orders had been sent via voller messengers to

Ortyg Coper and Kytun Dorn—true comrades both—in far Djanduin. When my ferocious Djang warriors joined me with their flutduin regiments they, too, would fly the blue flag with the golden zhantil emblazoned at its center. I guessed that Ortyg Coper would run Djanduin in my absence, as its civil head, and Kytun would fly with his warriors to fight at my side.

I was not wrong.

Kytun Kholin Dorn, his coppery hair flowing as wildly as ever, his four arms wide in a gigantic embrace, leaped from the first voller to touch down at our camp in a small bay to the east of the northern coastline of Tomboram. We were not too many dwaburs west of Jholaix here, for the army of Hamal pressed ever on from the west, overrunning Pando's own Kovnate of Bormark.

"Dray! King!" He enfolded me in three of his bear-like arms and I tensed my gut. He punched me there, so I punched him back with fifty percent of my arms, and his seventy-five percent hugged me while the other twenty-five rat-a-tatted against my stomach. "Dray! King! By Holy Djan himself!"

Well, such is the temper of my Djangs. I fancied my Valkans would find themselves in the company of their peers, if not their superiors, when it came to drinking, brawling, and fighting. A four-armed man holds a tremendous advantage over us two-armed types, I fear.

The Pachaks, with their two left arms, hold many advantages, also, and I had high hopes for the regiments of those we had brought, too.

Soon messengers from Tomboram arrived. We had timed it nicely, Kytun complaining boisterously of the long haul here, all the way up from Djanduin in the southwest corner of Havilfar, along the South Lohvian Sea and, avoiding the Sea of Chem, striking inland northeastward over the Orange River and Ordsmot. From there they'd flown north, skirting the badlands and that area where no flier or flyer would voluntarily go. Here Kytun made a face.

"These damned fliers aren't what they used to be, Dray! In the old days, by Djondalar, fliers flew! This new rubbish we bought from Hamal breaks down all the time!"

"There is this war, Kytun," I said gently, "which is being fought in part over that matter."

"Then let us get to it, by Asshurphas! We lost two good vollers over in the badlands, and Kodun Myklemair was flying one of 'em, a fine lad, may the Curse of Rig strike those cramphs of Hamal!"

I expressed my regret. Although I did not know the young Djang personally, his name was that of an honored family.

Kytun had brought his men in a wide sweep to avoid the Hamalians in South Pandahem and so, curving to the northwest around between the Koroles and Astar, had driven swiftly across Tomboram here.

The messengers from King Nemo of Tomboram—for that fat greasy rast still sat on the throne here, for all he quaked in his high black boots and his black bar mustache quivered with the fury of his ferocious and petty nature—assumed a high and mighty air of importance. I held down my rage. I had dealt with their kind before. I said, "You will wait until the Kov of Bormark or his messengers arrive."

The chief of these messengers from King Nemo was a hard-faced man, bulky, in the flamboyant robes of his kind. He bristled up, his hand to his rapier. His face was covered with purplish spots, and his nose was a mere bloated purple cauliflower.

"I am Lart Mosno, Kov of Memberensis, and my Kovnate does not lie beneath the heel of the invader! The King commands—"

"I have had dealings with your King Nemo before," I told him, very brisk. "I let him inspect my dagger. But if you must prattle, Kov Lart, tell me what you know of Kov Pando."

He laughed, nastily, like a leem sneezing.

"Better ask his mother, Tilda the Fair!"

I took his neck between my fingers. I did not choke him, much. I let him breathe. His fellows gaped at the swords in the hands of my people, ringing them.

"We have come here to assist you in fighting the Hamalians. You had best keep a civil tongue in your head. I will ask you only once more: What of Kov Pando?"

He gobbled a little and spittle ran down. He managed to blurt out: "His army was broken and he was forced to flee. The King has put a price on his head for treachery. As for his mother, Tilda of the Many Veils . . ."

"Yes?"

"She . . ." He swallowed and avoided my eyes, which I allow must have been glaring and mad. I thought of what Inch had told me.

"She drinks," I said. "I know that. Speak!"

"Yes, yes! They are hiding somewhere, I hear! My neck! I beg you, put me down!"

I hadn't realized I was lifting him off his feet, his face a bright and brilliant purple, his neck white under my grasp. I set him down with a crash that jarred his teeth. He moaned.

"The dowager Kovneva Tilda is drunk all the time, and the Kov Pando Marsilus, Kov of Bormark, has no army, no wealth, no friends, and is under interdict! If the King catches him in his skulking place he will be executed, by royal order!"

Chapter Nine

The Battle of Tomor Peak

I shook this Kov Lart.

"You are mistaken, onker! Kov Pando has an army, friends, and wealth! For they are here, surrounding you with steel! And if King Nemo harms a hair of his head, or his mother's, I shall hang him from the highest spire in his own damned palace! Is that clear?"

Only after I had shouted so passionately did I stop to consider what my men thought of all this. For they had traveled far to arrive here. They had expected to be met by friends, by an army, by a hospitable Kov and Kings, ready to go with them in arms against the enemy.

Instead, they had been met with a tale of disaster, possibly a tale of treachery, for some might think I had lured them here, knowing the situation, intending merely to use them as bargaining pieces. Translation difficulties ensue here, for I cannot say they might think I used them as pawns, for the pawn in Jikaida is called the swod, and,

78

indeed, so very many of these wild fighting men were swods in real life.

So harsh truth trips up all the fine euphemisms!

Kytun had no hesitation.

He ripped out his djangir, that short broad sword which symbolizes so much of the warrior Djangs, and waved it aloft.

"We came here to fight, Dray Prescot, King of Djanduin! Lead us to the enemy and we will thrash them!"

As usual, Kytun had struck at just the right psychological moment. The clustered warriors took up the shout and the soldiers, although no doubt looking a little askance at this calling of their prince a king, joined in, and so the moment passed, as so many moments pass on Kregen, in a shining forest of upraised blades, and a mighty shout of these men of mine to lead them on to the enemy.

So, complying with the wishes of my army, I shook this Kov Lart Mosno again.

"Where is Kov Pando hiding?"

"If I knew that, I would have had him dragged out by the heels."

"But you would not do such a foolish thing now, would you?"

He saw my face. "No, no I would not."

Turko the Shield, at my left side, half a pace in the rear, stepped forward. He put his handsome face up against Mosno's.

"You address the Prince Majister as Majister, nulsh!"

And Kytun, also outraged, stepped up and boomed, "You address the King as Majister, nidge!"

I kept my face iron-hard. As you know, titles mean nothing to me—except my being a Krozair of Zy, and that is not a title, anyway—but I did feel some relief that Turko had not bellowed that this quaking Kov should call me Prince, while Kytun had boomed that he should call me King.

I did not relish the set-to which would follow that little contretemps.

"Majister," said this miserable wight. I would not allow myself to feel sorry for him. "The last report from the King's scouts said he was hiding with the remnants of his army." He swallowed and choked a little.

I set him on his feet more firmly, patted his ornate uniform front in a mock cleaning-up way, smoothed a strand of hair from his gilt-encrusted shoulder. "Now take your time, Kov. Just think. And tell me."

"Yes, Majister." His eyes were unfocused and he was sweating. Probably he had never before been in such close proximity to such a gang of rascals as surrounded us now. And the chiefest rogue of all was myself.

"In the woods south of Tomor Peak. Yes, Majister. He must be hiding there for the enemy has sent a force to cut off what is left of the army of Bormark."

"You mean," I said, outraged, "that your miserable cramph of a King Nemo let Pando and his army fight alone?"

"It was the policy, Majister."

This was no time for furthering bickering. "How many in this force?"

He licked his lips. "We estimate at least twenty thousand."

I felt relief and I felt alarm. My warriors could surely overcome a force only this much stronger than they were, but now the fight would be against the iron legions of Hamal.

The effect of my demonstration with Balass the Hawk and Handon might strike shrewdly now. Not all of my men had witnessed that—a deliberate stratagem on my part—and most of these witnesses remained in Valka and were training a little more willingly with sword and shield. But enough here had seen . . .

There was no sense in saddling a fluttrell before you catch him, so I set at once about organizing the order of march.

I shouted so that as many men as possible might hear.

"We need a guide. The Kov Lart of Mamberensis knows the country and the whereabouts of the enemy! He volunteers to be our guide!"

Kov Lart sputtered. "But, Majister, I must return to the King and report!"

"Oh," I said. "He'll find out in due course, I have no doubt."

So we ended on a jest and could ready for the march in good spirits.

Belying the jest, however, I told one of Kov Lart's retinue to take a message to King Nemo. He was to come with forces to the woods south of Tomor Peak and be ready to fight Hamalese troops. I had little faith he would turn up; and if he did he might very well fight us over the question of Pando.

The main army of Hamal, meanwhile, still lay to the west, being held in play by an army consisting of the remnants escaped from those Pandahem countries already overrun, together with the main forces of King Nemo. If we were off on a sideshow it was a sideshow commensurate with our strength, and the taking out of twenty thousand men would surely embarrass the generals of Hamal. I thought of the Hamalian Kov Pereth, the Pallan of the Northern Front. He had been appointed during the time of my spying mission in Hamal; perhaps by now the intrigues within Queen Thyllis' court had deposed him and set up a fresh commander.

So we set off. We had a considerable quantity of baggage, mostly warlike stores. Of provisions we had only iron rations, for I fully intended my men to live off the country. They would do this anyway, even if the commissariat could give them roast vosk, taylynes, momolams and looshas pudding every day, followed by miscils and palines. All the infantry we could we crammed onto the baggage carts. The patient quoffas with their long faces and their hearth-rug appearance did not complain but sturdily hauled the creaking carts. The transports of Vallia had been designed well, massive craft nearer superior argenters than galleons. We did not lack for cavalry, and our aerial cavalry was the best, I had now persuaded myself, in all Havilfar.

The new regimental system of organization appeared to be working well, and the Jiktars knew they would have to face me if they fouled up. So we plodded along the country roads of Tomboram, heading south, and on the third day the country grew wilder of aspect, with mountains rising in the distance. On the fourth day we passed the site of a battle, most distressing, with corpses in grotesque attitudes, broken weapons and drums, tattered banners. I saw the blue flag and the golden zhantil there, as well as the purple and gold of Hamal, and I pondered. Whoever had fought here had retired swiftly after the defeat, and the victors had followed up with equal rapidity.

Flutduin patrols had not yet reported the presence of any enemy. I kept the voller force close. We marched on.

The mountains proved troublesome, but we found local guides only too pleased to show us the easiest ways through the passes, the hatred of Hamal evident in their vigor when they saw our banners and realized we fought for Tomboram. Down on the southern side we debouched from the last pass below Tomor Peak. Stones rattled under the hooves of the nikvoves, zorcas, and totrixes, and under the stout marching boots of the men. The quoffas trundled along and the carts creaked and protested. The men sang.

Before us stretched a wide plain, much forested, with the wink and glitter of watercourses. Interesting country to plan a battle. We marched on and the flutduin patrols came in with negative reports until, at last, one returned with news that he had spied a military encampment far off. Obeying my instructions, he had returned immediately.

So I took flight astride a flutduin, with Kytun and an escort, and we flew into the eyes of the suns, turned and came down to survey the camp.

Laid out neatly, as was to be expected of the Hamalians, the camp could contain the twenty thousand men reputed to be in the force facing us. I studied and made notes against the wind rush, then we turned and, undetected, returned to our own camp. I felt some pleasure as we touched down in a flurry of wings.

"We can take them, Dray," said Kytun. He removed his flying helmet with one hand, unlaced his leathers with another, took up a goblet of wine with the third, and reached for a camp chair with the fourth. That kind of behavior always made me blink.

"Yes, Kytun. But no mad chunkrah rush for us!"

"They have vollers."

"But not as many as I had expected. There must be scouts out, so we must have a patrol aloft at all times. But, still, remember this is a flank-force of the main army only, finishing up its business with Pando's army." I sighed. "Poor Pando! He needed a touch of a father's hand—a not so gentle hand—when he was young."

Pando, that young imp of Sicce, would be almost full grown now. I wondered if he would remember me. I thought he would, but you could never tell. As for Tilda the Beautiful, his mother, she'd remember . . . if she was sober. That, in absolute truth, was a tragedy.

We ate scanty rations that night, for the country had been poor, inevitably, through the mountains. Out on the plains we could find deer and fruits, and life would perk up. We marched at night, too, at a steady pace I had instituted as a regulation pace, not to be deviated from unless ordered, and we covered the ground steadily if not rapidly.

We were not observed, I felt reasonably sure, in the light of She of the Veils. The Twins came up after midnight and the Maiden with the Many Smiles only just before dawn. The three lesser moons of Kregen hurtled frantically across the sky, close to the ground, but the totality of light gave our wide-ranging patrols opportunity enough of counter-observing any Hamalese scouts.

Just before the Suns of Scorpio were due to rise we marched up to an extensive forest area, scouted and clear, so we could enter in among the trees to bivouac. Fires were lit under the strictest control, Hikdars being appointed to the task to ensure that no betraying smoke wafted away. I rested for a whik and then rode Snowy through the lanes between the trees to the forest's southern edge. For a long time I sat there looking out. One more night's march, I thought, and we would be in position to spring.

The day passed peacefully. The men saw to their weapons, animals, and vollers. This very quietness seduced a man. Tomorrow, with the dawn, we would turn into a pack of ravening beasts, seeking to slay and go on slaying before we were slain in our turn. Many thoughts thronged my brain, but of them all only the image of Delia rode with me, constantly. Only after her could I think of the strangeness of my life, of how I had been caught up out of humdrum nothingness on Earth to be transported four hundred light-years through space, to joy in the exhilaration of Kregen, to love and to battle—aye! and to hate!— on the surface of this wild and beautiful, lovely and horrible world of Kregen under Antares.

That night we left all unnecessary impedimenta in the camp among the trees. Stripped for action, with carts loaded with shafts to follow, we marched out under the moons of Kregen.

Pinkish moonlight showed us the way. We marched silently. Not a weapon chingled, not a man spoke. Direction was maintained by stellar navigation, and Jiktars marked the ends of our lines. A great ghostly array of men, marching on, timed to strike just as dawn broke in a blaze of emerald and crimson, we marched across the face of Kregen . . . and who of all those thousands could guess the man who led them had been born under the light of another sun—a single sun!

Kytun rode his zorca next to mine. He leaned over and his whisper reached me, harsh in the night:

"We are late, Dray! The Twins are already up!"

"The ground is softer here. It makes for heavier going for the infantry."

Then, to compound our troubles, a merker astride his fluttclepper flew swiftly in from the moonshot darkness landing with a great rustling. He alighted and ran swiftly across, to pace my zorca and so stare up, troubled of face.

"Well, Chan of the Wings?"

"We are observed, King. A voller—very fast—curved sharply away. He must have seen us." This Chan of the Wings was a most important man in a king's retinue, a man of secrets. "There was nothing we could do."

"Thank you, Chan of the Wings." This was the man who had first openly raised the call of "Notor Prescot, King of Djanduin!" With the Pallan Coper and Kytun, and the others with me in that old struggle to refashion Djanduin, Chan of the Wings had been an important man in banishing the phantom of Khokkak the Meddler from my scheming brain.

Well, my brain had been idle and shiftless then, even if full of careless schemes; now it must be filled with purpose, or my valiant warriors from Vallia and Djanduin were doomed.

And then a more sensible thought occurred to me as we advanced through the moon-drenched shadows. To attack a camp, a fortified camp at that, against superior numbers had not appealed to me. If we had been observed and our numbers counted, maybe the overconfident Hamalians would march out to confront us. We could bring our entire force to bear on one face of the camp, against locally inferior numbers. If the whole Hamalese force marched out, they could form their superior numbers in the old wing formation, to encircle and crush us. I perked up. Maybe this was not so disastrous a happening, after all.

From this last apparently paradoxical thought you will gather just how much reliance I placed in my thousand Bowmen of Loh, my half-thousand Valkan Longbowmen and the remainder of my Valkan Archers.

One day, I had vowed, there would be no difference between a Valkan Longbowman and a Valkan Archer, for everyone—except for a few reserved for fortress and aerial work—would use the great longbow.

So we marched on and I did not give the order to increase our speed to the full pace. The regulation pace would bring us to the spot I had selected in good time. The rising suns would shine obliquely down over our left shoulders. I grunted at Kytun to continue the march, then swung Snowy to canter off down the ranks just to reassure myself.

This little army was not the army I had promised myself I would one day create on Kregen. But we were a fine bunch, and a wildly mixed bunch, too. There were the Archers, there were the Chuliks, the Pachaks, a group of Rapas and another of Fristles—not marching together. There were the corps of cavalry, the zorcamen for recce work and the heavier warriors astride their nikvoves for the crunching shoulder-to-shoulder charge. I heard the creak of leather and the breathing of the men and animals as we pressed on. I pondered this little army. The Pachaks carried their shields on their two left arms. Because the Chuliks from the Chulik Islands southeast of Balintol are trained from near birth to fight with any weapons and use those of the master who hires them, these Chuliks carried rapiers, daggers, and glaives. There had just not been any shields in Vallia for their equipment. Trained to be mercenaries on their islands, the Chuliks were also trained in the same old ways in their own places of the Eye of the World. It is difficult, perhaps, to remember that if ordinary men and women called apims may live on the face of Kregen in ignorance that others of their kind live on other continents, the same is true of all the diffs also. Only a diff, Bleg, Numim, Chulik, or Rapa, would call himself ordinary, and we apims would be the halflings to him.

At the rear of the column tailed the baggage carts loaded with shafts and bolts for the varters. These trundled along on carriages drawn by teams of four totrixes, and there were far too miserably few of them for any well-balanced army. But I must make do with what I had. The varters would spit their venom when the time came.

When the dawn broke and the whole plain lit up with the fires of Antares, the green of grass and tree breaking into splendid color, the sky paling through all those marvelous changes of radiance, I halted the army and we rested for a while. Now was the time for those last-minute preparations: the rapier clean and easy in the scabbard, the main-gauche to hand, the Jiktar and the Hikdar. The glaive firmly socketed, the ash stave true and ungreasy. The helmet sitting well on the forehead, so that the brim did not tip up nor yet dip down over the eyes. The corselet not constricting the free play of the arms. And, in the case of those with this despised article, the shield fair and ready, resting on its grips. And, finally, the last check to make sure the high-laced marching boots with their studded soles were tightly secured, ready to afford that vital security of grip on the earth—this earth that was not my Earth but the wonderful world of Kregen.

Turko the Shield gently rode his zorca over as the men began to rise and stretch and take up their arms to move out to their appointed places. The light grew stronger mur by mur, and our twinned shadows stretched long.

"You will ride Stormcloud, Dray?"

"Later, I think. I'll need to be here and there at the beginning, so Snowy will be better."

"I'll tell Xarmon." Xarmon was the groom I had brought, a man from Xuntal like Balass the Hawk, a man who loved zorcas and nikvoves. He even liked totrixes, which proved his love of the steeds of Kregen.

I would not fly a flutduin, despite the advantages of aerial observation, because of the disadvantages of being cut off from the giving of immediately obeyed orders and also because I did not wish to deprive the fighting air cavalry of a single mount. The air smelled crisp and sweet, a tiny breeze started up, which all the bowmen would feel in their bones.

Some people say that one battle is much like another and I suppose if you are in the ranks and it is all a red mist of cutting, thrusting, and bashing on—or running—then there is truth in this. But no two battles are really alike. There is always some factor that gives each battle its individual flavor. I think this battle, which became known as the Battle of Tomor Peak, was marked by the first full realization by my Valkans of the power of the shield in battles of this nature.

Tom ti Vulheim, who had fought with me in the Battle of the Crimson Missals, gave orders similar to the ones I had given then. But now we had pitifully few shieldmen. The Pachaks must not fail us. They strung out in the first ranks, grim, hard men, among the most intensely loyal of all the mercenary warriors of Kregen. They held their shields high in their two left hands, their single right hands gripping thraxters or spears; their tail hands, flicking evilly this way and that or shooting diabolically between their legs, grasped bladed steel. The archers formed their battle wedges. The rapier and dagger men lined out, ready to drive in when the first gaps appeared and, like sensible fellows, they would use their glaives until the stout ash shafts broke.

Over all, the aerial patrols curved against the sky. Up there the first important maneuvers would be carried out. I cocked my head up. Then I looked to the wings where the zorca and nikvove cavalry waited, their lances all aligned, the brave blue pennons flying. We did not wear Vallian buff, but the blue of Pandahem: blue shirts and tunics hastily sewn up for us by the sempstresses of Vallia. We still wore buff Valkan breeches and boots, or buff breechclouts held by broad belts with dependent bronze and leather pteruges, and high-thonged military boots. But I admit I took little comfort that we did not fight in scarlet and that my own flag, Old Superb, did not fly above us.

The Hamalians lined up, ready for us.

They made a brave showing. I studied them, watching how they formed, judging their efficiency, even their morale, by the way they marched into position. Already, even as the final preparations were made in this earliest of light, the flyers clashed. The aerial fighting swirled this way and that, each side attempting to break through above the opposing army and shower down their shafts. And each side sought to throw back the hostile waves of screeching fighting men of the air.

I felt that Kytun had the thrashing of the Hamalians, and the few vollers we had could hold their own against the vollers of Hamal, for this flank force was not overly well supplied with air power. I guessed Kov Pereth, the Pallan of the Northern Front, kept the majority of his air for his own use with the main army. But, make no mistake, although this may have been a sideshow, it was a most grim and bloody affair.

The armies clashed in a first flowering of shafts. Crossbow bolts rose from the massed ranks of the enemy, and our shafts cut the air in reply. The sheer mass of the enemy meant we could not halt them, as we had halted the Canops, by an overwhelming deluge of arrows. But even so the superior rate of discharge of the longbows and the compound bows more than compensated for our inferiority of numbers.

I had checked every point. We had successfully kept the air above us clear. The cavalry waited for the orders to charge. I positioned myself in the center, astride Snowy, and Turko hovered at my side, his shield ready. With his superb Khamorro skills and muscular control, he could pick up the flight of a shaft and take it out of the air with a casual-seeming flick of the shield. This meant that I could concentrate on the battle instead of constantly watching for the shaft that would slay me.

Kytun had done wonders. We were able to shoot coolly and methodically. When it came to hand strokes, the shield walls of the Hamalese brigades held firmly at first, but the longbows tore huge gaps in their ranks, which immediately closed up, only to be ripped apart again. The Pachaks and the Chuliks roared into action, thirsting not only to earn their pay but also for glory to be won, the possible achievement of the honor of being dubbed *paktun*. The armies clashed along the center, and I saw the Hamalese wings begin their circling movement.

"Hanitch! Hanitch!" screeched the soldiers of Hamal, iron men advancing in their might, yelling their war cries. "Hanitch! Hamal!"

I marked a regiment with flowing colors born on ahead, standards larger than those of the other regiments of infantry, colors that glowed with purple and gold, and so knew them for an imperial regiment dedicated to Queen Thyllis. Above the closer yells and screams I heard this regiment's deep-toned yells: "Hanitch! Thyllis! Thyllis! Hanitch!"

My men responded with yells, too, and among all the shouts for "Bormark!" and "Tomboram!" I heard the old familiar cries. When men march forward into battle, their weapons in their fists, their heads down, and their helmets clanging with the steel tips of the birds of war, they tend to forget subterfuges and shout out what they are accustomed to yelling. "Vallia! Vallia!" they bellowed. "Valka! Valka!" And, of course, "Dray Prescot!"

Most of the mercenaries managed to remember to shout for Bormark and Tomboram.

Just as I marked that arrogant purple and gold regiment yelling for Queen Thyllis, I saw Tom ti Vulheim ride out astride a zorca, waving his sword in command. His men released their shafts in a superb display of controlled shooting. I thought Seg would have gained pleasure from that sight. Queen Thyllis' regiment shrank. The crossbow bolts came back, hard and lethally, but as the armies clashed with the iron clangor of hand-to-hand combat I saw with great satisfaction that, indeed, the superior rate of discharge and the longer range of the longbows had once again played their part.

Dust rose as thousands of booted feet stamped in the throes of conflict. Thraxter and shield clashed with glaive, or with sword and shield. My rapier men fought like leems, sliding in and out, not holding firm ranks but using their mobility and individual skills to the utmost, exploiting the gaps torn by the bowmen. The battle swayed. I surveyed the field and, as always, keyed up to that kind of pitch in which every detail limns clear, and yet the whole is one vast blur of action. Soon the climax would come, soon I must make the decision. Too soon and disaster; too late and disaster.

The noise spurted high into the glowing air. A flight of mirvols swooped over the struggle, their riders attempting to shoot down, and a savage flight of flutduins followed them, mercilessly feathering them from the air. Men reeled from the fight, torn and bloodied. The noise grew to a prodigious long, drawn-out howl. And still those Hamalese cavalry wings circled around us, not drawing in yet, biding their time.

"Xarmon," I said. "I will ride Stormcloud now."

"Here, Majister."

I hopped off Snowy with a pat to his sleek white neck and took a grip on the harness of Stormcloud. He was a splendid steed. He was not a vove—one of those glorious russet mounts of the Great Plains of Segesthes, chargers full of fire and spirit, all horns and fangs and pumping hearts that would never surrender save in death. Stormcloud was a glossy black nikvove, a half-vove, smaller than a true vove and without the fangs and horns. But he did have the eight legs of the vove and a loyal heart; he was a king's steed for any man.

Delia had given me a rich set of trappings for Stormcloud over the schabracque of zhantil skin, and first-quality lesten hide studded with bronze and scarrons. The rich gleam of the bronze and the brilliant sparkle of the scarlet scarrons, all matched and perfect, against that jet coat made an inspiring and martial picture.

I saw the high polish on my black boot as I stuck it into

the stirrup, and I saw a little ant crawling there. I mounted up and sat firmly, and I let the ant take his chances on my boot. He and I, would ride together today.

Any general must have a corps of aides and messengers. To young Nath Byant, who was an Elten in his own right, his father being a Trylon of Vallia, I said: "To Chuktar Erling. My compliments. He may begin his advance. Tell him from me, may Opaz ride with him and all his men this day."

Elten Nath Byant, who rode as an aide out of sheer zest for adventure, bashed his right arm across his breast-plate in salute, yelled, his voice rather shrill, "At once, my Prince!" and was off like a shaft from a Lohvian longbow astride his zorca. The left-hand squadrons would commence their charge at the vital moment, led by Chuktar Erling.

Turko had mounted up astride his nikvove. Also riding closer on a nikvove was Planath Pe-Na, my personal standard-bearer who had been with me since the affair of the Burned Man at Twin Forks.* Planath, being a Pachak, could carry the standard and also swing a mean sword at the same time. As for the standard—as I say, the old scarlet and yellow remained at home in Esser Rarioch. I rode beneath a confection of blue, green, and crimson with a great deal of gold bullion for tassels. It was a gaudy object, but it would serve its purpose and identify my position in the field. As for the great flag of Bormark, that was carried into action alongside my own color by a specially selected Hikdar from the regiments. The honor he achieved was great. These are high and serious matters in any army which fights hand to hand.

The chief of the corps of trumpeters was now Kodar ti Vakkansmot, for old Naghan had contracted an eye infection and had been unable to march with us. Kodar had been with me at the Battle of the Crimson Missals.

So it remained only to don the Mask of Recognition.

Xarmon handed the blazing golden mask up. I fitted it in place beneath my helmet brim, covering my features, the sights and breaths less than adequate but providing a discomfort I would have to put up with. This great mask

---

Nikvove. The word *nik*, when used as a prefix seems to mean *half*. When used as a suffix it carries a more general meaning of *small* or *diminutive*. I believe this to be a correct interpretation of Prescot's use of the word. As for Planath Pe-Na, the Pachak, and the affair of the Burned Man at Twin Forks, this is lost.   A.B.A.

might afford some slight protection against a shaft; I tended to doubt that. Its main function was to make me instantly recognizable to my men. An auxiliary function and one which I valued was to conceal my features from those who did not know me.

All these preparations assumed a heightened significance.

The tall and heavy lance with its golden pennon slanted in the rays of the Suns of Scorpio. I said, the words booming and hollow: "We ride to victory. Opaz is with us."

"Aye," said Turko, with that mockery clearly evident. "And you stay close to my shield. I have made a promise."

No need to ask who had taken that promise willingly given.

We wheeled to the right. The right-hand squadrons of nikvove cavalry saw me riding to lead them and let rip an enormous cheer. This heartened me. I pointed at the enemy cavalry, at the junction with the infantry flank about to come into action against our right flank consisting of Rapas. The enemy clearly intended to roll us up from the right, and yet his left wing cavalry persisted in advancing against us. Either the general in command was a goodly way off, was a fool, or was dead. I did not think he was either of the first two, and so that cheered me up no end.

"Forward!" I shouted. My voice clanged resonantly. "Follow me!"

This is no way for a general to behave in a battle. I know.

The only regret I had as we smashed in a mighty avalanche of flesh and blood and steel into the roaring racket of the charge was that my own flag, Old Superb, did not wave over me and I did not wear the old brave scarlet.

I saw two regiments of Hamalese cavalry—they were zorcas, a crime in itself—haul out to face us and we went through them as—to say like a hot knife through butter is to give no adequate picture. For the poor zorcas simply sprayed away from our charge, like chips ripping from a buzz saw. We smashed on with such thorough ground-shaking power that we scarcely noticed the zorcamen. They bounced and were whiffed away.

Beyond them three regiments of totrixes attempted to stand. For a space their courage held and a wild excitement of whirling brands and piercing lances ensued;

then they broke and we roared on, unstoppable. And we rode only nikvoves!

My men followed me as we carried out the tricky operation of changing front in a charge. The angle was not great, a mere partial wheel to the left, and it was carried out to perfection. We hit the Hamalese infantry in their left flank and we began to roll them up as the furniture men roll up a stair carpet.

That proved the turning point of the battle.

The moment chosen was the correct one. An earlier charge would have exposed us to the crossbow bolts of unbroken infantry—a prospect to send shudders down any cavalryman's spine—and against uncommitted cavalry. A later charge would just have been too late. Our left wing also enjoyed success and then—then—it was the turn of the zorcamen to go in and pile on the agony in the flying pursuit, not allowing infantry to reform and stand, catching stragglers, routing any and everything Hamalese that had fought on the field of Tomor Peak.

The rest of the day was administration, that and the caring for the wounded and the burying of the dead. We had lost men, good men; but the Hamalese force had ceased to exist.

One indispensable part of the aftermath was the herding of the prisoners into stockades built from their own ripped-apart camp fortifications. That and the recognition of bravery by my men, the awards of the medals I had instituted, the battlefield promotions, the gifts and the congratulations. Over the moans of the dying rose the fierce battle songs. Oh, we cared for the wounded, friend and foe alike, for I would have it no other way; but my men knew what we had accomplished, and we were still an intact force, ready to turn and join with our new comrades of Pandahem and struggle again with the foes from Hamal.

A Chuktar strode up, bluff, beefy, his helmet under his arm and showing a dint in the crown, its blue feathers half shorn away. He looked drunk on glory. "My Prince!" he bellowed.

I looked up from the camp table where the lists were being prepared. "Chuktar Erling! I am overjoyed you live."

"My Prince, I have found a young fambly who says you want to see him. A thin, scruffy urchin, with a drunken slut. . . ."

But I knew as they were wheeled up by a guard party of Pachaks, as always to be trusted in times of victory as well as defeat, I knew so I sighed and stood up and braced myself for the ordeal of meeting Pando, the Kov of Bormark, and his mother, Tilda of the Many Veils.

Chapter
Ten

"*Hamun! By Krun! Hamun!*"

Tilda—and Pando!

How I wish Inch could be here now.

Pando had fleshed out, growing tall and straight in the seasons between now and our last meeting. He still carried that cheeky air about him, the urchin description perfectly apt, and I saw that he was short of his full stature of growth and short too, I fancied, in his full stature as a Kov. But imp of Sicce though he was, I had known him as a nine year old, a scamp, but a lad full of brightness and good humor, untidy, mischievous, and lovable.

And Tilda. My heart sank as I looked on Tilda the Beautiful. I remembered her as a genuinely beautiful woman, with that black hair floating around her as she swirled, black and lush as an impiter's wing. I recalled those violet eyes that could flash into scorn or love, into hatred and mockery, and those sweet luscious lips, soft and melting. Her figure had been marvelous, firm and voluptuous and calculated to drive any mortal man to madness. She had not plagued me, only at the very end, there in the palace of Pomdermam, the capital of Tomboram, just before the Scorpion and the blue radiance had snatched me back to Earth. And no woman can touch me now, not one, not when I hold the form and face of my Delia with me.

So I stood looking at them as they trailed up, and I

saw how Pando had changed and knew that with wise
counsel he would become good in life. But Tilda! Her face
was as beautiful as ever, even if betraying lines showed
around her eyes and mouth. But her hair hung lank and
bedraggled. And that glorious figure had coarsened, grown
fat around the waist, sagging, and she walked in a slovenly
slouch that I knew instinctively was not merely because
she had been captured. Both of them were dressed in
rags, the tattered remnants of finery.

After the battle I had washed and changed into a
simple short tunic of finest white linen—that linen called
verss—but pandering to old times Delia had caused to be
stitched around neck, arms, and hem an inch-wide band
of brilliant scarlet. So, I, Dray Prescot, Lord of Strombor,
stood cool, clean, and bathed, to greet these two, my
friends, in their dirt, misery, and despair.

"Fetch a chair for the Kovneva," I said. "The Kov may
stand."

Pando glared at me defiantly, finding spirit to drag
himself out of his misery and curse me by the gross Armi-
pand.

At the sound of my voice Tilda looked up sluggishly;
then a Pachak swod pushed a folding chair forward and
she sank down, grateful to rest.

"You were captured, I take it," I said. "Tell me about
it."

Pando forced his shoulders back. And I recalled him
as a nine year old, running, shouting, and tumbling in
the dust with the other urchins of Pa Mejab.

"Those cramphs of Hamal beat our army. And now
you come to take us prisoner in your turn. If you want
money in ransom, you whom men called Prince Majister,
then you are unlucky. I suggest you have our heads off
now. That is what princes do, as I know full well."

You couldn't say much to that.

Chuktar Erling grunted and spoke up in his parade
ground bellow. "They were chained up among the calsanys."

I made a face. I knew as well as anyone on Kregen
what calsanys did when they were upset. No wonder
these two filled the air odoriferously.

"There is an old apim with them who says he is a Pallan. He is being carried in, being extremely fragile."

"That is Pallan Nicomeyn, an old and valued friend!"
snapped out Pando.

I could guess that the miserable King Nemo had in some way disgraced Pallan Nicomeyn, who had helped Tilda in the days when we sought to prove Pando's right to the title of Kov of Bormark. He must have gone to Pando for help and protection.

"See to the Pallan," I said. "Let him rest. Give him eat and drink and have him bathed and give him clothes. He is to be treated with respect."

"At once, my Prince!" Erling bellowed and dashed off to give the orders.

I had a shrewd suspicion that even if these two poor wights here did not recognize me, Pallan Nicomeyn would, and quickly.

As though something of her old witchery at reading men and their inmost secret thoughts returned to Tilda, she lifted her head, somewhat drunkenly, for the Hamalese guards had let her drink—no doubt with evil intentions—and regarded me.

"I knew a man, once," she said, slurring her words. "A man—he looked a little like you, although tougher and harder and leaner—and he wouldn't—wouldn't—" She forgot what she was saying, wiped her lips, and started over. "This man I knew, he cared for Pando'n me. If he was here now he'd knock you down as soon as look at you, grand and a prince though you are."

I felt like a get-onker.

She might be talking about her husband, she might be talking about Meldi, who had cared for her and Pando, she might be talking about any man she had known recently. . . . I fancied she was talking about me.

I said, "I am told your husband, Marker Marsilus, was a fine soldier and a good man. It is fitting you should think of him."

"Onker!" she said. Something of her fire flashed. "For what business it is of yours, you lord of Vallia, I loved my husband and we gave up our separate lives for each other. I have loved no man since. . . . " Her drunken voice droned on, telling things she would keep fast locked if she was sober. She did not fall off the chair, and her poise was that of the great lady. It boiled down to a maudlin recital of lost hopes and fading memories, of her husband and of her great days on the stage—for she had been a justly famed actress—of memories of this man she talked about so wistfully, this man who had been me, so that I turned to Pando, with a look on my face that made him start back.

Before I could flare out what boiled in me, telling them it was I, their old Dray Prescot, who stood before them, Tilda rambled on, her voice rising: "So between Hamal and Vallia we are crushed like a grain in the mill. Well, so be it. Pandrite knows the whole of it; with Opaz is the right. Have done with us as my son commands, and let Vallia pick over the corpses."

"You do not like Vallians?"

"I hate and detest them!"

"Yet you have not looked at the banners we fly."

Pando laughed most scornfully, his lip curling. "A mere trick, Vallian, to deceive. The blue flag with the zhantil is *my* flag. Mine! Had I my strength and my army I would make you rue the day you flaunted the flag of Bormark, which is a sign given by this same man of whom my mother speaks."

He moved forward, passionate, and the Pachaks tensed up a little, their deadly tails quivering.

"You have the power now. You have the position, the treasures, and the army. Bormark is gone, gulped by the cramphs of Hamal. And now Vallia stoops in to claw the corpse. A fitting act for a vile nation."

"By Vox!" I said. "You're still a confounded spitfire!"

"And I would shoot fire-arrows into your eyes if I could."

"Hikdar Re-Po!" I bellowed as loudly as the Chuktar had. The Pachak Hikdar of the guard stiffened up, his straw-yellow hair beneath the smooth round helmet of his race glimmering in the suns' light. "Hikdar! Clear these two off to be bathed and clothed decently. Give them food! I do not want to see them again until they are no longer an offense in a man's nostrils, and until the Kovneva is sober!"

The Hikdar's tail flashed in the Pachak salute. He turned to march his detail off and I shouted, very passionate, despising myself: "And treat them with respect. See that the Kovneva is cared for, for she is a great lady."

"Yes, my Prince!" bellowed Hikdar Re-Po, and Pando was politely invited to step between the ranks of armored men, and his mother was carefully assisted away. I glared after them. By Zair! I should have found time to come back to Bormark and make sure Pando developed like a proper Kov. It was all my fault, and I was not prepared to blame my Delia or any of my friends or enemies who had detained me in Valka or Havilfar.

But, I vowed, I would have Tilda dried out, and I'd talk to that young rip Pando and sort him out—I would! It was a task I had withdrawn from for far too long. And if you ask why I considered this my business at all, then you have no understanding of the madman who is Dray Prescot.

My own despicable action lay, of course, in that I had not come straight out with it and let them see who I was. But I felt this would shame them as much as it would me. Relationships are prickly bedfellows. Once they were bathed and well fed and dressed fittingly, feeling more human, then would be the time to let them know that the lordly and puissant Prince Majister of Vallia was only their old friend and helpmeet Dray Prescot.

As it happened there was inevitably so much to do after the battle that I could not spare a thought for Pando and Tilda for most of the day. Hikdar Re-Po sent an ob-Deldar to inform me that my orders had been carried out, that the prisoners—guests—were sleeping fast, for they were exhausted. I sent the ob-Deldar back with orders that they were not to be disturbed, but that I was to be informed two burs after they awoke, by which time I indicated I expected them refreshed, filled with a good meal, ready to meet me—and sober.

One of my concerns meanwhile lay with Kytun, who reported in his losses, shaking his head. He brightened up as he described the flyers and fliers he had captured. What with the masses of zorcas and totrixes we rounded up, and the saddle-birds and vollers Kytun brought in, we were reasonably well provided. I told Chuktar Tom ti Vulheim that we would mount up a goodly proportion of the footmen, turn them into mounted infantry. I cocked my head on one side. Tom ti Vulheim had served well and faithfully in those dark and harrowing days when we had cleansed Valka, all of which you may hear in the great song: *The Fetching of Drak na Valka.*

"Tom," I said, and I spoke in my no-nonsense voice, so that he braced up. "Tom. You struggled against being made a Chuktar. You run the foot soldiers perfectly. Your Archers are a wonder. Yet you refuse a second name. Why?"

He stared at me, nonplussed. He was a blade comrade. "Do I need a whole raggle-taggle tail of names?"

"You do not, and neither do I. Yet, for my sins, I have been saddled with a rainbow of pretty names. I wish to unload some of my sinfulness upon your head."

He knew I had something in my mind, so he smiled and nodded and waited for the ax to fall.

"We have just gained a victory—oh, it was not one of the greatest battles in all history—but it was a smart little win, all the same. Beneath Tomor Peak. And, too, there is a nice estate not too far from Vulheim, a place of samphron bushes and nectarine plantations, a charming place called Avanar—"

"I know it."

"Well, Tom ti Vulheim, whether you like it or not, whether you own it or not, from henceforth you are Tom Tomor, Elten of Avanar, with all the rights and duties of your rank and all the goodness of your estate for yourself—save what the law requires you to part with in the way of taxes and imperial dues."

He bowed. He actually bowed. "I thank you, Prince." Most formal, this, for Tom ti Vulheim, who was now an Elten! "I accept with all gratitude, and I do so for the sake of Bibi, the granddaughter of Theirson and Thisi the Fair." I nodded at this, the memories rising. "And, if it pleases you, I will call myself Tom Tomor ti Vulheim."

"And you, Tom, the man who mocked a string of names!"

But I understood his meaning.

Well, as you may imagine, all this was highly gratifying to me, in the old selfish way. I'd make all my friends princes and princesses, if that was possible. Mind you, on Kregen, it is entirely possible, entirely. . . .

I mentioned, earlier that I had instituted a mark of valor within the Valkan regiments. A silversmith of Vandayha, one Eckermin the Graver, had designed a round medal showing the little valkavol flying above and the symbol of Valka in the center, the trident shooting up from the bow. Below was a scroll of leaves and sacred plants and, on the reverse, a space for the name of the recipient, the place, and occasion. These medals were more like phalerae and those men who distinguished themselves in battle received them at my hands and proudly wore them on their war harness. Well, petty it may have been, but it seemed the least I could do, that and the addition of tidily heavy bags of golden talens.

My men called these phalerae "bobs." This was a typical ranker's way of contracting and abbreviating their full name, which was of the order of "The Strom's Medal for the Valor of a Warrior Heart."

I had not, needless to say, chosen that name myself. The High Council of Elders of Valka, warming to my suggestion, had given the name. I like the swods, preferred bobs.

So we worked all that day. With the sinking of Antares I took up a cup of Vela's Tears and drank deeply, preparing to plunge afresh into the reorganization and forward planning of my little army. We must not be trapped by the vastly superior forces of Hamal before I had made proper contact with the King of Tomboram, who had not turned up, as I had expected. Mind you, he had his hands full elsewhere. Now we must march and throw ourselves into the battleline alongside him. Kytun Kholin Dorn and Tom Tomor would handle the troops; I had no fears on that score. So I planned and, the night being hot, threw off the white tunic and sat in a plain blue breechclout, drinking, and working by the mellow gleam of the samphron-oil lamp within my tent.

Stretching, I yawned. The close air clogged my lungs, so I rose and, hitching a fine Vallian rapier and main-gauche about me, strode outside the tent for a breath of fresh air. The guard slapped his glaive across as I went out and I spoke a few words to him. I wandered along in the fuzzy pink moonlight, with the camp about me filled with those nocturnal noises of a sleeping army. . . .

A shadow moved against a darkened tent. I halted at once but the shadow had gone. I went on quietly and saw a guard—a Chulik—sleeping peacefully on the ground. About to bellow at him to stand up and get on guard, he'd face a charge in the morning, I held my tongue. A thin thread of dark blood trickled down behind his ear. He was not dead. I straightened up, looking around, and the pink moonlight fell full on my face.

I heard a gasp. Then a voice spoke, a blustery lion-voice that strove to whisper in that moonshot darkness.

"Hamun! By Krun! Hamun!"

Chapter Eleven

Escape under the Moons of Kregen

The rapier went back into the scabbard with a snick.

I said, "If you shout loudly, enough, Rees, you fambly, the whole camp will know we have escaped."

"By Krun!" said the Trylon Rees of the Golden Wind, stepping forward and looking around him. "You are a changed man from our days in Ruathytu, so help me Opaz!"

"And you, too, Rees, old fellow. Has Opaz then conquered you? What of Havil the Green?"

"This is no time to argue theology, Hamun! For the good graces of Hanitcha the Harrower, let us get out of here!"

This was to be expected. The plan that had instantly flown into my head demanded a few murs alone, and yet I should have known that Rees, that glorious golden Numim who—I counted myself fortunate—was a friend as well as an enemy, would be full of energy and resolve. He wouldn't hang around when he could escape.

I said, "I am overjoyed to see you, Rees, by Krun! I did not know you were with the army here."

"And I had no idea you were either, old fellow. Now where are you going?"

"I will fetch weapons and clothes." I had seen he wore the wreck of a uniform, and he carried a stone in his hand with which he had knocked the Chulik out. "Wait quietly!"

"Don't be long. They are as efficient a pack of scoundrels here as any I've known."

"Oh, yes," I said. "These rasts of Tomboram are a fine fighting bunch."

"Tomboram? These are cramphs of Vallia!"

So that meant I'd blown up one pretty little scheme.

Still, I would not have my friend Rees slain out of hand. He and I had ruffled it together in the Sacred Quarter of Ruathytu, when I was spying in Hamal; with Chido we had had some fine old brawls and roistered the night away. He thought I had been captured and escaped, as he had. Now I would put that to my advantage, for there were outstanding items in Hamal.

You may imagine the speed with which I ran.

"Tom!" I said into his ear, and he was awake on the instant. "I am going to Hamal. Do not question. You and Kytun must do what we planned with the army. I trust you. If there is any difficulty at all with the rast of a King of Tomboram—any difficulty at all—then pull out. Use the transports and the vollers and get the men safely away. No questions. Tell Kytun. Tell him I trust you both and if you argue too much, one with the other, I'll knock both your heads together."

"But Dray—!"

But I was gone.

In my own tent I ripped out a clean blue shirt for Rees and a loincloth. I snatched up a fine matched pair of rapier and main-gauche and then, on my way out, paused. I turned back, snatched up the longsword, and at top speed again fled into the moonlight.

I saw Rees hiding in the shadows of the tent. As I came fairly close to him a Chulik guard stepped out into the fuzzy pink and golden glow of moonlight. He started to snap his spear across in salute and to bellow out, "All's well—" He would have finished that with, "My Prince!"

I leaped for him, took him by the throat, hissed in his ear: "Silence! Shut up! Stand still!" Then I tapped him alongside the head, just under the brim of his helmet. "Fall down and lie still, my friend!"

He fell down and he lay still.

Rees got up and whistled. "A different man from that Amak Hamun I rescued from the Rapas and the burning building, by Krun!"

"Here are clothes, here are weapons. Now let us find a voller."

Rees stared at the longsword. "That bar of iron—is that a weapon?"

"I found it in a tent and thought it might serve."

"I fancy I might wield it passing well."

101

"We stole a voller and made good our escape."

"I fancy so, too. But for now I think I will carry it. It pleases me."

Rees shook that golden head of his so that his mane fluttered under the golden moonsglow. "A different man."

We crept cautiously away.

"Not so, Rees. I am still the same Hamun ham Farthytu, the Amak of Paline Valley. But I have been in a battle and I see things a little differently now."

We reached the voller lines. I had to be far more careful now than even Rees realized. I most certainly would not slay one of my own men, not even for a scheme of importance, but Rees would be elated if he could dispatch a hated Vallian to the Ice Floes of Sicce.

A thought occurred to me, so, as we eased up to a voller with our eyes glaring out at the guard, a Rapa who paced some fifty yards away, I said: "And Chido? Is he here, too?"

"Now, old feller! D'you think I'd sneak off and leave old Chido a prisoner? No, he was not taken, thanks to Opaz."

I noted this use of Opaz by a Hamalian who in theory should stick to his state religion of Havil the Green, and who by belief and predilection professed Krun. I shook my head.

"Of course not. I am glad he is safe." I was sincere.

How can a man be friends with men who are enemies of his country? It is a puzzle and a torment.

In any event we stole a voller—not a prime example, I was glad to see—and we made good our escape, successfully eluding the guards. Much though this pleased me—we had not had to fight, so I was saved the agony that would have caused me—I was also hotly angry that my guards had allowed it. On one hand my pleasure was genuine as we flew swiftly through the pink-streaming moonlight, and on the other I was ragingly angry at the slackness of discipline. I would have something to say to the guard commanders when I got back, that I promised. To jump ahead, and also to explain much of what had happened, I should now say that Tom Tomor had sprung out of his bed, rushed out, and seen my attack on the Chulik. The Chulik had repeated my words. So Tom gave immediate orders that a mock pursuit was to take place. He understood just enough to assume I knew what I was doing, maniacal though that appeared. But then my chiefs of Valka are accustomed to a maniac leading them. . . .

In my own overweening pride I had decided that any attempt to fake the escape would alert Rees. Probably, in one way, that was right. But now I think that if Tom had not given his orders, Rees and I would never have escaped so easily.

During that flight through the night sky of Kregen with the moons casting down their pinkish golden light, Rees told me what had happened in his life since I had last seen him, a gravely ill man, near death's door. He spoke of his daughter Saffi, the glorious golden lion-maid, and his thanks for her rescue were given in gruff, harsh tones, but simple, direct, and from the heart. She had reached Ruathytu safely with Doctor Larghos the Needle and Jiktar Horan. She had been full of her escapade when, kidnapped by Vad Garnath and his Kataki Strom, she had been taken as a bargaining counter to the Manhounds of Faol. Apparently she had described the fight in the voller, when I had just about keeled over from loss of blood, to her father as a High Jikai. Well, it had been a little Jikai, I suppose; I remember nothing of it, as I said.*

Rees looked back. "Those yetches of Vallia do not follow." As he turned to me his golden face with that fierce lion-look glowed in the moonlight. "Hamun, old son. I owe you much, so much that I know I can never repay you, but—"

"You can repay me, Rees."

"How?"

"Promise me you will hold out your hand in friendship to me."

"Well, of course! May Hanitcha harrow me else!"

"In friendship, Rees, no matter what happens."

"By Krun! This makes me glad to promise."

Would a promise, the feeling of gratitude to me for the life of his adored daughter, weigh in the balance when he discovered I was a hated enemy, a Vallian and, much worse, the damned Prince Majister of those cramphs of Vallians? I wondered.

And, at that moment, I felt a great partiality for Rees, for hadn't he dragged me off from poring over figures and plans—fascinating in themselves, of course—and

---

*See *Avenger of Antares*, Dray Prescot # 10.

hauled me into headlong action, haring over the surface of Kregen into more adventures, flying under the moons?

What Rees had to say about the Battle of Tomor Peak intrigued me, but he clearly did not relish talking about it. This, at least, was a comfort, because I only had to mumble something about joining at the last minute by voller, not really knowing Rees was there but finally wishing to join his regiment, and being caught up in the battle. I could not forbear adding, "And how did the regiment behave?"

His fists clenched. He looked unhappy and guilty, which pained me.

"You always hinted, more than hinted, about my beautiful zorcas. My lovely regiment! We trotted out, every lance aligned, all in perfect formation—oh, Hamun, the regiment looked grand!"

I did not speak but busied myself unnecessarily with the voller controls. Presently Rees went on in a slow, leaden voice, reliving those moments of scarlet horror.

"We were trotting out, ready to charge, having those yetches on the run. The infantry was attacking. We picked up speed, yelling: 'Hanitch! Hanitch! Hamal!' in the old way. And then . . . then a crazy mob of maniacs astride animals—nikvoves, I believe they are called—smashed at us. My beautiful zorcas!"

He did not go on. He could not, I think, go on.

I said, "But the totrix regiments were smashed, also."

"Aye. It is a sad day for us. What the Queen will say . . ."

"Will you reform the regiment?"

"Again?"

"The war still goes on."

"Aye, old fellow, the damned war still goes on. And the Queen will not be pleased. We have suffered a reverse. And I think her treasury does not have a never-ending supply of deldys."

This was heartening. I prodded. "Do you think she would come to some arrangement? Not sue for peace, but desist from the fighting while arrangements are made?"

"Now that the rasts of Vallians have come in, maybe that will stay her hand. She has a fear of Vallia, for all they are a miserable lot, too stupid to build their own vollers."

By Vox! It was true!

"And," went on Rees, visibly growing warmer, "did you

see the crazy man who led the charge? A big man, broad in the shoulder like you. His face was covered by a blazing golden mask. He came in at the head of the nikvoves like Hanitcha himself."

I said, with perfect truth, "No. I did not see him."

A breeze of alarm touched me. That golden mask was a mere toy, designed to mark me out so that my own men might know and follow. It had served here in that Rees had not seen my face. But suppose some imp of memory stirred, some mannerism betrayed me? Then common sense reasserted itself. How could the Trylon Rees possibly equate his bumbling friend Amak Hamun, for all he had picked up a few sworder's tricks lately, with the puissant majesty of the Prince Majister of Vallia?

For Rees knew who that man riding like the thunderclouds in his golden mask was.

"A feller called Prescot. Prince Majister of Vallia. I'd like to have him at the point of my rapier!"

I coughed and twitched the controls. The airboat flew up and swooped, and Rees, thrown off balance, yelped, "What in the name of Hakki are you playing at?"

"A shadow, there under the moon . . . It is gone now."

He peered but could see nothing. "We should be up with the remnants of the army soon."

"Would you give the Jikai to the Vallians for their victory?"

He looked at me as though I had sprouted devil's horns.

"The Jikai? To nulshes of Vallia! Are you off your head?"

"They beat us, fair and square."

He chewed on that. His hand brushed his golden mane. He did not like the thought. I pressed on relentlessly. "If they march to fight the main army, they might overthrow that, also. Kov Pereth—"

Luckily he burst in then, interrupting me, fortunately concealing my lack of up-to-date knowledge out of Hamal.

"Yes! The Queen threw Kov Pereth into a dungeon in the Hanitch! That idiot Kov Hangol is Pallan of the armies of the north now. I know him! A bungler, but he knows how to fawn on the Queen, Havil take him!"

"She'll run out of Kovs soon."

"You may jest, Hamun. But you have a sorry truth in the jest."

"Then she may turn to a Trylon, perhaps the Trylon of the Golden Wind."

106

"She knows I have never toadied to her, and dangerous that has been, fool that I am. No, old friend, I think we know each other well enough by now for me to tell you that the King himself frowns on his wife's follies. Of course he is powerless, but one day . . . who knows?"

"The King?" I said, surprised. "But he is a mere puppet."

"Today, yes. If the war goes on . . . then tomorrow, who's to say?"

As you may imagine, I digested all this very thoroughly. It would not be as easy as all that. Queen Thyllis was seated very firmly on the throne—she and the Opaz-forsaken manhounds that lolled on her golden steps. The King her husband was a mere cipher. If the Queen was to be deposed, I hoped for little from the King. Anyway, as soon as a great and suitable opportunity arose, a mighty victory, for instance, then Queen Thyllis was going to hold her triumphal procession and have herself crowned Empress of Hamal. She was hard, and evil, and power-crazed.

Mind you, she would make exactly the same insults about the Emperor of Vallia and his son-in-law. I could guess.

Rees pointed down over the wooden coaming.

"There they are. We'll have to go down at once, before they shoot at us."

I swung the flier around and set the control levers for a rapid descent. In the vitals of the craft the sturm-wood orbits would be turning and the silver boxes would be rotating around each other, their power directing and upholding the flier. Down we plunged. I still had plans about vollers and silver boxes in Hamal, and this time I would not be put off by a miserable farce of dirt and air. No, by Zair! For this time I was armed with knowledge I believed had been sent to me by direct intervention of the Star Lords or the Savanti.

Any help from them was like a gallon of water in the Owlarh Waste—something not to be believed.

But this time I believed, the water was no mirage.

So we slanted in and landed, quickly ringed by fierce, hot-eyed men of Hamal, soldiers who had lost a battle and did not care for the experience. Units were mixed up, but discipline still held together, and we were passed through to the Chuktar who had taken command after the general had been slain.

These remnants were on their way north and west to join up with Kov Hangol, the new commander in chief. Our story excited little comment, even though we were the only two to escape after being made prisoner, as far as I could determine. I'd have something to say to my own men later if there had been others.

Chido said that, by Krun! he'd given Rees up for dead. Of course, dear old Chido, he said Wees for Rees. He stared at me as though I was a ghost. He goggled at me, his cheerful, flap-eared, chinless face alight with fellow feeling.

I said, "Chido, you old rascal. How happy I am to see you alive!"

We spent two miserable days with these miserable men, and then a merker came with orders for Rees to take himself and what remained of his officers back to Ruathytu. I went also. I believed Rees would have need of friends. Other officers who had fought and lost were also to report back. The men were to rejoin the main army and then be distributed into other regiments. The flank force had been wiped out.

On the flight back no one spoke much. They all acted like a bunch of misbehaving midshipmen up on first lieutenant's report—only those poor devils suspected heads would roll.

It is, I assure you, a painfully curious and sobering experience to share the suffering of men who go to meet a harsh and unjust fate, knowing you are the prime mover, the person responsible for their suffering. Believe me.

There also flew with me the memory of the blood, smoking and hot, which had been so lavishly spilled on the battlefield of Tomor Peak. I had seen men pierced through, men whose limbs had been hacked half off; I had seen zorcas screaming in agony; I had seen whole regiments smashed away to a red pulp. In the arrow storm I had watched all this—and sitting in the voller on the way to Ruathytu, capital of Hamal, I wondered just how much of the reality a vindictive queen could comprehend. What she saw in her foul Jikhorkdun paled beside the reality of a battlefield.

How many of these officers would end up in the arena, spilling their guts in the Jikhorkdun for the sadistic pleasure of the crowd and their evil ruler?

So, of course, the danger rose in my mind and mocked me.

I had borne at least three names in Hamal that could identify me, clean or dirty, bearded or clean-shaven: Chaadur. Bagor ti Hemlad. Amak Hamun Farthytu.

Well, I was Hamun now and had no wish at all to be Bagor ti Hemlad again, for he had run afoul of Queen Thyllis and for a time had been her plaything. That cramph of a King Doghamrei had attempted to have Bagor slain by setting him alight and dumping him out of a Hamalese skyship down onto the decks of a galleon of Vallia. One galleon had burned. This crazy onker Bagor, with his trousers on fire had wrecked the two Hamalese skyships in a midair collision, and then had taken passage aboard the other galleon to further adventures.*

All this I knew. My rear still itched when I thought of that fight and my trousers burning.

As for Chaadur, it was wrongly said that he had slain the Kovneva Esme, when he had in reality merely set that despicable woman—for whom one could only feel a tiny pang of pity—in silver chains, as she had kept her own girls in chains that galled them. The Kov her husband had raged after Chaadur, who had been a gul working in the voller manufactory of Sumbakir, run by Ornol ham Feoste, the Kov of Apulad. I had never met Ornol ham Feoste in Ruathytu, for Sumbakir lay at a considerable distance, but I had always been on the lookout for him—he would know Chaadur when he saw him**

Also, a minor worry: those two rascals Avec and Ilter who had named Chaadur knew that Chaadur's real name was Dray Prescot.

Ruathytu looked pretty much as that sinful brawling city had always looked, except for a pervasive air of dinginess, dustiness, a down-at-the heels lethargy that, product of the war though it was, depressed me. We were carried swiftly from the voller landing park to the north of the River Havilthytus in a procession of zorca riders silent except for the clitter-clatter of polished hooves against the stones. The Queen allowed only the most important people and super-urgent messengers to land on her palace island where the evil pile of Hammabi el Lamma rose in spires, peaks, and turrets against the sky. The whole northern area of Ruathytu through which we passed was given

---

*See *Bladesman of Antares*, Dray Prescot # 9.
**See *Fliers of Antares*, Dray Prescot # 8.

over to the soldiers' barracks. There had once been a merry little fire up there . . . another story. At the river we were ferried across to the palace island, the boats thunking into the ocher flood. The rowers at the oars were being reminded that they were slaves by the lashes in the hands of the whip-Deldars. I noticed there were far more diffs in Ruathytu now. The Queen was spending the country's money prodigiously in hiring mercenaries. The emperor in Vallia was having to dig deep, too, to counter all this.

There were few preliminaries at the palace before we were shuffled into line and ushered through into the Hall of Notor Zan. This was not the impressive audience chamber in which I had encountered Queen Thyllis before. That chamber had been dominated by the enormous crystal throne, the golden steps, the golden-chained Chail Sheom, and, perhaps most of all, dominated by the somnolent but savagely vicious forms of the jiklos, Manhounds of Faol used as throne-step pets. There also lay in that resplendent high-ceiled chamber a hole in the marble floor beneath which grew a syatra, that leprous-white man-eating plant.

It soon became clear that Queen Thyllis had no intention of thrusting these officers down to her pet syatra.

The Hall of Notor Zan opened before us and we shuffled through to stand in a bunch on the left of the tall balass doors. The whole chamber was robed in black. The ceiling was not very tall, as such things are measured in palaces, and the room was out of proportion to the extent that its length was overly long to its width. Black cloths cloaked the ceiling and black drapes covered the walls. Samphron-oil lamps shed a clear, unwavering light. There were no windows. At the far end, sitting on a giant black basaltic throne, the Queen clenched her arms on the fur coverings—a dramatic and dynamic picture of a woman/queen worked up to a pitch of anger. There were no Chail Sheom in evidence here for the grim work ahead, but three manhounds dozed on the black and shining steps. I sniffed. Incense burned, and incense is calculated to make a man throw up.

The Queen's guard stood to either hand beside the throne in close mesh mail. Marshals and chamberlains, all dressed in sober black, fussed around, ready to open the proceedings.

And the Queen? Queen Thyllis? She sat erect and leaning a little forward, dressed all in black—as she had been when I first saw her during that little folly, clutched in the grip of flutsmen. Her face blazed white now, her green eyes diamonds to match the fire of Genodras. That rich red mouth of hers which could firm instantly to killing hardness was set now like a trap, with a corner of her lip caught up between her white pointed teeth.

She had never failed to make an impression, this Queen Thyllis, the Empress of Hamal.

The stillness held. I admit to feeling the effectiveness of the stage-setting. If I been a Hamalese officer laden with guilt for having lost a battle, no doubt I'd have felt as sick as these poor devils around me.

A marshal spoke to us after a while, a prickly, stupid little man, waving a sheet of paper.

"When your name is called out go forward. The Queen will hear the charge against you and give judgment. If you are adjudged not guilty return here and stand to the right of the door. Although, for myself, I think she will send you all to the Jikhorkdun."

The names were called. Men went forward. They were mostly regimental commanders, Jiktars, or pastang commanders, Hikdars. Of the first ten only one was reprieved to go stand by the right of the door. Seven were condemned to the Jikhorkdun and one was condemned to a hanging. One was given—there and then!—to the jiklos, who arose in fearsome bestiality and tore him to pieces. The blood was left to shine greasily on the black marble of the floor in front of the throne.

About then the thought occurred to me, for I had been absorbed by the Queen's flummery in overawing her soldiers, that my name would not be on the paper prepared according to the rigid laws of Hamal. I had not been a member of the army and so could not be written down. Eventually, everyone else would be called forward to face their judgment. I would be left to stand alone!

Then, surely then, the evil Queen could not fail to recognize in this man claiming to be Hamun ham Farthytu, Amak of Paline Valley, that same wild leem Bagor ti Hemlad who had rescued her, then refused to bend to her whims, and one day disappeared from her dark palace of Hammabi el Lamma!

How she would smile when she had me once more in her clutches!

Chapter Twelve

In the Hall of Notor Zan

As that macabre and horrific scene went on, I stood there calculating my chances. Although I did not sweat I grew decidedly warm. Another screaming wretch was thrown to the manhounds. These jiklos had been well trained, for they disposed of him in a cat-like, playful, obscene way. When he was dead they did not eat him, crunching on his bones with their jagged teeth; instead they pushed the mangled body aside and looked up, sniffing, their tongues lolling, waiting for the next victim.

"The army does not deserve this!" breathed a Jiktar next to Rees.

Rees the lion-man said, "The army lost. We were defeated. That is a personal affront to the Queen."

I carefully edged a little away from Rees and Chido. Our weapons had been taken from us, but we had been tricked out in fancy new uniforms. Our baggage, what there was of it after the rout of the army, had been brought back and warehoused in the soldiers' quarters. I had stuffed the longsword down into a roll of blankets and swathed a military cloak around the whole.

The feel of that longsword hilt in my hands would have been highly comforting now. The mailed guards, the manhounds . . . if I fought, it would most likely be my last fight of all. There had to be a better way to get out of this than simple fighting. Brains and cunning rather than swords and brawn, now . . .

The Queen would rejoice to humiliate and torture this Bagor ti Hemlad, who was me, and her revenge would surpass the terror of the manhounds.

In accordance with the strict laws of Hamal the offending officers were called up in alphabetical order—needless to say the Kregish alphabet does not begin with an *a* and end with a *z*—with the pastang Hikdars grouped after their Jiktar. The Chuktar who had taken command after the death of the commanding general featured in the group of many men whose names began with *h*. He went forward, upright, dour, already believing himself condemned.

"I think, Chuktar Hingleson," said the Queen after the man's supposed crimes had been read out, "that you deserve great ill at my hands."

"We fought, Majestrix. We were defeated."

"I am minded to let my pretty jiklos try their teeth on you."

"As the Queen commands."

He was a brave old fellow, if somewhat lacking in the knowledge needful in a successful commander. He held himself upright in that black room of horror, and he did not flinch.

"Because of you my army was beaten."

He didn't dare contradict her, except for his life. He said, "The army was already defeated when I took command. This I swear, my Queen, by the light of the Silver One."

I knew what he was talking about.

Lem the Silver Leem!

That foul religion wormed its way into the very heart of evil societies and now held sway over the Queen. And this Chuktar was a devotee. Maybe, just maybe he would come out of this with a whole skin. I watched, fascinated. I remembered the scene so vividly, the men around me shaking in their shoes, the black light-absorbing drapes on the walls, the tall, unwavering flames of the lamps, the black throne, and the hideous forms of the manhounds slavering for more now they had tasted blood. And over all, the vibrant form of the Queen, all in black, with her white face brooding on her judgments, her green eyes emerald fires of hatred and power!

"You may go to stand by the right of the door, Chuktar Hingleson. You will report to me when I send for you. Hold yourself in readiness."

"My Queen!" He bellowed it out in parade-ground fashion, and that snapped my mood. I realized I had to do something or else be faced with the prospect of forming a manhound's supper, if nothing worse.

The Chuktar stomped back and it was the turn of the next Jiktar. Rees would be next. I realized how selfish I had been in thinking only of my own skin, when Rees and Chido would be striding over the black marble to their destinies. I saw the Chuktar halfway back. All eyes were fixed on him as he turned and performed the full incline bow. I moved very quietly and very smoothly from the left of the door to the right. The man to whose side I stepped moved forward to see better as the Chuktar straightened up. He murmured, so low the words were a mere hum. "He is a dead man."

I said nothing. The Chuktar joined us at the right of the door. In the ensuing shuffle so that he might stand at the front, I became integrated with the others who had been reprieved.

When Rees stepped forward I sent up a prayer to Zair for him.

Zair, that deity who inhabits the red sun Zim, smiled; Rees was discharged from obloquy and, with his officers, including Chido, was sent to stand at the right of the door.

Then it was over and we could escape into the fresh air of Ruathytu and Rees could say to me, puzzled, "I did not hear your name called, Hamun."

To which I replied, "I think many of us missed a great deal, when the names were called. Did you see the Chuktar?"

The question set him off and, with Chido, we went to find a wet, talking away about the experience like a drove of fluttrells. We all knew we had brushed death by, there in the black Hall of Notor Zan in the Hammabi el Lamma.

I did not know whether or not the little ant that had crawled on my boot when I mounted Stormcloud to lead the charge in the Battle of Tomor Peak had survived. Perhaps he had tumbled off somewhere in the trampled grass and run to hide among the corpses. Well, perhaps something of his stature belonged to me during those moments in the Hall of Notor Zan. I had taken a crazy chance for if a man had been seen crossing from the left to the right, he would have been arrested instantly to face all manner of unmentionable horrors. But there had been nothing else to do. Yes, I hoped that little ant had lived, as I had.

We did not feel like patronizing the Golden Talu, for

the atmosphere in that high-class tavern, as I have said, was most respectable. We sought out a much more robust, coarse, hard-drinking den—not a dopa den—and swung together through the low portals of the Scented Sylvie. With the jug upon the sturm-wood table and our glasses filled, Chido had a fit of the shakes, remembering. Rees, too, looked unhealthily sallow. They were suffering from the aftereffects of what they had been through, and I suffered with them. With a few coarse oaths and more drink, and the sight of the dancing girls—marvelous Fristle fifis of incredible lissomeness and lasciviousness— they perked up. We sat back to carouse the night away.

This did not suit my plans, but I wanted to ask questions anyway, and I might find loosened tongues in a low tavern where men grew merry. The quality of the company was not low—there were two Kovs and three Trylons there—but the atmosphere was conducive to erratic behavior, hard drinking, wenching, and a fuddlement of the senses. As I had found out, when you act as a spy you must employ what weapons come to hand.

Looking around the low-ceiled tavern with the wine-drenched tables, the scurrying serving wenches, the flushed faces of boisterous revelers, I found it extraordinarily difficult to realize all that had happened to me since I had spent my nights in Ruathytu in just this fashion. But not whole nights—when the others had staggered off to their homes I had gone leaping over the rooftops, my cloak flaring, a mask covering my features, a rapier glittering ready to spit the first person who tried to stop me. Now I was going about exactly the same task in a different way.

And only because I had rescued Rees's daughter, the glorious lion-maid Saffi, from a hideous death in Far Faol. The mad dash to save Saffi had not been a hindrance to my plans, had not been an interruption in my search for the secrets of the vollers. If I had not gone after Saffi I would not have come into possession of the information I had through a narrow air shaft, a fragment of a conversation between that cramph Vad Garnath and his agent, the Chuktar Strom, Rosil na Morcray who was a vile Kataki, and Phu-si-Yantong, a Wizard of Loh, a man of whom I was to know far more later, to my cost.

For one thing, this Wizard of Loh fancied he was going to take over Hamal from Queen Thyllis, that is, if I had heard him correctly. And he intended to use me,

Dray Prescot, as his pawn in taking secret command of the Vallian Empire when the Emperor was gone. This was megalomania. At least, that is what I thought then. Later I came to know this Phu-si-Yantong better and to understand he was in deadly earnest.

Yantong had also said I was not to be assassinated, so he had not sent the stikitches who had attacked Delia, the twins, and myself in our walled garden of Esser Rarioch.

He had mentioned the Nine Faceless Ones of Hamal as appointing the nobles to their duties in connection with voller manufacture. The secrets were well understood to be secrets and were well kept. I believed exactly the same precautions were taken in Hyrklana, where Queen Fahia would have me dragged into her arena and butchered for the crowds if I showed myself.

So, with the smell of spilled wine about me, men arguing in half-drunken ways, the girls dancing, and the air filled with shouts, there in the Scented Sylvie, I marked one of the Kovs talking to a Trylon. Both were of Hamal, hard men, filled with the vigor of full growth. Their faces severe even as they felt the wine working on their senses, they were men who knew their high positions and would not tolerate a single infringement upon their pride or their dignity. The pride of a noble is fanatical in most countries of Kregen. This I knew.

Outside in the moons-shot darkness they would have their preysany litters waiting with their link slaves and a retinue of guards, fierce predatory men—diffs, apims— who would delight in smashing a few heads to clear a path for their master.

The tavern was well patronized by diffs, I noticed and, even as Rees turned to me, I saw a fresh party of Kataki officers stride in, their tails bare, laughing, shouting, clearly already very merry from previous taverns. Other halflings sat at the sturm-wood tables, Chuliks, Rapas, Blegs—many and many a member of the diffs on Kregen, many of races I have not even mentioned yet, for the reason that they have not figured largely in my story up to this time. This was clear proof, if proof was needed, that Queen Thyllis had been pouring out her coffers to hire mercenaries. Bankers like Casmas the Deldy had lent her vast sums, to be rewarded by patents of nobility, favors or prerequisites within an administration which was corrupt despite all the rigid laws of Hamal. This reeking tavern, the Scented Sylvie, had evidently become a favorite haunt of the halflings in Ruathytu.

"Damned diffs," the Kov was saying, his face a deep plum purple, as he lifted his glass.

Rees saw my look and turned to me, saying, "You don't want to take too much notice of what old Nath the Crafty says, but, by Krun, you must watch your back if you cross him."

"Nath ham Livahan," said Chido, and bent his goggle-eyed face back to his glass. "Kov of Thoth Uppwe. We call him old Nath the Crafty—"

"And, by Krun," chipped in Rees, "never a man better deserved it!"

"He don't like diffs," Chido said, laughed, and drank.

Well, there were many men on Kregen who disliked every other man not of their race. This was inevitable, I suppose, given xenophobia. A Chulik does not get on with a Fristle. A Rapa gets on with very few other races. Blegs will draw swords against Mystiges without excuse. And apims like Chido and myself—there probably being more apims than any other race on Kregen—often came in for hatreds from every quarter.

The presence of so many Katakis intrigued me, for previously, as far as I was aware, they had seldom ventured far from their homes in the Shrouded Sea and elsewhere. The only reason I could advance for their presence was the prospect of enormous hauls of slaves, for Katakis are slave-masters *par excellence*.

The noise racketed on and the girls danced; wine and beer were spilled, and men cursed by a medley of gods and spirits. More than once, listening, I heard the name of Lem spurt from the seething mass. Rees touched me on the forearm.

"Leave him be, Hamun. He is in a nasty mood."

For quite humorous reasons, I could not explain to Rees that I wished to discuss the problems of the Nine Faceless Ones and the secrets of the vollers with this Nath the Crafty, this Kov of Thoth Uppwe, so I sat back in the chair. Nath the Crafty suddenly jerked up as his arm was jogged, and a stream of wine—the best the house afforded although not Jholaix—spattered the front of his gray shirt and the ling fur of his pelisse. Kov Nath leaped to his feet, his harsh features convulsed. He dragged out his thraxter.

The Bleg who had jostled him, about to apologize,

snapped into the fiercely angry rage of that race and whipped his sword out in turn.

"Cramph!" bellowed Kov Nath. "Rast! You will pay for that!"

A Kataki about to sit at the next table, his tail curved over his shoulder, whipped a hand into his sash and flashed out a wickedly bladed dagger. The thing was strapped to his tail in a twinkling. Other diffs were brandishing weapons. The moment spurted a dark and horrible fire.

"To me, apims!" screeched Nath the Crafty. What craftiness there was now about his conduct I couldn't see.

A Rapa hurled a knife. A Kataki whistled his bladed tail. "Kill the apim yetch!" yelled a Chulik, his tusks catching the oil lamps' gleam and glistening.

In the next mur the tavern turned into a boil of action and fighting, a frenzied, murderous brawl.

We three, Rees, Chido, and myself, sat at our table shoved up against the wall.

I said, "If an apim tries to stick you, Rees, we will help you dispose of him."

"And," said Rees, "if a Numim does likewise, likewise."

The tavern exploded with action. Men were reeling around, many more than half drunk, blinded by the glitter of sword and rapier. Daggers thunked home. The Katakis whistled their tails about and the wicked blades sliced and slashed. I sat still. I meant what I had said to Rees for one thing. For another, every man slain here meant a fighting man less for Hamal to fling against my country.

A Numim staggered from the press, a rapier still transfixing his body, and reeled to crash full-length on our table.

Rees pushed him off to die on the floor.

"Naghan Largismore," he said. "He should have known better."

Blood sprayed from an apim as he sprawled past, his neck efficiently slashed by a Kataki tail.

The Kov of Thorth Uppwe, this Nath ham Livahan men called Nath the Crafty, fought with a terrible cold fury which had swiftly succeeded his hectoring words and hot-tempered anger. But there were more diffs than apims. Another apim sprawled to the floor, grasping his neck and looking surprised as the blood spurted between his fingers. The Kataki who had flicked his tail with such virulent purpose swerved to get at another young apim whose thraxter glistened with fresh blood.

It was increasingly difficult for me to sit. I cannot analyze my feelings. I glanced at Rees. He looked disgusted with the whole proceedings. I wondered . . . suppose Rees had been with other Numims this night, instead of two apim friends? How often we behave so vastly differently with different company!

But I felt I could not sit much longer and watch young apims being slaughtered by Katakis and Chuliks.

A man stood in the doorway. I had not seen him enter. I looked at him from the tail of my eye—and I knew! I knew!

I knew what he would do and I knew the brand he wielded. Under an enveloping black cloak he wore hunting leathers, with the addition of a gray shirt. As he burst forward into the fray I saw his sword, that Savanti sword of superb balance and inconceivably cunning design, fashioned of steel far surpassing anything we have so far forged.

A man serving the Savanti! He had not been thrown out of Paradise, as I had. He had gone through all the tests and had been proved fit to be numbered among the elect. Now he worked with great purpose for the Savanti in their high designs for Kregen.

I admit I felt all the pangs I had thought dead and buried as I watched this man go about the business for which he had been selected, tested, and trained: to alter fate.

Once on a beach in Valka I had seen a young man try to do what the Savanti required, and fail. And so I had come into the possession of Alex Hunter's Savanti sword. Do you wonder that I gazed at this man who had come from the Swinging City, and hungered for his blade?

Oh, yes, of course there were all the other reasons. But although I did not harbor a grudge against the Savanti for so contemptuously dismissing me from Aphrasöe, the Swinging City, I felt under no obligation to go out of my way for them; rather I would go on doing what I had always done, knowing that much of it paralleled what the Savanti were attempting to do on Kregen.

The fight did not last too long after that. This man was no novice, no amateur like Alex Hunter. He kept his eyes open and ducked the thrown knife, the wickedly flicking

119

tail. He had been trained well. And he had a great deal of experience.

Soon the diffs were calling it a day and running. The tavern's occupants boiled out into the street, here in the Sacred Quarter where brawls were a way of life, running and shouting and hullabalooing. In any second the watch and the police would be here, and the laws of Hamal would swing into action.

I stood up.

"Right gladly, Hamun," said Rees.

Kov Nath stood, shaking a little, staring around at the carnage. The Trylon with him, holding a bloody arm, looked sick.

Rees and Chido made for the door. Going with them, for I had no wish to tangle with the law again, I watched the man sent by the Savanti. He walked quickly to the door, waited for Rees and Chido to pass out—had he raised his marvelous blade against Rees he would have been a dead man, for my rapier was loose in the scabbard —and swiftly followed. I went after them.

The street, indifferently lighted here, with the moons casting enough light to see sufficiently well not to trip over the first corpse on the doorstep, showed blank and empty. The link slaves had run. The guards had fought among themselves. I may be cynical, but I felt sorrow over that.

Fully prepared to make my own opening, Chido saved me the gambit.

"Warm work, dom," he said in his shrill voice.

"Aye," said this man, swirling his black cape about him, "for a tavern fight."

"Do you hate us so much then?" Rees spoke heavily.

"It were better you did not ask that question, Numim."

Walking up, I said, "Do you have a bed for the night, dom?"

"No. I am but newly arrived."

I could believe that.

"I have rooms," I said. "You would be welcome."

Rees stared at me. I hated to hurt him, but I fancied he would remember our words in the voller. No explanation was possible.

The man from the Savanti hesitated only a moment, then said, "I am grateful, dom."

"As for me, I am for home," said Rees.

"And I," piped up Chido. "I will walk with you."

Rees did not say good night or remberee. I was grateful for that. What I was about to do would betray Hamun ham Farthytu, and I had spent a lot of time and pain building up that young man.

When Rees and Chido had gone he walked the other way. We had gone perhaps six paces when I heard the shouts and I yelled "Run!"

He ran without question. The Savanti train well.

We eluded the watch and the patrols and so walked to my old inn, the Kyr Nath and the Fifi. Absences in time of war are a common occurrence, and Nulty had seen to payment for the rooms. How was he faring in Paline Valley? We went up to my room and I closed the door. The man from the Savanti unclasped his cape and threw it swirling on the bed. I looked at him.

He smiled. He was apim, of course, with thick fair hair and a square-set face, exceedingly grim as to the set of the jaw. I liked the brightness of his eye and the laugh lines at the corners of his mouth. Strongly built, as, of course, he must be, he looked like what he was, a powerful, professional fighting man.

I said, "Happy Swinging. And how are things in Aphrasöe?"

Before I had even finished, that superb, deadly Savanti blade had flashed from the scabbard and the point pricked my throat.

"Speak, rast! What do you know of Aphrasöe? Speak quickly and speak the truth—or you are a dead man!"

Chapter Thirteen

Of a Savapim and the Savanti

Could I take this man? A fighting man trained by the Savanti, in ferocious form as I had seen a man on a hair-trigger of violence? And, moreover, a man armed with that Savanti sword which is, I truly believe, the most perfect sword on the face of Kregen, not excepting the fantastic Krozair longsword? Could I take him?

"Hurry, rast! My patience wears thin! Speak up!"

I jerked my head back. I saw—a mere glance in passing—a drop of my blood on the gleaming blade he had so thoroughly cleaned on dead men's clothes.

He took that as a signal of treachery and drove in instantly.

I had only a rapier and main-gauche. There was scarcely time to explain to him that I was not in the habit of speaking up with a sword at my throat—not, that is, unless absolutely no other course lay open. The other course here was starkly plain. I could get my fool self killed.

I skipped back and the main-gauche came out of its scabbard seemingly of its own volition; his blade screeched against it. The following rapier thrust—the rapier had leaped into my hand, out of the scabbard, and pointed at him as though alive—passed through thin air. He danced away.

"You fight well. But I think you are a dead man."

Could I possibly face a man armed with a Savanti sword? I had never done so before except in practice in Aphrasöe, and that, clearly, was a different kettle of fish.

"Damn!" I burst out. "You're a bunch of rogues in Aphrasöe these days! Can't a fellow wish you Happy Swinging without a sword at his throat?"

"Tell me what you know of Aphrasöe and I will not slay you."

"And if you don't speak civilly I'll have to teach you a lesson! Do you know Maspero?"

"Yes." The brand gleamed in the lamplight as he let it drop a fraction.

"He was my tutor."

"*You* are a Savapim?"

I had never heard the word before. It must mean a man who was an agent of the Savanti. Boldly, then, lying in my teeth, I said, "Of course, you damned great onker! What is your name?"

"Oh, no. You tell me your name, onker."

Well, at least we were past the sword stage and to the probably more fruitful arguing stage. I did not laugh. I do not laugh easily outside the company of Delia, my children, and a few close friends, as you know.

122

Anyway, what confounded name should I give? The old and always amusing question popped up again. The Savanti could not have realized I was in the tavern when they had dispatched this man—one of their Savapims—to sort out the quarrel. Unlike the Star Lords, who dumped me down in the middle of a problem of life and death stark naked and weaponless, the Savanti at least equipped their agents with clothes and weapons. The Star Lords are altogether a starker group, starker, darker, and far more deadly.

This fellow could always make a few inquiries here and quickly discover I was the Amak of Paline Valley. Always assuming, of course, that I let him live that long.

So I said: "I am the Amak Hamun ham Farthytu."

"An Amak! You must have gone through Aphrasöe before my time."

"You get a thousand years," I said meaningfully.

"Yes. I am Wolfgang . . ." Then he paused. After a moment he went on, "Wolfgang. That is enough. And where is your sword?"

"Wolfgang?" I said. "My sword is in another place." And, by Zair, that was true!

"You would not understand Wolfgang. The name is strange to you, I have no doubt."

If he was about to launch into a garbled explanation that he came from one of the lights in the sky and a place there called Germany, he would be badly trained. He did not.

"Very strange." I prodded. "Where is your home, then, before you came to Aphrasöe down the River Aph?"

This seemed to reassure him. He did not enlighten me apart from a vague reference to a "distant place."

"I am from Hamal," I said. "And my labors are here. You?"

"I cannot understand why you were not used. I am tired lately, I have been very busy." He grumbled on about the missions which had occupied him while he put the sword up and I found some wine—reasonable stuff Nulty had left, a middling Stuvan—and we drank. The tension lessened. He explained that he had been in so many fights lately that he'd upset his tutor, a man he called Harding, because of the great quantity of deaths he had caused. I wondered, as you may imagine.

"My training taught me that life is sacred."

"Of course! That is just the point! It is a dispute that

cannot be resolved. Kregen must be civilized, as the Savanti decree." He waxed excited and perhaps the wine did the trick.

"The doves watch well." He sat on my bed cradling the wine glass. I kept it hospitably filled. He was talking about the white Savanti dove that had flown over me many times on Kregen to spy on me and report back to the Savanti. "There are so many diffs on this terrible world . . . "

I prodded, for I had not completed the course in Aphrasöe.

"The halflings live here as well as we apims."

"But have they always? I am considered high in the Savapim. This mission was given to me as an emergency, at the last minute. I should be in Aphrasöe now, happily swinging. But as for the diffs, of course there are many of them, how could it be otherwise? This is not Earth—" He checked himself, put the glass down, and added, "My home."

"Earth?" I said. "Is that in Havilfar?"

"You would not understand."

"Maybe not. Tell me about the latest reports in Aphrasöe concerning the diff question. The problem is acute."

We talked for a while about Aphrasöe, that marvelous city in the lake of the River Aph, and of the pool of baptism in the River Zelph where a dip will confer a thousand years of life, tremendous resistance to disease, and rapid recovery from wounds. I fully demonstrated that I knew what I was talking about, and his guard slipped; he drank a little more. Of course there were many different kinds of halflings, beast-men, men-beasts, on this world. It was an alien world. Would you expect to find men exactly the same as Madison Avenue advertising executives if you penetrated the jungles of Central America, the ice floes of the north? Some idiot might cavil at so many different kinds of men; the variety of nature is so enormous that it is this Earth with only one kind of dominant man that is strange and odd. Here on Kregen one kind of man had not obtained an ascendancy over all the others. And, too, this Wolfgang also believed that many of the species and races had come from other planets, as we had done ourselves, although I did not tell him that.

In an alien setting only the most stupid of blinkered idiots could say that they would not expect to see many

124

different kinds of life. Differences in numbers of arms and legs, in facial and skull structures, are the most common ways in which diffs vary from apims, but they are only the outward show. The most significant differences are those of psychology rather than physiology, of racial outlooks rather than morphology. At least this Wolfgang was not such an onker as to be eternally surprised at the multifarious faces of nature.

And suppose the Star Lords *had* scoured the galaxy to find different forms of life and placed them all here arbitrarily? What was their purpose? Why did they use me, Dray Prescot? One day, I promised myself, one day I'd find out.

Wouldn't a Pachak, with his tail hand, think an apim a most crippled mortal? Wouldn't a Djang, with his four powerful arms, think an apim practically armless? Who is to say who differs from whom?

The closed mind is always the most frightening horror in any world.

"Anyway," said this Savapim, who came from Germany on a spot of dirt circling a spot of light all but invisible from Kregen, "I am tired and it is late. Tomorrow I must continue my task. I envy you resident Savapims." He glanced at me sharply. "Although, if you are doing your job properly, why was I needed here at all?"

"There are many fresh diffs in Ruathytu just now," I said diplomatically.

He could sleep in Nulty's room. I saw to his wants, and he stretched out. "As I say," he said, yawning, "we now believe that the distribution of diffs and flora and fauna has clearly been carried out deliberately. And with a lot of snarl-ups. Has it been done to plan or arbitrarily? Has the initial distribution been completed, or is it a continuous process? And how long ago was it begun?" He yawned again. "And is evolution taking care of those species placed down in locales not suitable for them?"

I nodded. "I think that must be so."

Wolfgang licked his lips as I went to the door.

"It's all a puzzle." His voice softened and slurred. "Thank you for your hospitality. I welcome it. Kregen is a world very hard on the stranger at times. I have found many strange peoples in many places and I have already assumed they must have been placed here; at

125

least it is a strong possibility, and only an idiot would comment adversely on the continuing occurrence of new peoples on a new world."

I did not point out to him that he was talking to a man who said he came from Havilfar and therefore to whom Kregen would hardly be a new world. As I closed the door he said through a huge and final yawn, "So who the devil *is* putting these damned diffs here on Kregen, anyway?"

And that made me, Dray Prescot, Lord of Strombor and Krozair of Zy, smile. It was a hard, cynical smile. I thought the Star Lords controlled Kregen. I could be wrong, but at least I knew a little more than this Savapim.

The gaining of my information had been extraordinarily painful, that I will admit.

When I awoke in the morning and looked into Nulty's room, Wolfgang the Savapim was gone.

Pinned by one of my daggers to the wall was a note. I tore it down. The paper—ah, the paper! Savanti paper! Of first quality, beautiful, crisp, white. I had not asked Wolfgang about the Savanti paper and its important function. Now it was too late. The note was brief.

"Lahal Amak: Thank you for the wine and the bed. We will go hunting the graint together, on the plains."

It was written in that beautiful flowing Kregan script, very pure, and instead of the usual *remberee* was written *Happy Swinging*.

"Happy Swinging to you, too," I said, and burned the note.

Chapter Fourteen

How Rees and Chido assisted the Star Lords

Chido said, "Y'know, old feller, Wees ain't half cut up about last night."

"Did he roar?"

"By Krun! He roared like a chunkrah with hoofache!"

"Let us go and take the Baths of the Nine."

So we went to the best establishment in the Sacred Quarter. The Baths of the Nine are extraordinarily decadent and luxurious in Ruathytu, as you may imagine, and we steamed and soaked. We found Rees moodily stretched on a slab with a Numim girl carefull brushing his glorious golden fur.

"Huh," he said when he saw us. "You apims and your naked skins! Oil and strigils! Barbarous!"

So we imagined he was back to form, which was a relief.

"Anyway, Hamun!" he bellowed. "Who was that Havilorsaken man?"

"I have no idea," I said. "He cleared off quickly this morning before I was up. He didn't speak much."

"I'll bet he didn't."

We stretched out next to Rees and two Fristle fifis started in on us with oils, unguents, and scrapers. I leaned my head close to Rees in the warm scented room.

Now nine is one of the most sacred numbers on Kregen. I was to perform wonders with the aid of a magic square based on nine, but that remains to be told. So I leaned toward Rees and I said, "The Nine have been asking questions."

He looked at me blankly.

I said, "Do you know what I'm talking about?"

127

"No, by Krun! I do not."

If he knew about the Nine Faceless Ones, he might not vouchsafe that information, bound by prior vows.

I said, "They are faceless, Rees."

"Faceless! Bodyless! Specters! I need a drink!"

Later, as we sat on the terrace overlooking the largest pool and watched the swimming and diving, I said, very lazily, acting my part as a chinless goggler like Chido, "Do you know anyone connected with the vollers, Rees?"

"Only that cramph Vad Garnath, and if he shows his face I shall kill him."

Now I did not think Garnath was involved with voller manufacture. He had mentioned that he might form a skyship flight or a voller squadron. That was not what I wanted.

I tried for what I promised myself would be the penultimate time.

"I don't mean that, Rees. I mean making the damned things."

He looked over at me, his glass half raised. "Now, old son! You don't want to go around talking about these things. It ain't healthy."

"Downright unhealthy," said Chido, going red.

"I thought I could help the war effort."

"If they want you to help, they'll ask you to help." He drained his glass and bellowed, "Fill her up, you little fifi! Run!" And, to me: "You ought to join the regiment. I'm reforming. Better than ever. This time no damn regiment of monstrosities will overset us—"

"Zorcas?"

He chuckled and watched as the Fristle girl filled the glass.

"No, Hamun. Totrixes! Damn contrary beasts, the most uncomfortable ride, apart from sleeths, that is."

So how could I not say I would ride with him in his fine new regiment?

To get around that I shouted for more to drink. It was not wine but the fine sherbert-like drink much favored in the warmer parts of Havilfar. It was called sazz, from the fizzing, I suppose, and I drank half of it off before I spoke.

"Let me first go to Paline Valley. Nulty might welcome a visit."

Chido snorted. "Since when has a Crebent ever welcomed a visit from his master?"

"Ah," I said, "but Nulty is a special kind of Crebent."

This was a mere interlude. I could not simply idle time away in Ruathytu now, ruffling and roistering, drinking and singing, carousing from tavern to tavern. Nor could I go with Rees and the new regiment he was forming, even though they were now to be mounted on totrixes. I knew my nikvove squadrons would have cut through Rees's regiment at the Battle of Tomor Peak, totrixes or no totrixes, as they had in fact scythed down the three totrix regiments Hamal already had mounted.

Poor Rees! This great blustering Numim, this Rees ham Harshur, Trylon of the Golden Wind, loved a good fight and a good laugh. This great golden lion-man had worn the Queen's colors and fought for her during the rebellion which had seated her on the crystal throne, and now he was badly out of favor with that evil, scheming woman. Yes, indeed, poor Rees, for he had lost his way. I knew that. I do not think Chido could see it as clearly, for he saw with different eyes; but as we ate miscils and caught the crumbs as those tiny delicious cakes melted in our mouths, as we lazily picked up plines and savored them, I saw that Rees was troubled. Oh, he was forming a regiment and this time of totrixes, not zorcas. But for all the feeling I had for him I ached to see him acting so vivaciously to maintain his habitual lion-like bellowing and roaring.

Once again concern over a friend had seduced me from my true work. Concern over an enemy had made me forget he was a Hamalian, an enemy, a man who was fighting the men of my own country of Vallia. Curse all wars!

So, speaking, I admit, with a greater heaviness than I wished to show, I said, "I'll ride out with you, old fellow, as soon as can be. We'll see what a totrix regiment can do."

It doesn't matter, we are told, if you lie to your enemy. I'd lie and cheat and do the dirtiest tricks possible on my enemies to assist my friends. As we sat in the scented air overlooking the pool with the happy sounds of splashing and diving, though, and I looked across as Rees took up a handful of palines and I saw his pleased look, knowing I had lied to him, I had no love at all for the life of a spy.

I must get on with spying, though. . . .

I had been in Ruathytu less than a day. Adding on our travel time from Pandahem I fancied Tom Tomor and

Kytun would have the army on the move heading north-west, I judged they would only have gone a short distance. As for Pando and Tilda, they must wait on the icy slab of anticipation for my return.

I had not shaved this morning, and resisted the attempts of a charming little apim girl to shave me during the bathing ritual.

Rees stood up, flinging the last paline into the air and catching it in his lion-mouth, his golden mane flowing. "You look as scruffy as the back end of a quoffa, Hamun!"

Chido guffawed and, in his turn, stood up.

But all the same, as Chido rose his eyes caught mine and he made a face which said, very clearly, "Poor old Wees is badly off color."

The cause might be that idiot called Nath the Crafty and his obsessive hatred of diffs, but I was not at all sure of that. It could just be that Rees felt more than a little humiliated that his gorgeous regiment of zorcamen had failed again so disastrously. The first zorca regiment he had raised had been tumbled over by a regiment of Pandahem hersanymen. It could be.

Well, it was no use trying to saddle a fluttrell before you catch it. And, equally, I had my own zhantil to saddle.

Many of our old friends and acquaintances of the Sacred Quarter had gone off to war, and the place festered with a sleazy gaiety that displeased me, notwithstanding the place was the capital city of an enemy country. The presence of so many diffs also posed an unsettling problem: there were many more fights centered on racial differences than there had ever been. At the time—I admit with all due shame, now—this had no power to worry me. The more fighting men of Hamal who were put *hors de combat* at their own hands, before they got to battle with my warriors of Valka and Djanduin, the better.

By Krun! Yes!

A fistfight broke out among a noisy group of bathers below the terrace as we turned to leave. Shouts and yells spurted up, bouncing from the high fire-crystal roof. Other people avoided the ugly scene, knowing the guards would quickly arrive. Rees turned back, looking down with hot eyes. Chido let out a *tchh* of annoyance.

"There is that onker Gordano! He only came in from

his volgendrin last night, for he called on me and left a note, and here he is brawling with Fristles."

"He should have found you last night at the Scented Sylvie," said Rees, his voice growling. "Maybe a damned Kataki would have slashed his throat open with his tail blade."

I did not like this at all. But I caught at that word Chido used, *volgendrin*. I had heard men speak of them, as I have indicated, but I had not bothered, being busy about other pursuits. But the word must have a meaning over and above what I supposed.

Chido turned back and leaned over the terrace parapet. The fight down there waxed warm and two men went headfirst into the pool. From one of them redness drifted into the water, chill and ominous.

"Run, Gordano, you fambly!" yelled Chido. "Run!" But, being Chido, he shouted, "Wun!"

Rees shouted something, but in such a way that his meaning was lost. He strode out, flinging his towel around his golden mane. I looked with Chido down at the poolside, at the greenery growing lushly in ceramic pots and hanging from the multi-planed rafters supporting the fireglass roof. A pot smashed, and an apim and a Numim, fighting furiously, rolled into the water in an almighty splash. I did not know which of the men fighting down there might be Gordano. I looked back over my shoulder. Rees had gone. Then Chido gripped my arm.

"By Krun, Hamun! The guards have them!"

The guards sorted out apim and diff and trundled them off in different directions. Chido let go my arm and wiped his forehead. "And Gordano's arrested. The law will deal with him, the great onker."

"What does he do?" I said to Chido as we trailed after Rees.

"Gordano has some sort of job—Havil knows what— over on his volgendrin. He don't talk about it. Mysterious feller, even if he is my cousin and a Vad."

I pondered. When I had heard those three evil men plotting with their voices rising to me through the bronze grill there in the fortress of Smerdislad in Faol, I had more particularly marked their plans for me, for Vallia, for Hamal. They had said they would recruit more guards, if necessary, to take care of the volgendrins. Why should they do that? I had been taken to that fateful meeting only because I had followed Saffi to rescue her.

131

I truly believed I had done that because the Star Lords—or the Savanti—had arranged it. Now I felt strongly again that the Star Lords—or the Savanti—had arranged this poolside fight purely for my benefit. Much was to grow from that fight. So much that it was no coincidence but must have been a carefully arranged scenario for the furtherance of the plans of the Star Lords—scarcely the Savanti—and an opportunity I must not miss. The Star Lords, of whom I then knew just about nothing at all, normally cared for me not one whit. But some force had put me in the way of overhearing that conversation in Smerdislad, and some force had directed that fight with its consequences to take place as I sat on the terrace directly above.

Chido and I walked off to the guardhouse to find out what we could of his cousin Gordano.

The Hikdar in charge, fat and imposing behind a balass desk, peered at us myopically, and then back to the ledger before him. "Gordano? No, Horters, no Gordano has been brought in."

Chido made a face and turned away, clearly considering that his cousin had managed to run from the guards. The fight had resulted in deaths, so the laws of Hamal would come into full force. The bleak local guard building, an unhappy piece of architecture, solid-walled and squat, had been designed to withstand a siege. One could see why. I walked off after Chido and saw him pause, then start to walk on again. Only this time he turned off the corridor down a side passage. I followed.

"Quiet, old feller. There's that fambly Gordano, and he's up to something."

If the fight was indeed no coincidence but the chance I believed given to me by the Star Lords, it would be a single chance. From now on I must work alone. If I failed in this, I might easily be hurled back to the Earth of my birth, flung in a blue radiance fashioned after the likeness of a monstrous scorpion, sent packing four hundred light-years away from all I held dear on Kregen. No wonder I stepped lightly!

This Gordano, rapidly and fluently talking to a somewhat thick-headed guard, a dwa-Deldar, looked far more like the usual Hamalian than ever young Chido could. I could not hear what he was saying, but I saw the wink of silver as a handful of dhems passed, to be clutched and stuffed away with practiced ease.

132

Chido opened his mouth. Gordano saw him and his voice rose to continue effortlessly: "Lahal, Nath! I've just been telling this good fellow that as I am Naghan Lamahan it is essential I write a letter. Now that you are here you can deliver it for me."

Chido gaped. I could imagine the wheels revolving in his mind. He was no Nath, by Krun! And this was Gordano ham Thafey, the Vad of Unlorlan, the son of Chido's father's brother, and who in a Herrelldrin hell was this Naghan Lamahan?

"Lahal, Naghan," I answered. "Nath and I will see your letter safely delivered."

This Gordano ham Thafey, the Vad of Unlorlan, gave me a pretty close stare, I can tell you. My dirty wisp of chin beard could not have impressed him, but the guard and Chido both spoke at once, then, and we had to sort out the babble.

"You must hurry, Horters. The Hikdar will be yelling for me any mur!"

"Very well. A mur only, then." Gordano drew Chido aside.

At that moment a bull voice roared along the passage. "Deldar! Where in Havil's name have you got to, you cramph of an onker!"

"By Havil!" gasped the Deldar. He bolted across the corridor to grab Gordano. That worthy, a dark-skinned man with a smooth complexion and exceedingly bright eyes, still wearing the lounging clothes he had donned after his arrest at the pool, smiled with a wide glitter and went peacefully. I saw Chido stuffing a piece of paper into his back pocket. So we walked back out of the guard station with blank and highly respectable citizens' faces covering our thoughts.

You have probably already guessed what ensued. Again, I stress, I did not think this was coincidence. Chido showed me the letter. Heavily sealed, it had clearly not just been written and was not a plea for help from a man in prison. "Gordano says it must reach the hands of Pallan Horosh in person, and at once; if it does not then Gordano will be stuck down in a dungeon of the Hanitchik and never see the lights of day again."

"There is no problem there. Let us take it to this Horosh and then——"

"But, Hamun! I am contracted to join Rees's new regiment. He is going to his estates of the Golden Wind to-morrow."

I did not fully understand yet, you see, so I made some observation into which Chido broke fretfully: "But Pallan Horosh will be at the volgendrin—Gordano says it is the Volgendrin of the Bridge. Rees cannot wait that long. You know how he is. He feels for the defeat his regiment suffered."

"I know that." I had to be a trifle careful here, for all that Chido was a chinless goggler he might think it strange that a fellow Hamalian, a fellow noble, did not know of the volgendrins.

To get out of that and to take two korfs with one shaft, as Seg would say, I spoke with gravity, impressing Chido: "I will take the letter for your cousin. It is the least I can do out of friendship. Just give me full instructions on how to reach Pallan Horosh and I will go." I added as an afterthought, "Doubtless there is a pass-word to bring me directly to him."

"We-ell," said Chido.

"Come on, old son, hand it over and tell me."

By Makki-Grodno's worm-infested intestines! I said—but to myself—wild risks must be taken to get my itchy fingers on a letter like this. It had to be important. I just knew it had to be. Otherwise why the coincidences that were not coincidences?

Chido hesitated. "Gordano said he didn't dare go through the official channels—he's not supposed to be here in Ruathytu at all, only came for some fun, get-onker that he is—and I'm supposed to say he's been taken ill. Can't let him down. We had a few good romps when we were young."

"I won't let you down, old feller."

Well, I said these things and planned what I would do, and I took no joy from it. Except—and here the joy welled fierce and deep—except that I was absolutely certain I was on to a further revelation of the silver boxes, the vaol and the paol boxes that powered fliers.

In the end, with many cautions, Chido handed the letter over. We were walking along in the blue shadows of the colonnades of the Kyro of the Vadvars, and out in the blinding light of Antares the zorca riders and the young onkers astride sleeths and all the many varieties of carriages and litters passed and repassed.

The light burned into my eyes and I looked back to

see Chido as a red-limned blur. "Well, and how do I find this Horosh?"

He gave me my directions, and I realized that the volgendrins lay to the west, right up to the Mountains of the West and the sparsely populated lands there.

"And, Hamun, you won't get a voller now. The Queen has commandeered every last one for military and governmental use."

"Well, by Krun!" I said. "I don't fancy a fluttrell. I'll buy or hire a mirvol."

Neither of us even so much as contemplated my getting a clepper of any kind; all the fiuttcleppers and volcleppers would be pressed into military service. And the little money I had left would not run to a zhyan. So, in any event, it was arranged. I did not see Rees before I left. I sent him my best felicitations by Chido and then, having gone up to the barracks to collect my gear including at least one most important article, I took off for the Mountains of the West.

Chido did not call remberee. Instead, just before the mirvol bashed its wings down in that powerful muscular beat at the beginning of a flight, he called out, "By Krun, Hamun. May the Light of Opaz shine on you."

One of the handlers in the voldrome looked somewhat curious, so to cover all that and warming to Chido, I yelled down: "May the Greenness of Havil cover you in benediction!"

Then I was up and away, soaring out over Ruathytu with the familiar streets, avenues, and boulevards spread below, with the Kyros and their radiating arteries of traffic, the Jikhorkduns doing brisk business, the merezos with the races already beginning. All the domes, arcades, and towers speared up, then fell away and away and the wind rushed in my ears and the mirvol bore me high up into the sky of Hamal.

Chapter Fifteen

I sing with swods

Wind-bluster battered past my ears. The close-fitting leather flying cap was devoid of feathers or ornamentation. I bent low to the neck of the mirvol as we hurtled on through the air over Hamal, the fields and watercourses passing away below in a long stream of checkered browns, reds, and yellows threaded with blue. Forests sprawled beneath, the trees mere toy lumps of greenery. This mirvol was a sturdy beast, not overly fast, but I had picked him out in the voldrome with an eye to reliability and stamina. His deep keel chest indicated he would fly well and for a long time. His coloring, too, was a mere speckled brown, with nothing of the flamboyance of some flying animals of Havilfar. I liked him, and his name was Liance.

Chido had not been standing at my side all the time I had made my preparations. But, even so, I had not opened the letter. He could easily have asked to see it before I took off, just to make sure I had it. He had not done so, but might have. My way lay south of west, almost three hundred dwaburs away. In theory the mirvol could cover that vast distance in something like forty-eight burs, the length of the Kregan day-and-night cycle. But that was in theory only. The beast would need to rest and eat, for a flying animal consumes enormous quantities of energy and must replenish its vital faculties with adequate supplies of food. Mirvols, like many flying animals, eat some meat, but the nut of the tsu-tsu tree and those fat and nourishing beans the Hamalians call dyrolains are the favorites of the mirvols; those and a sweet thick syrup they like dripped on just about anything they eat, including meat. Feeding flying animals is often more involved than merely turning them out to graze, although they forage on their own account most efficiently. I thought of the groves of dyrolains growing in my Delia's estates of Delphond. Vallia could feed her aerial cavalry when the time came.

Planning to reach the Volgendrin of the Bridge just after the suns set on the next day, I touched down at a tiny dusty mining town where the local inn turned out to be surprisingly well stocked on beers and sazz, if not wine. I partook of an enormous meal there and saw to it that Liance filled his belly, also. I relied on the cunning strength of his wings.

The plans went well and I slanted down from the sky with all the forward horizon sheets and pinnacles of color as the twin suns sank beyond the Mountains of the West. The mountains bulked against that glowing sky, black edges of menace. The coruscations of fire, all ruby and emerald with orange and yellow shooting through in a glowing pyrotechnic display that formed one of those breathtaking suns' settings of Kregen, could not diminish the stark jaggedness of those peaks; neither could the beauty conceal the horrors I knew lurked byond the mountains ready to fly in to lay waste and destroy. Was I not the Amak of Paline Valley?

The letter had been opened and read.

I had done not this at the mining camp, which I left with much good-humored abuse ringing in my ears, but later, coming to earth by a grove of trees where a river edged the beginning of the barren plain that led up to the mountains here. Much of the eastward face of the mountains and the land immediately below it is smothered in heavy forest, subtropical, dangerous country. But equally as dangerous were the areas where the rivers did not run, where the rain shadows caused barrens. Where I was going, following Chido's instructions, was clearly a semi-desert.

I opened the letter with some skill, although the seal was broken in the process, for I was over-hasty. I would deal with that problem when it arose. A single sheet of paper, yellow and finely made by hand, folded in half, rewarded my larceny. It was covered with rows of figures. Apart from the heading which read *The First Month of the Maiden with the Many Smiles*, that was all.

It seemed fairly clear what the figures must be. If my suspicions were right—and I was going on a mishmash of whispers, overheard conversations, and coincidences that were not coincidences, but engineered by the Star Lords; and also on the very reasons I was here at all—then these figures must refer to production targets. I believed they would be targets, for completion reports would be flying in the opposite direction. And, that being so, the product of which these figures were the subject must be connected with the silver boxes, must in all probability be a mineral, and, if I was lucky, one of the four minerals we in Vallia had not identified and so had been unable to use. If I could discover what the actual stuff was, instead of merely giving San Evold Scavander a name he did not recognize, then we might produce vollers which would travel and steer instead of merely float up in the air.

The paper, correctly folded, went back into the wrapper. I pushed the split seal together, then I threw the packet on the ground and jumped on it. A few crumples and bashings and it looked as though it had gone through a charge by wild chunkrahs.

So, as I slanted down looking for the Volgendrin of the Bridge, I had to believe that Pallan Horosh would take my story for gospel. I'd have a bit of swordplay on my hands if he did not, unless they killed me first.

The feel of the great longsword on my back came as a comfort.

With a final outburst of orange fire streaked with the stained green, the Suns of Scorpio sank beyond the mountains. In the dying moments of that burning glow I saw the marker I looked for: a gigantic cleft in the rock shone and coruscated in flashing reflections of the sunset, flaming in orange, red, and jade fires for murs after the suns had vanished beyond the peaks.

What happened next was so typical of Kregen, and happened just as Chido had told me Gordano had explained to him, that I felt my craggy old lips thin out into a semblance of a smile.

The air around me filled with the rustling forms of flying beasts. They curved in with swift and brutal efficiency, swerving to hem me in so that escape without a fight was not possible.

I knew these beasts and their riders.

These were the same bandy-legged diffs, squat, malefic with energy, with square, clamped mouths, who had welcomed me when I'd been flown into that hellhole called the Heavenly Mines. These were the Gerawin of

138

Gilarna the Barren. They flew with consummate skill on tyryvols whose glistening black and ocher scales were dulled now by the onset of night. But I knew the Gerawin well enough, and knew the efficiency with which they guarded slaves for the Empire of Hamal.

Parked like a slice of vosk in a sandwich of Kregen bread, I flew on. We did not fly down to land. We flew on straight for the mountains. A black mass, indistinct and vague in the darkness, loomed above. My mirvol, Liance, behaved perfectly, for all that a tyryvol with its whip tail and scales can unsettle practically any other flying animal or bird. We were landing. The ground felt soft and spongy as, with a soothing word to Liance, I alighted.

The Gerawin did not land with me but curved up and away, their tridents dark lances of menace, circling like upthrown leaves away into the enveloping gloom. Men advanced toward me. I held up my hand in greeting. "Lahal," I said, speaking firmly and loudly. "Lahal. I must see Pallan Horosh at once."

A slender luminousness pervaded the scene as She of the Veils rose in the eastern sky. For that little space we had been living through a period of Notor Zan. The Tenth Lord would not rise tonight, for after She of the Veils the Twins would rise and we would have light enough. If I do say so myself, I had timed my arrival nicely.

"This way." The voice was cold and businesslike. A torch flared. The guard party were apims, clad in normal Hamalese armor, bearing stuxes, swords, and shields. She of the Veils touched the black and ocher plumes of their helmets, the same colors at that time favored by the Gerawin. I went with them.

The ground possessed an odd and unsettling feeling and I could not quite accustom myself to land again. I felt like a sailor stepping ashore for the first time after six months at sea. And this was strange, for I had not experienced this when I'd touched down on the way here. Vague fancies about earthquakes and rock slides took me as we went through an overhanging forest of branches, hanging with fruits I did not know. The path squelched. Everything was conducted as I had expected it would be, with the full ritual observance of the dread laws of Hamal.

All the same, the deadliness of the effect, the hardness, the queasy feeling underfoot, the silence of these men and the odd surroundings, affected me . . . affected me power-

139

fully, so that my hand rested on the pommel of my rapier and I wriggled my shoulder blades to make sure the longsword still hung there.

The tunnel-like avenue through the hanging branches and the dependent fruit broadened and we came to a wooden guardhouse. Torches were flaring, soldiers talking, and the smell of food cooking. I could eat again, having grown accustomed to Kregen ideas on the correct number of meals per day. I wore a dark cloak which I left hanging over my left shoulder; it was pushed back and clipped on the right, just in case.

On my right shoulder under the cloak I wore a sheath containing six terchicks, the deadly throwing knives. Six men would die before I drew the longsword. . . .

Nothing of these bloodthirsty thoughts showed on my ugly old face as the Hikdar walked out from the wooden hut to inspect me. He carried a chicken bone in his hand. He saw I did not wear a uniform beneath the cloak and was prepared to be unpleasant. He was an ord-Hikdar, which meant he was of pretty high rank to catch guard duty, or so I thought then.

"Now, then, by Barfurd! What have we here?" He walked around me, peering, exaggerating. Any soldierman gets tired and irritated on distant guard duty; I did not blame the Hikdar for acting like this, for it was in his nature, but I gave him up to the time I counted ten, then I would deal with him.

"Pallan Horosh, Hikdar," I said. "The password is Thyllis the Magnificent." Then I forgot all about counting to ten and added with a look that made him drop the chicken bone, "And if you don't jump, onker, and unglue your wings you'll be a swod with a brush and pan in your fists!"

There was little delay after that. The nearest an Earthly expression can get to the flavor of "unglue your wings" in the Havilfarese flying culture is "get the lead out of your pants!"

I will not go into the various substances often alluded to as causing the gluing up of wings.

The moons now cast enough light for me to see the undulating plain-like expanse, covered with a thick growth of yellow grass, which extended from the guard hut to a bulging hill about half an ulm off. There was something almighty strange about this land. Away in the distance the moons shone on the Mountains of the West, the whiteness of their peaks glazed with gold and pink. I went with the detail toward the humped hill. A door opened in the vine-like growth and we went inside.

The place had been constructed, I thought, from beams and crossties of wood in the natural state, that is, the bark had not been removed and the wood had not been split or sawn. Canvas coverings formed the walls. Carpets covered the floor, which alone had been constructed from carpentered wood. The noise of habitation came up with the familiar sensations an old soldier experienced on entering barracks. The strains of song wafted along as we went through to a door guarded by two Pachaks. The song was, I remember, *Tyr Korgan and the Mermaid*. As we passed between the two Pachak guards to enter the Pallan's opulent quarters, those swods down there had reached the fourth verse, where Tyr Korgan draws his fourth great breath and dives to take the mermaid's hand.

The Pallan's quarters were those with which one would expect a man of culture and refinement to furnish himself on a distant assignment in a rough and barren land. This Horosh liked his comfort. All the evidences of hedonistic living met my gaze, and perhaps only the predominance of black and purple—in rugs and feathered hangings—indicated any particular local affiliations. I stood looking at the Pallan, who sat at a balass-wood desk, gilt and enamel in the panels, writing with a quill. He glanced up.

Pallan Horosh's look reminded me of the malefic face of the Devil of the Ice-Wind who guards the north shore of Gundarlo.

"Your name?"

His voice grated like an unoiled wheel.

"Naghan Lamahan." It amused me to give the name Gordano had used in the police watch station.

His head went up. His nostrils pinched, whitely.

"You address me as Notor, nulsh."

I, Dray Prescot, Prince Majister of Vallia and King of Djanduin—and much else besides—remained fast. I did not blink an eye. I said: "Notor."

"Give me the letter."

When he saw its condition he opened his mouth and I said, smooth and quick, "There was an accident. Flutsmen." I would have gone on but he waved me down and took the letter. His hands were long and slender, missing the middle finger of the left hand.

141

"I care nothing for your experiences."

He did not have to break the seal. He threw the wrapper to the carpet and fell to reading the figures. After a space he looked up, saw me, growled out, "You still here, nulsh? Get out." He added, quite unnecessarily, "Schtump!"

I said, "Notor," turned, and marched off.

I had enjoyed myself—maybe you can understand a little more now the coldness which was entering my heart when I dealt with these heartless men of Hamal.

My plans were really no plans. I had followed coincidences, believing them not to be coincidences. Here I was, in the Volgendrin of the Bridge. I had had one chance and I'd taken it with both hands. Here, with the moons sailing past above and the night breeze redolent with the scents of secretly opening flowers, I went with the detail to my assigned quarters. What to do now? One thing remained certain in a shifting world: I should not tarry here overlong. If the Star Lords had thrown me this gnawed bone and refused me the meat, then I would fly back to my little army and joy in seeing Tom Tomor and Kytun once more.

Naghan Lamahan. In Hamal that was like saying Charles Robinson on Earth.

The detail left and I waited for half a bur before going off prowling, with all my gear still on me. I wandered down to the corridor where I'd heard the strains of song. Down there they'd begun on the *Canticles of the Rose City,* that famous song-cycle celebrating the mythical doings of the man-god Drak. When I pushed through into the mess they were still nowhere near the end. Apart from one or two flushed faces turned in my direction, the men went on lustily bellowing it out, all of it, taking a great joy in their singing. Of course, much of the mythical story followed different forms, for the legendary Drak is very much a god-hero of Vallia, and these Hamalians changed things accordingly.

I settled down and a Matoc shoved an earthenware pot into my hand. I thanked him and drank the beer and so joined in the singing. This, to me, assuaged a great drought.

Why is it that, in general, the ordinary common soldier, when he is not drunk on alcohol or the red killing fury of battle, is such a quiet, cheerful, decent sort of fellow? Maybe it is because, as so many would-be pundits have

142

said, a good soldier is devoid of imagination. I tend to doubt that, but it is unfortunately so often true as to have become a byword.

The song finished and my earthenware pot was replenished. The wooden walls reverberated to the strains, of *Sogandar the Upright and the Sylvie*. The first lines of this go something like: "Now Upright Sogandar had no idea at all, and thought the Sylvie wanted just to see his Painted Hall," and from then on it is all downhill. There is much jocose repetition of "No idea at all, at all, no idea at all." This always sends these tough old warriors into fits of laughter at the naiveté of Sogandar the Upright.

One thing was certain: these Hamalians wouldn't sing *The Bowmen of Loh*.

I talked to them as the jugs went around between songs, the apims and the Numims, the Pachaks and Brokelsh. Chuliks usually regard singing as a decadence. A little Och staggered up and gave us a charming solo: *The Cup Song of the Och Kings*. He fell flat on his face just before he finished, his six limbs twitching. A black-bristle Brokelsh poured a jug of beer over him as he lay; he did not stir.

Talking to them, lazily asking questions so it appeared I had no interest in the answers, drinking and singing, I spent the best part of three burs in the swods' mess. The Matoc—a very low grade of noncom—who had pressed the first beer on me, had been grumbling away, in between singing, and I had understood him to be worried about what he called the drift.

A Numim, his golden fur somewhat torn and his mane in shreds, belched and said, "Aye, dom! The drift this time has been real bad. Them mountings is a sight mortal close."

"If I know the way of it," said the Matoc, grumbling. "The binhoys will be late. By Kuerden the Merciless! I'd as lief be sent to the northern front."

"Yes," agreed an apim, leering. "Plenty of loot up there."

Reaching over the jug, I said in a companionable voice, "I hear tell the army's bogged down, up in Pandahem."

They were interested. I managed to avoid the immediate charge of being a peace-monger, but I sowed a few seeds I hoped would grow to the discomfort of Hamal.

But they were back to the drift again, cursing the Volgen-drin of the Bridge.

They were also most crude in their comments about flyers they called exorcs. They wondered in their cheer-fully rough way if the exorcs' parents—which they called cows—would be blown away, and hoping by Krun they would. They had no time, that was very plain, for these exorcs.

The wooden mess hall shuddered abruptly. I heard the noise of the wind, which had been steadily growing in volume, rising now with unmistakable ferocity. Again the wooden walls shook. The Matoc drained his jug and threw it aside, making no effort to refill it. "May Keurden the Merciless take 'em all!" he burst out. "It'll be fencing for us this night, mark my words."

"I never understand it," said the Brokelsh, shaking his head. "The damned vo'drin's not supposed to care about wind."

"No more it don't," said the apim who wished to go to the northern front. "It's just the drift and our bad luck."

"Anyway," shouted the Numim, scratching his torn fur. "Who'd be a Gerawin on a night like this, huh, lads?"

They all chuckled at this, most evilly, I thought, and I realized they were taking some sour pleasure from think-ing of other swods worse off than themselves.

An ob-Deldar stuck his head in the door and bel-lowed.

That, after all, is what ob-Deldars exist to do.

"All out! Wenda!"* In the lamplight the ob-Deldar's face exhibited an incipient case of apoplexy. The swods scrambled for the door. They took only their thraxters for weapons, leaving their stuxes and shields. They knew what they were being called out for.

The ob-Deldar saw me.

"You! Nit that crawls on a fluttrell's back! Out!"

I went across to him and looked at him.

"I am not a soldier, dom. Hurry about your business. The Hikdar appeared to me to be a man of hasty temper."

"By Keurden the Merciless! You are right, he is a very devil."

The wooden walls shook—no, the floor shook!

The Deldar took a fresh grip on his thraxter and pushed his helmet straight. "Look out for yourself," he

---

*Wenda: Let's go. Hurry.

said. "You messengers don't know half of it." He ran out, already bellowing fearsomely for the men to get topside.

When I reached the door the men were already gone. I stepped out and gasped. The wind reached for me with burning fingers. Flat and level, the wind coursed across the ground, swirling dead leaves and twigs, scraps, rubbish, dust. I bent my head into it and tried to see what was going on. The four major moons were up, but drifting clouds broke the light and threw intermittent shadows on the earth.

The wind blew with the furnace breath of the desert. I peered through slitted eyes and saw the trees bending. I also saw, but did not realize then the full significance of what I saw, the unripe fruit being torn from the trees and hurled through the air, squashing and dripping, wasted.

A fresh party of soldiers ran up and the Hikdar, having lost all appetite for chicken, was bellowing them on. He saw me and was about to push past. I said, "I will help."

"You will be welcome. We go to mend the windbreaks. The fruit is being destroyed."

I could understand that. Heads down, our capes billowing, we struggled against the wind across that fruit-strewn ground. And I thought—I thought!—the ground moved beneath me with the violence of the wind.

After a time the fences showed before us. Tall constructs of wood and lath, they were tightly woven to give shelter to the fruit trees. Now there were grinning gaps torn in their orderly ranks. Even as we came up a whole section a full hundred paces long ripped away and flailed concertina-like for a moment, then broke and splintered. The air was filled with the whirring, deadly slivers of wood.

"On! On!" yelled the Hikdar, as though he led a regimental charge against swordsmen. A number of low huts against the fence contained repair materials. We were going to have to rebuild the damned fence if the gale persisted much longer. Soon I was employed lugging out lengths of lumber and running with them to the men propping the fences, reinforcing the props that had snapped, reweaving fresh withes between the uprights and diagonals to form fresh panels. It was damned hot work with that biting, burning wind scouring the air in the lungs and frying the eyes in the head. And, over all, the moons of Kregen shone down through the gale-torn gaps in the clouds. It did not rain.

Other men were there helping, and I realized that reinforcements had been brought up from somewhere, for these new arrivals were slaves. They were lashed into the work, while the soldiers labored through their own discipline.

A voller sliced down from above, riding on an even keel and without discomfort in the shriek of the gale. It was very clearly of that class of flier that moves independently of the wind, the forces in its silver boxes surrounding the voller with its own sphere of influence. A man in a blue cape gestured and the anger in his gesture was plain. The Hikdar yelled more fiercely over the wind and the slave overseers plied their whips.

Staggering up carrying a timber balk against the wind I cannonned into a Brokelsh who, with the crudity of that race, grabbed me for mutual support. He seized the other end of the balk and together we ran it across to the soldiers where they struggled to hold up a section of fence against the wind. In the lee of the half-raised fence the cessation of violence, streaming wind, and blattering noise cut and snuffed, I paused for a quick breather. The Brokelsh spat.

"These onkers'll never get a section as big as this up. Look at 'em . . . onkers!"

"It's a tough one," I said. A few paces further along the fence lay flat on the ground, rippling with the wind flow. Men clustered like flies on a honeyed rope as they sought to shove the fence up with their poles. A pole slipped from the upright against which it thrust. It ripped through the withes, tearing them like tissue as wind pressure smashed the fence down. Men jumped out of the way and the wind hit us again.

Ropes lay neatly coiled here and there. I had once been a sailor on the seas of Earth and had long experience in handling enormous weights and dealing with wind pressures, with the only power at my disposal the muscles of men.

The blustering yell of the wind made normal speech impossible. If I started to do what I intended others would follow . . . that is always the way. Once a man takes the lead there are always those who will follow. It just needs the right man in the right place at the right time. How all the gods of Kregen must have guffawed! How the

146

Star Lords and the Savanti, if they were watching, must have snickered!

They say pride comes before a fall.

I, Dray Prescot, Krozair of Zy, jumped up and ran head-down into the wind. I snatched up the end of a coil of rope and sprinted for the flat section of fence. Once over that I could loop the rope around an upright and then, with the men I knew would follow my example, we could haul back and so raise the fence in proper ship-shape fashion.

I saw the Deldar waving his arms at me, his face a most wonderful color, much like an overripe shonage, and his mouth opening and opening as he bellowed all silently in the wind rush.

I waved my arm back, reassuringly. The rope felt thick and bristly in my hands. It felt wonderfully reassuring, also, bringing back many salty moments of the past. Running forward, bent over, I scarcely heeded where I was going. Just to get around the end of the fence and loop the rope up onto an upright, that was my task. I'd show these onkers of Hamal how a sailorman handled the wind!

As I say, pride goes before a fall.

I lurched against the wind past the end of the fence and for a moment I put my hand against the wood. I looked down.

To this day, as I sit here talking into this microphone, I can recall the utter shock of disbelief that thrilled through me.

The wind shrieked past my ears, the wood felt thick and sleazy in one hand, and the rope thick and bristly in the other—and I looked down. I stood on the very lip of a precipice. The edge of ground broke sheer away. At that instant the clouds parted. The four great moons of Kregen shone forth.

And I saw.

I saw.

Far far below I saw the ground. I saw the ground moving past below. The sharp edge of the precipice did not join that ground; I stood on ground that soared above the earth like a flier. I yelled. The very shock of it, the incredible fact of it, hit me shrewdly. Land that flew through the air!

Volgendrin!

And then I slipped and pitched forward, spinning out into thin air.

Chapter Sixteen

The Volgendrin of the Bridge

I fell.

The wind smashed at me. The world spun upside down and right side up, with the moons hurtling between my feet and the volgendrin catherine-wheeling above me and then the hard earth far far below flicking into view over my head.

The rope burned through my hand.

My other hand came across as though I drew my rapier to face a treacherous attack from a Bravo fighter, and gripped. My two hands pained with a tearing agony that lanced up my arms and into my brain, but I held on. I held on and dangled. Now the distant earth was below me and above me the volgendrin showed its sheer side and the black rock crust. Above that the moons cast down their mingled pinkish light and I was rising and lifting in the air as willing hands hauled me back from death.

"By Havil!" said the Brokelsh as they hauled me over the lip. "And how were the Ice Floes of Sicce?"

"Cold."

They landed me as a fisher lands a fish and I rolled over on the ground, getting my breath back. The wind had sensibly decreased in violence. The longsword poked out awkwardly as I sat up sideways and so rose to my feet.

"That is a strange cross on your shoulder, dom," said the Brokelsh. The Deldar moved up, shouting, and we

148

could hear what he was saying, the usual farago of obscenities and orders to get back to work.

"Aye," I said. "And here is the obbie."

The ob-Deldar lashed his men on and, in that remarkable way these men have, requested me most politely, although at the top of his voice, if I would mind lending a hand. So we pitched in to reerect the fences.

The whole time, as we labored and the wind dropped, sighed a few fitful gusts, then died altogether, I marveled at just where I was. So the word *volgendrin* held a precise meaning! I had not suspected the full truth, but, looking back, and with a little hindsight, I realized I had been blind. In all probability you who listen to these tapes will long ago have fathomed out just what a volgendrin is.

No one went to their beds that night until the last fence had been firmly staked, lashed, and propped. It was now clear why the wind had risen so rapidly and then so rapidly died away: the volgendrin had passed from the lee of one mountain into the open maw of a pass before reaching the shelter of the next peak. Those barren, burning wastes of arid mountain sides with the wind funneling through had poured that burning gale on us. Now the volgendrin in its eternal circling movement would swing around and away from the mountains before its course once more brought it back into the funnel of the wind.

Just how high up we soared through the air was not too easy to determine; I thought we held the thousand-foot mark. With the earliest light of the next day I was up, ostensibly to fly back, in actuality to find out as much as I could about this marvel, this flying island, this volgendrin.

And the first thing I saw with the suns was another flying island an ulm away, floating through the air like a cloud.

Beyond that floated others. I had no idea how many there were or how far they extended. The land below, barren and poor, would not reveal by stunted growths the path of the islands' shadows. One thing was very clear: the agency which held these masses in the air must be closely allied to the forces within the vaol and paol boxes. The wind had no effect on them in the sense that they floated independently of it, although it could wash across them, as we had seen last night. I spent some time just walking around the flying island, following the perimeter fence and climbing up to the watchtowers studding the rim. I saw why this volgendrin had been given its name.

From its northern side the next volgendrin was joined by a seething mass of writhing vegetation, from bottom to bottom. That undulating floor of creeping vines stretched between the two volgendrins, and I judged it to be at least a hundred feet thick, against the apparent three hundred foot thickness of the islands themselves. Across the gap stretched the bridge.

A thin, spidery construction, it looked frail and flimsy. It was still there, though, after the wind of the previous night.

To give a revoltingly crude image, imagine two thick slices of bread resting on a plate of spaghetti, with a hair stretching between them—there you have the volgendrins, the undulating mat of vines, and the bridge spanning that horrific gap.

Men were continually crossing the Bridge carrying burdens, or marching from slave quarters to work in the orchards. Near at hand a gang worked a chain pump fetching water up from the cavernous reservoirs deep below. The orchards thrived. The land below burned barren and desiccated under the Suns of Scorpio and under the eternal orbiting of the volgendrins around a continually shifting locus.

The volgendrins remain in their orbits, like planets circling a sun, although for them the locus is an invisibility. The wind cannot move them. They remain there, close to the Mountains of the West of Hamal. There are other volgendrins on Kregen, which I was to visit in the fullness of time, but I do not believe any of them shocked me with such a sense of wonder as that one time when I discovered the Volgendrin of the Bridge.

Why had the chain of events instigated by the Star Lords brought me here?

When I went along to see about food, I felt it politic to go to the swods' mess. That Hikdar might have thought about the way I had treated him. As it happened, the Matoc in charge of the group I had sung with was not at all surprised to see me. He smiled a snaggle-toothed smile as I helped myself to roast ponsho and momolans—not as fine as those served in Delphond, but tasty all the same —with a right-angled section of squish pie which I took with what memories and hopes you may imagine. I truly felt that I had not wasted my time here so far, for a recce is always valuable. But time was running out. Soon I must return to Pandahem and the army. If the Star Lords had given me this one chance and I was too blind and too stupid to see in which direction I must go, then I must once again trust myself to Oxkalin the Blind Spirit.

So I said: "Tell me, Matoc, has production been good recently? The war makes heavy demands on us all."

He wiped his plate clean with a chunk of bread, the heavy somewhat doughy bread much favored in Hamal, and stuffed the dripping mass into his mouth. With the flavorsome chunk pushed into his cheek, bulging and shining, he said, "I thought you merkers knew all the secrets in the world."

I made myself laugh. "Oh, aye, Matoc. That is what is said."

He gave a few perfunctory chews and swallowed with a fine acrobatic display from his Adam's apple. Already he was pulling out a wad of cham wrapped in its leaves from his pouch. "Well, now, this wind won't do production any good. The pashams were rolling every which way, like Ochs' heads after a cavalry charge."

That image made him laugh in his turn.

I said, "Yes. I saw plenty of fruit rolling around in the wind." I had to contain myself. Who the blazes was interested in their fresh fruit production? I wanted to know about the mineral that went into the silver boxes of the vollers. I opened my mouth and started to say, "That's all very well, but the army of Hamal requires bigger production. How many binhoys can you fill in—" And then I paused. Could it be?

He had the cham in his mouth now and was working it up into a succulent wad that would last him through better than two burs.

So it was somewhat indistinctly that he said: "What they do with 'em I do not know, by Krun! They taste like the sweepings of a totrix stable. And you never see 'em sold in the markets."

This emboldened me to say, "I've never seen any pashams in the markets of Ruathytu."

"I come from Dovad. I'd sooner be there than here."

"I know Dovad," I said. "A charming town and the waterfall is most impressive."

"Ah!" he said, chewing. "Many's the time I've taken a pretty little shishi on a trip to the falls. Well, no one then believed you could ever go as far as the Mountains of the West." He spat, the cham working up nicely. "And they're right, by Havil's Greenness! I've no wish to serve on a vo'drin, and that's a fact."

There was no difficulty at all in picking up a pasham. The slaves were being flogged into clearing up and I simply walked past the collecting bins. The bins were running with a green juice that had called forth all manner of obscenities, for the fruit was not ripe and was useless. The juice ran down, smelling of old sweaty socks. I picked up a reasonably undamaged pasham, making a face, and wrapped it in leaves. This I stowed away in the lower pockets of the green dolman I wore slung over my left shoulder under the cloak.

The fruit looked to be as large as a grapefruit and would probably swell into melon size—honey melon, that is—when ripe. If it was not edible and yet was so assiduously cultivated and provided with soldiers to act as guards, then it must be connected to voller production. It could simply be that the pasham was pressed for oil, for lubrication, for example. But I hankered after my unfounded belief in the Star Lords. They had used me as their puppet and I had resisted them. Of late they had left me alone. I knew that at any minute I could find myself caught up in the mistiness of that radiant blue scorpion and go head over heels back four hundred light-years to Earth. But, despite the aloofness of the Everoinye, I persisted in my notion that they had sent me here, for a purpose connected with the vollers. That being so, pashams had to be the answer.

From my previous experiences with the management of voller production in Hamal I surmised that the people here would simply grow and pack the pashams. After that the binhoys, those huge flat barge-like fliers, would take the fruits to be processed at another plant. Then they would go on somewhere else and then—the thought occurred to me with no excitement but only a dull feeling of my own ineffectiveness—they could be dried and ground into a powder, a powder I had previously thought of as a mineral.

There were four minerals we had not found in Vallia, for all San Evold Scavander's researches and the field trips of Ornol. The iron-masters of Vallia did not know. Coal was known and used; the coal-masters did not know. Nor did the masters of the various chemical works, all in a relatively primitive state, to be sure, know. The dyers threw up their hands and shrugged. So perhaps one of the mystery minerals was no mineral at all, but a dried and powdered fruit.

In the past, Vallia had bought everything she required except her navy from the traders of the world of Kregen under Antares.

Now the Hamalians were clamping down, and it was high time I returned to my army in Pandahem. There was one other question, and then I would be off.

The binhoys were late, as the Matoc had foretold. I wandered down to the lowest open sections of cliff face, fenced in, and looked down at the writhing mat of vines and tendrils below, stretching out to join the other volgendrin which was, really, a part of the whole, the whole Volgendrin of the Bridge.

Away to my left another volgendrin drifted along, partly shielded by the island across the Bridge. I walked along the rail walkway above the mat of vines, walking quietly, coming up to the Hikdar who stood there, overseeing his overseers as they flogged on a line of slaves hard at work. I did not know what they were doing. The Bridge extended out from the cliff face above our heads, casting two pencil-thin lines from the twin suns. Something glittered on the distant flying island and I looked across, between the two halves of the Volgendrin of the Bridge.

The Hikdar saw me.

"That's where we'd all like to be, Naghan Lamahan. Over there having a good time."

I nodded and forced a grimace of a smile. It looked like a town over there on the other island, with domes and towers.

"About time the binhoys were here," I said, leaning on the wooden rail at his elbow and looking down at the slaves.

"Aye, Havil take 'em!"

"The ripe crop . . ."

He laughed, a bitter laugh. "What there is of it. We have little enough to show, and the other vo'drins not much more, I'll wager."

As I asked my next question I was fully prepared to upend him over the rail and see him well on the way to his death before I raised the alarm and shouted the equivalent of "Man overboard!"

"What about the other end?" I said. "The destination of the binhoys, they'll be going mad."

153

"Well, let them! Hanitcha may harrow them for all I care. If they don't know our troubles we don't give a fluttrell feather for theirs!"

"I believe you. You've never been there?"

He fleered a look at me. "Who has? And I wouldn't have the knowledge you have in your heart, Horter. I remember my vows. I want to know nothing more beyond my duties here."

He seemed to bear me no ill will for the way I had treated him when I'd first arrived. He would have put all that down to the high and mighty ways of merkers, who notoriously consider themselves above the normal ruck of men, having access to secrets.

So I commented on the slaves and he grunted and said the wind had weakened a guy rope of the Bridge. If that was not put right—now!—Pallan Horosh would be dealing out a few of the nasty punishments of Hamal, and every one legal. I spent a few more murs in conversation so that those exchanges dealing with the destination of the binhoy loads of pashams would not stand too starkly in his memory, and then bid him remberee.

In a culture as hard and authoritarian as Hamal, and many another country of Kregen, there are of necessity many cruel words shouted at slaves and workers, words that mean hurry up, get a move on, and all that intemperate display of power being ruthlessly used. So far I have adhered to English, but one word the Hamalians favored is, in the Kregish, *grak*. I can tell you the air above the Volgendrin of the Bridge resounded with "Grak! Grak! You yetches! Grak!" It is an ugly word, harsh and unpleasant, and I have seen a slave jump as though scalded with the lash when the overseer bellowed "Grak" at him.

The shout of "Grak!" and the crack of the lash are inseparable.

The sky-god of draft beasts in Magdag is called Grakki-Grodno, as you know, and those Grodnims of the northern shore of the inner sea know what they are doing when it comes to making slaves run and haul and work. Among the megaliths of Magdag, as among the warrens and the swifters, the yells of "Grak" resound to the misery of those in bondage. Well, one day I would revisit the Eye of the World away there to the west of Turismond, and how I would joy to see my two oar comrades again, Nath

154

and Zolta! How we three would roister through all the succulent taverns of bright Sanurkazz!

I do not forget I am a Krozair brother, a Krozair of Zy.

There were family plans to be made . . . and when I thought of what Delia would say to what I proposed I hastily turned to thinking about something else.

These volgendrins floated in the air like massy clouds, drifting in their own silent rhythms in vast orbits for dwabur after dwabur that covered many a kool of land beneath. The sight of their blocky hardness against the real white clouds high above, the wind catching a tree here or a high platform there, the very implacable nature of their onward progress, all these things combined to impress the volgendrins most forcibly on my brain.

We had drifted far enough now to leave the worst of the barrens to the north and the Mountains of the West a good few dwaburs off; below us a river tumbled along, still white and rapid from the hills. Scattered vegetation showed, gradually clumping and thickening. One could find a living down there, but I saw no single sign of any habitation. The volgendrins moved, I judged, at about five knots. At that speed they would tire a man on foot to keep up. The speed also meant that their shadows, never exactly the same on any following orbit, did not stunt or destroy the vegetation below.

Before I went to report to Pallan Horosh for orders I saw four separate clumps of Gerawin flying high, their tridents winking brilliantly in the streaming light of the suns. They were watchful, prowling, on patrol. I noticed that every soldier from time to time cocked his head aloft and searched the bright bowl of the sky.

I, the Amak of Paline Valley, had no need to be told for whom—or what—they watched so carefully.

As I went through into the Pallan's quarters, the Pachaks passing me through without comment, I heard Horosh talking about that selfsame threat to a man who stood with his back to me.

"Three times like leems, during the last month of the Maiden with the Many Smiles!" Horosh sounded fretful, angry, and a little fearful. I fancied he was not frightened of the wild men who flew over the Mountains of the West from the Wild Lands beyond to lay waste. Rather, he was frightened of the queen in Ruathytu when his production schedules slipped. "My Gerawin fight bravely; indeed, they are fearsome warriors. And my soldiers are brave, as is any soldier of Hamal. But those wild ones still attack us, like werstings foaming at the mouth."

"I know about werstings," said the man with his back to me.

I stood stock still. I knew about werstings, also, and I knew this man who stood talking about them. The last time I'd heard him he'd been bellowing and screeching at the door of a voller manufactory, blaming me for the death of his wife, the Kovneve Esme, and threatening to let his pack of slavering werstings rip me limb from limb, until he'd thought of a better way of dealing with me.

"Come out, you Kovneva-murdering rast! Come out so I can plunge my hands into your guts and rip out your evil stinking heart!" That's what this man, this Ornol ham Feoste, this Kov of Apulad, had shouted and screamed at me there in Sumbakir.

He would know me as Chaadur, the gul, the worker on vollers.

I half turned to leave but Pallan Horosh, looking past Ornol ham Feoste, called, "Ah, Horter Lamahan. You are late, sir! Here are the reports! Use your best speed back."

Half turned, I hesitated. There was a chance . . .

And those reports would be going to the place where they processed pashams. The risk was worth the prize, for Vallia. . . .

Swinging back and hunching my right shoulder a fraction against the Kov of Apulad, I went to the desk. Horosh lifted the wrapper with its shining seal.

The Kov of Apulad said, "As Malahak is my witness! Chaadur! The murdering nulsh who slew my wife!"

His thraxter cleared the scabbard with a screech of steel.

I made a grab for the wrapped report; Horosh jerked it back as he stumbled to his feet with a startled oath. The thraxter lunged for my midriff. I knocked it away with my right hand and, there being two Pachaks at my back, whirled away intending to grab that report and then do what was necessary.

Action exploded in that sumptuous apartment.

Chapter
Seventeen

Of vines and exorcs

"The man's a maniac!" I bellowed, leaping away from that swishing thraxter. "He's mistaken me for somebody else!"

"I'd know you, Chaadur, in the mists of the Ice Floes themselves! Take him alive! Guards! Guards!"

"No, no, you onker!" I shouted, and the two Pachaks came running in, shields up, thraxters out, their tail blades coiled above their close-fitting helmets. If I couldn't convince Pallan Horosh in the next half-mur that this Kov was mistaken, the Pachaks would attack and seek to overpower me.

"I know you, gul! Sumbakir knows you! You may have run away to Ruathytu and joined the political guls there—call yourself a Horter now, do you! By Hanitcha the Harrower! I'll fry your liver for breakfast and gnaw on your bones for supper."

He was quite possessed. Given that his wife had indeed been foully murdered—with her own dagger at the hands of Floy, the Fristle girl who had been one of Esme's Chail Sheom—he was entitled to be angry to the point of madness. That he had proved himself to be a most evil Kov, joying in his power for the capacity it gave him for the infliction of pain, meant that sympathy for him came hard.

One last try: "Pallan Horosh! Call this madman off or I will not be answerable for the consequences!"

There was little time to finish what I was saying as ham Feoste hurled away the chair that impeded his progress and lunged after me with his thraxter. I had to avoid that dangerous implement and watch out for the Pachaks. They were looking at the Pallan for orders.

157

Kov Ornol ham Feoste clinched it when he bellowed: "You know me, Hennard! I'm your cousin's son! I am the Kov of Apulad! This is a gul, a cramph, calling himself a Horter—"

I really believe it was mainly my own odd behavior since arrival here that tipped Horosh's decision, that and the fact that the man calling for my head was a relation and a Kov.

"Take him, guards!"

So, feeling sorry for the Pachaks, I was finally forced into an action I had sought to avoid.

The two Pachaks slumped to the carpets with a sighing wheeze from one and nothing at all from the other. Each Pachak wore a terchik through the eye.

"In Havil's name!" screeched the Pallan, completely shattered, horrified. He began to yell for guards in a voice that quavered up and down the scale. The Kov of Apulad bolted for the door. He did not yell until he was well outside; he saved all his breath for running. I let him go.

To the Pallan I said, "I'll take that report now, and do my duty. You will have to explain the dead guards." The Pallan stopped shouting to look at me, dazed. "They were good men. It is the fault of that foul Kov, and yours, that they are dead."

"You . . . you . . ." He was trying to breath, to get the breath down into his lungs, wheezing and gasping. His head was hunched down between his shoulder blades and he rested both his hands, his arms at full extent, on the desk. He glared up at me and his eyes showed red-rimmed. "You . . . Naghan Lamahan . . . you are a dead man."

I picked up the report. "Not yet, and you look out for yourself—Hennard, was it? A most distinguished name."

Outside I composed myself and looked swiftly around. Soldiers were running up from the left, over the yellow grass. Leading them, the Kov was still waving his thraxter and shrieking. He must have felt naked without his pet werstings.

The path to the right into the orchards lay open so I ran that way. The report I had thrust down into the breast of my shirt and the pasham in my pocket were far more important than an exhilarating interlude of swordsmanship now. As for the Kov of Apulad, the man was a blot, but I did not feel called on to deal with him. It could safely be left to the next slave revolt to see him off.

All the laws on Hamal wouldn't save him then.

I ran.

I ran into the orchard, with a definite plan in my head.

There were crossbowmen back there and a few bolts whispered past through the leaves. I jinked left-handed and so pelted on, through the leaves and their dependent pashams, still green and unripe. No time to stop to pick a basketful now.

The Kov was still yelling, his voice coming faintly and most irritatingly, like that of a nagging wife through closed doors, destroying the harmony of a home. "I'll have you, Chaadur! You'll wish you'd never been born! I'll—" Well, thinking about it, I will not repeat his threats. They possessed nothing of originality to make them worth remembering.

The orchards here were planted for ease of upkeep, with wide lanes. I had to hurdle the bent forms of slaves as they weeded. Weeds drank too much water, which was precious on a volgendrin. The pack bayed after.

There would be no hope of reaching Liance. The mirvol would immediately be ringed by soldiers waiting for me to run that way. As you know, I can look after myself reasonably well in a little fight like this and can usually, although not always, make a break for freedom. The problem is always that of numbers. However hard a normal human being fights, in the end he can be swamped by numbers. It is only the heroes of myths and fables, the giant men of the dawn and the phantasms of sick minds, who can fight and fight and never be beaten.

And, anyway, if a hero can never be beaten, where is the interest, where the chivalry, where the sport, in hearing of his adventures?

I've always considered Achilles a real heel in comparison with Hector.

You who have been listening to these tapes will know that I am merely making excuses for myself for what happened very soon after that. . . .

The grass padded by underfoot. I wore the military boot of the Horter class, tall, black, and shiny, not too well adapted for running. The trees passed backward with hypnotic effect. It was highly desirable to jink from row to row to stop a clear shot, and soon the swods spread out to take a shot at me in whichever row of trees I ran.

When a bolt thwunked a trunk ahead of me, shredding bark and a yellow sliver of wood, I put on a burst of speed, angling through the trees, coming into each open row fast enough to be gone before the crossbows could be loosed. The way brought me to the very edge of the volgendrin, with a wooden fence rearing up before me. Beyond that fence lay thin air.

Up over the fence, with a grip and a twist, and I let myself down on the other side. There was perhaps a pace of ground here to give sufficient purchase for the fence stakes.

I looked down.

It was a long long way to the ground.

A river trended slowly past below, with the green of trees and the lighter green of open spaces. I thought I could see a glimpse of sleek brown forms running, but it could have been a trick of the eye.

I started to climb down the sheer face, which afforded jagged hand- and footholds in the striated strata of the flying island. Down I went, hand under hand, feet feeling for a purchase, down and down, and I looked aloft for the first fierce face to show over the fence.

This was a pretty little fix! I felt like a fly in amber. It seemed to me I climbed down that serrated cliff edge with all the speed and activity of a nonagenarian negotiating his seat from bed to bathchair. I didn't dare take any chances.

"By the Black Chunkrah!" I said to myself. "The cramphs won't get to me before I'm out of sight!"

In any event, only three crossbow bolts spattered down before I found a scooped hole in the rock. Here rainwater had gouged out a hollow in softer rock between shales. I flopped in, rested my back, and cursed. The moment I put my head out they'd shoot down. Some swod with an eye would feather his quarrel in my skull.

A slight overhang enabled me to look down, even if I could not in safety look up. So I looked down.

The ground seemed no nearer, but there were definitely animals running through the open spaces down there. I saw they were animals very much like the cattle of Kregen, somewhat smaller than Earthly cattle, with short horns and, in this wild state, of uncertain temper. These were very much like the fine fat cattle that grazed so peacefully in Delphond.

The shadow of the volgendrin, moving like a demarcation line across the terrain, seemed to drive them to fearful flight, for they ran and ran to stay in the suns' shine.

I admit I dwelt with some philosophical rancor on my plight. I do not run away very often or very easily. The old Dray Prescot would have stood his ground, unscabbarded the great longsword, and simply slugged it out . . . until he was rapped on the head and all the Bells of Beng Kishi rang in that thick and stupid skull of his.

Well, by using what brains I imagined I possessed, in running in order to escape with the report and the pasham, how had I improved matters?

This position was not even a standoff.

I knew what they would do. A voller would ghost along the cliff edge—and a flight or two of Gerawin as well, in all probability—and they'd simply shoot me full of quarrels.

The angle of the suns, hidden by the bulk of the flying island, told me there were far too many burs before nightfall for me to last that long without discovery.

The lust for revenge consuming the Kov of Apulad escaped my calculations.

A voller ghosted into view, flying along the edge of the volgendrin from left to right. It flew perhaps ten feet below the level of the hollow. I drew back. Maybe, just maybe, there would be a chance for life.

They saw me.

The voller eased up. Gerawin, their purple and black feathers flying in the wind of their passage, circled ready to plunge in. Crossbowmen packed the deck of the voller. They had mantlets erected so as the craft rose level the men vanished from my view behind the shields; all I could see of them were the heads of the quarrels through shooting slits.

With a grunt I reached up and drew out the longsword. This was not a genuine Krozair longsword. This weapon had been created by Naghan the Gnat and myself in the smithy of Esser Rarioch. It was a superlative weapon, built as closely as I could make it to pure Krozair lines, of perfect balance and heft, with a pair of superb cutting edges. It would do enormous damage. But it was not a true Krozair longsword.

With the silver wire-wound hilt gripped in the cunning Krozair fashion, right hand up to the quillons, left hand to the pommel, with that spread of leverage between them, I stood up on the lip of crumbling rock and prepared to fight the last fight.

With the sword angled before me and vertical, I could

bat away the flying bolts by quick delicate flicks of the wrist. They loosed, but the bolts hissed past on either side and not one came near enough to touch me. Bits of rock chippings flew.

A voice hailed from the voller.

"Chaadur, you who call yourself Naghan Lamahan. You have no chance. Give yourself up to the law as is proper."

I considered this. Oh, yes, I, Dray Prescot, tried to decide if I should fling back defiance and fight until death, or if I should risk present capture for later escape.

The struggle between the Dray Prescots that are me—at least, at the very least, two of them!—was, believe me, of far greater virulence than any fight with steel swords could ever be.

First I tried to stick to my guns. "I am Naghan Lamahan. That mad Kov is mistaken. Who is this Chaddur?"

"I know you, yetch!" That was the Kov, foaming at the mouth most likely. "Do you think I could ever forget *you?*"

He would have gone on, but I heard another voice, then whispers, then nothing as their voices sank. But I could guess easily enough that they were trying to calm the Kov so as not to excite me. I did not laugh, but this was a ripe occasion for a real belly laugh, if ever there was one.

"Give yourself up, Chaadur!"

The voller inched in. Another foot or so and I could leap the gap.

"Not while that cramph of a Kov remains out of a madhouse!"

More shouts and whisperings, and the voller edging closer, the watchful Gerawin circling. . . .

"You have no chance of escape, Chaadur!"

About that time, realizing I had no bow, they took down a couple of the mantlets. I could see the Hikdar yelling at me, the pressing mass of bowmen, and Kov Ornol ham Feoste, too, shaking his thraxter at me, all on the deck of the voller.

No Hikdar, even an ord-Hikdar, was going to argue overlong with a Kov.

And the voller inched in. . . .

I had to consider the Gerawin most carefully. They would see the impossible situation in which I was held, and would know escape was impossible. All the same, being guards by nature, they would still be ready to hurtle down at the first suspicion that something had gone wrong.

So I watched them circling for a while and, looking down, saw a couple spiraling up with great speed. Far below these two I saw other flyers spinning down to the ground, leveling off, planing with wings I felt my eyes must be deceiving me as to their span. I could see no riders astride their backs. The flyers' wings were short, yes, but they were heavily ribbed with deep vees at the trailing edges between the ribs. They appeared to be hardly moving as the flyers planed down. Long whip tails flicked out into hard rearward-pointing spears.

They were aimed for a large open clearing among the trees in which the cattle animals—wild ordels—ran in a breaking smother of heaving brown backs and upthrust horns.

My eyes switched back, before whatever was going to happen down there took place, to the Gerawin and then to the voller.

The thing had stopped moving in. It hung just too far off for a certain leap without a running takeoff.

The men aboard were all looking away from me. The Gerawin were swirling up, clumping together, stringing out from the lumps into fighting patrol vees.

No one needed to tell the Amak of Paline Valley, which lies close to the Mountains of the West to the north of these volgendrins, what was happening.

I heard sharp yells from the voller, sounds of violent argument. No genius needed to guess what that was!

Kov Ornol ham Feoste appeared on the coaming, one foot up and the leg flexed. He held a crossbow. Deliberately, he aimed at me. When the bolt flew I was ready and swatted it away. It caromed against the rock and fell far out, dwindling into a mere black speck before it vanished.

The voller was moving.

The Hikdar shouted, impassioned, "He will stay, Kov, until we return! He cannot climb down! And if he climbs up . . ."

The Kov of Apulad had reloaded. He was not very quick. He took another shot and again I batted the bolt away. The voller rose faster now, the Gerawin up there in their fighting vees heading back across the volgendrin. The flier moving faster and rose out of my view.

I was left alone, perfectly trapped, to await the return of the soldiers and the law of Hamal.

Well, not perfectly trapped. I could go on climbing down and fall off the bottom of the volgendrin. I could climb up and be taken prisoner by the guards waiting for me as I climbed over the fence.

The deep booming gong-tones of bells reached me. Now the other volgendrins took up the alarm. The air vibrated with the tocsin notes. At Paline Valley we had our alarm gongs, also, and our watchmen with hammers and strong arms.

Then, gazing up into the brilliant sky of Kregen, squinting at an angle against the streaming mingled light of the twin Suns of Scorpio, I saw the oncoming black dots. The suns threw all my side of the volgendrin into shadow. But the brilliance of the sky by contrast made me squint hard. Yes. Yes, there flew the Wild Men from the Wild Lands. They had many names, mostly obscene. I clenced my fists on the longsword. These were men similar to those who had laid waste Paline Valley. Many of them were not really men at all; many were more kin to those dreadful crofermen living on the outer skirts of the Stratemsk in Turismond.

My place was at the side of men fighting to protect their lives and their property from the Wild Men. And here I was, skulking in a hole in the side of a flying island in the sky!

There had really only been two possible alternatives when the alarm bells rang and the Gerawin massed for battle. The attackers might have been flutsmen up there, those reiving mercenaries of the skies, or Wild Men. It would have been better by far for the Volgendrin of the Bridge and the other local flying islands if those alarm bells had heralded flutsmen! By far and far!

I remembered how I had promised to take the name of Hamun ham Farthytu in Hamal. Names are precious. I had brought some honor to that name, in the end, after all the playacting, and a marble monument existed in the Palace of Names in Ruathytu to the greater glory of Havil the Green and ham Farthytu. I think you will understand that the Havil part was anathema to me; the ham Farthytu I had come to regard with a strange affection, considering it was the name of a family of a country that was an enemy to my own country of Vallia.

So, with a blistering Makki-Grodno oath to clear the vocal chords, a dolloping spit on the hands, the longsword thrust away on my back, I started the climb again.

I climbed down.

I deliberately chose to leave that battle against the Wild Men from over the mountains. I deliberately chose to continue my quest for the secrets of the vollers and for the good of Vallia.

Now that another chance had been given me I moved with exquisite caution. I tried not to tear my hands on the rock and I tried not to rip out my fingernails. My boots were inevitably ripped and, very shortly, now that haste had gone, I took off the boots and pitched them overside. They took a mortal long time to fall away to nothing.

I saw one of the mysterious winged flyers pounce on a boot and miss, then go planing on past, its little wings stiffly outstretched, deeply curved, supported on thick wingroots that sprouted like columns from its shoulder blades.

If they were the exorcs the soldiers had mentioned, with dislike, they appeared singularly clumsy. . . .

I climbed down three hundred feet. Toward the end the way became extraordinarily difficult as the overhang of the island increased and the bottom rounded into a dish shape. Over the years any sharp edges had been worn away, here at the bottom, and I had to grip, cling, and worm my way along fissures with my body braced, hands and elbows, knees and feet. Occasionally I had to pause and dig away to form a handhold with that sailor's knife from the scabbard over my right hip. I persevered, there under that floating mass of earth and rock, and at last was rewarded. Sweat clung thickly to my forehead. I felt my arms had long since been wrenched from their sockets and were held only by the shirt. That shirt, the green dolman, the dark cloak, all were ripped and covered with rock/dust and the mildewed droppings of the woflovols which inhabited every crevice.

But at last I saw what I searched for.

That spreading mass of vines and creepers which grew under the volgendrins and, in the case of the Volgendrin of the Bridge, joined two together, grew thin and brittle here at the edge. Most of the vines were dead. As I handed myself along I had to be most careful not to trust to a grip on a tendril that was brittle. The ground beneath would be damned hard. Soon the mat of vines increased in thickness and fresh plants showed green, some with orange and dirty-white flowers, here in the shadows, growing strongly with roots penetrating many feet into the rocky crevices, seeking the dirt and moisture there.

Now the way was much easier.

Animal life inhabited the vines. I had a short, sharp fight with a spiny creature with six suckered feet; I dispatched it with the main-gauche. The place deepened with plant growth and became infested with insect life. This was about as far as I wished to go. Much later on in my story you will hear of what lay further into the viny jungle beneath the volgendrins, but at this time I was not interested in exploring.

I found a good solid trunk of vine, as thick as a roston's trunk, and swiped away until I had made a comfortable nest. Sitting there and looking down I could see the ground flowing past beneath my feet, that steady five knots taking us over river, lake, and forest, trending southward and eastward in the long Keplerian orbits of the volgendrins.

The first few hundred feet of vine was easy to find, merely by hauling it in and testing each length carefully. Some of it came away from its roots without trouble. To get some of it I had to crawl through the twisted jungly mass, most of the time upside down, and hack away with the dagger or the knife to free it. The rope lengthened. I took off all my gear, leaving myself clad only in a blue breechclout, a once-clean one I had taken from my rooms in the Kyr Nath and the Fifi. The longsword, the shirt, the dolman, the rapier and the cloak were all bundled up and securely lashed to the end of the vine. Then I lowered it down until it hung and dangled in the breeze. Then it was back to more vine cutting, hauling, and tying. A sailor uses a sailor's knots; I had no fear the knots would slip, only that the vine might part.

I had to judge the length carefully. If the bundle of my possessions caught on a tree, not only would I lose the lot, but the line might part anywhere up its length.

Finally, shoving the dagger and knife away—neither had broken, for which I gave thanks to Zair—I coiled about five fathoms of vine up around my shoulders.

The Breath I took was a deep one.

A thousand feet, hand under hand, feet clamping as I went down! A long way. A damned long way. But down there the bundle swayed and gyrated at the end of the line, seemingly flying unattached through the air, as the line was barely visible at that distance.

Down I went.

My breath came raggedly and the sweat slicked thick and greasy. I took deep draughts of air, pausing more and more frequently. The wind swung me around and I revolved dizzyingly, praying the lashings above would not part. A roston's trunk is mighty thick, but the strains I was imposing were tremendous. Down I climbed, hand under hand, and the ground slowly rose to meet me.

I paused, dragging thick lungfuls of air past my opened lips, flicked the back of my hand across my forehead and eyes, and looked down. I studied the landscape.

Trees, a river, those brown humped-back wild ordels, grass, more trees. I wanted to pick my spot. A few feet further down and my legs wrapped around my bundle. I looked up. What a monstrous sight! A massive oval black shape, square in the sky, soaring up there, disdaining the pull of gravity! The volgendrin! Insupportable weight drifting through the air light as thistledown. The line vanished some distance before the twisted interlacement of vines at the bottom of the floating island.

I caught the wind on my cheeks, looked down and ahead, and chose my spot. The knot with which I lashed the line over my shoulder to the main line was made with painstaking care. I did not wish to slip at this last point. The bundle was cut free. I hung on as we sailed over a tree, and then I cast my five fathoms down.

It did not reach the ground. Wind pressure curved the line away. I cursed. But there was nothing I could do about it. Down I would have to go. . . .

I was concentrating so hard on the length of line, my bundle, the ground rushing past, that the first sign of the exorcs' attack came with a harsh croaking cry.

My head snapped up.

A thing like a cat, the size of a large dog, with a green leathery skin, hook-clawed webbed feet, pricked pointed ears, a gaping mouth scarlet as the mouth of hell, fanged with four enormous canine teeth, and eyes like crimson pits, lanced ferociously at me. I got up my left arm and the thing spun away, screeching. I was astonished to see the left-hand dagger in that fist.

The exorc's wings were almost rudimentary. Those thick columns rose from just behind its shoulder blades, one on either side of the spine, and the wings branched from them more like the antlers of a deer than the wings of a bat, but the likeness was plain. It could not fly back up at me. It planed on past, screeching, and the second one followed, hissing. I saw the whiplike tails, barbed, coiling for a slash, but the range was too great.

These exorcs were mere gliders: they could launch themselves from the volgendrins, but they could never fly back.

So that explained the reference to the cows.

Taking a fresh grip on the rope, jamming the main-gauche between my teeth, my lips ricked back in the old way, I shimmied down the last length of vine. I wanted to get onto terra firma as rapidly as possible right now!

A tree nearly got me but I lifted with bulging muscles and stuck my feet straight out. I received no more than I had often suffered at the hands of the bosun over a gun breech.

The open space had gone, but another appeared ahead just past the trees. Even at five knots and with the wind I seemed to be racing over the ground. A river appeared and disappeared. I went down lower and braced myself, trying to remember to relax. Further down the grass hissed away. A stupid wild ordel rushed away before me, then a herd of them, running in panic. I was down now and they wouldn't get out of the way. I felt the ground coming up with sudden treacherous speed and I didn't bother to look up. The vine had parted. I was falling. I fell perhaps four feet to land astride an ordel, running, plunging, and racing in blind panic. It felt me on its back and it went wild as I grasped a chunk of mane.

Like a bucking bronco it carried me crazily across the grass.

Trees showed ahead. I took a much firmer grip, bashed in my naked heels, yelled in the ordel's ear and swerved him away. In the next second I was flying through the air—again—and rolling head over heels on the grass, winded and bruised but very much alive!

I sat up.

The ordels had reached some kind of sanctuary among the trees. They would have to come out to graze, and then the exorcs would get at them again. I looked up. Already the volgendrin was sailing on past. It was already beginning to take on the appearance of a black cloud in the sky, and other flying islands showed to left and right, bringing the perspectives into proportion. The suns blazed down gloriously.

I stood up.

"The exorcs swarmed down to attack."

It seemed a good idea to put the clothes on, to put the dolman on as a pelisse, to fashion the cloak up loosely around my left arm, to see to the rapier and main-gauche, and then grasp the longsword in that cunning Krozair grip.

I did all this . . . and only just in time.

The exorcs swarmed down to attack.

They glided in, hissing, their fanged jaws wide, their ruby eyes like the lights of hell.

The longsword could deal with them, shearing wings, heads, and legs. Four legs they had, with those nasty hooked claws, webbed, leathery, vicious. I took cuts; but the clothes were ripped and blood marked my body. But the sword kept a ring of steel about my head, and dead and writhing exorcs littered the ground. I saw them running off on all fours, like cats after a fight with a dog, running to the monstrous cows which flew down to pick them up. These were the mothers. They could really fly. The exorcs hooked onto the cow's underside and the broad wings flapped and away up to the nests under the volgendrin they went, so that their offspring could be launched once again to make the kill. The mother cow would then return to pick up the killers who could not fly and to feed on the kill.

Covered in blood, ripped, scratched, weary, at last I saw the stream of exorcs dwindle. The volgendrin had passed too far and they were attacking a bunch of short-horned cattle in the next open space. I put the point of the longsword into the ground and leaned forward on the pommel, gasping for air.

I suppose a four-armed Djang might have been ready for fresh combat instantly. I admit I felt wrung out. The strain of climbing down the vine had taxed me, the fight in its sheer insensate ferocity had drained me. I am, after all, only human. Those exorcs had glided in hissing like a constant succession of paper darts launched at my head. There had been no single instant when I could pause for breath. So I leaned and drew enormous gulps of air, my head hanging.

I heard the rustling and I lifted my head, which felt as though a damned volgendrin itself rested on my neck.

The Gerawin handled it all very smoothly, very professionally.

They alighted in a ring about me.

They had crossbows. Their tridents glittered in the light of the Suns of Scorpio.

The leader advanced, his feathers flaring, his leggings tightly strapped around his bandy legs.

"You fight well, dom."

"Aye," I said hating the pant in my voice. "Do you wish to find out how well?"

"I do not think so. I would prefer, if you wish it, to put a score of shafts into you."

"That might be preferable."

He snickered. They are good guards, the Gerawin, if very much on the predatory side. Also, they consider their tyryvols to be the best flyers in all Havilfar. I believed my Djangs and their flutduins would disabuse them of that idea, but there were no friendly Djangs around their king now. There was only me, that onker Dray Prescot, who had escaped into captivity.

They made a rush at me from the front and I put up the longsword ready to take a few of their heads off. Their tridents flashed but they withdrew and the leader yelled, "Now, Genarnin the Chank!"

I swung around sluggishly. The iron links knocked me down. The iron chains wrapped me up. The longsword spun away. I was on my hands and knees, and chain after chain lapped me. Then I felt the grass against my cheek. I welcomed the dark advances of Notor Zan, but only to conceal from myself my own foolishness.

Chapter Eighteen

A longsword falls

"You nurdling get-onker!" The Gerawin's voice hammered close to my ear and I opened my eyes, feeling as sluggish as Tyr Nath after he'd drunk the sylvie's poisoned cup in the Grotto of the Trell Kings. I was being carried along like a rolled-up carpet, swaying from side to side. I cocked an eye down.

Below me lay a windswept, empty space beyond the slats and ropes; below that was the undulating mass of creepers and vines.

So I knew that Gerawin were carrying me across the bridge that gave this volgendrin its name.

We halted and the bandy-legged flyer thus addressed shouted something about no sane man having to cope with such a bar of iron. His yells were the furious and desperate shouts of a man seeing vast unpleasantnesses fast approaching.

"You have only yourself to blame, Genarnin the Chank!"

The chank is that vicious white shark of the Outer Oceans of Kregen, a somewhat smaller cousin of the chank of the Eye of the World. The nickname is often given to men who possess that swift and deadly ferocity that marks them for small-sized killers.

Breeze fleered the trappings of the Gerawin, there on the bridge over the vine jungle far below. I felt the blood painfully pulsating in my body. My head rang with Beng Kishi's finest reverberations. The bar of iron had caused trouble. I did not laugh, but the thought was in my head, somewhere, mixed with the woolly balls of fuzz that scrambled my brains. The Gerawin stopped and the leader bent his head to stare at one of the bracing rope uprights. It was slashed through, hanging by a single thread. So the old longsword still possessed an edge, then. . . .

The Gerawin who carried the sword in so awkward a fashion looked properly horrified by what he had done. A mere single upright keeping the hand-rope fixed to the side-rope would never bring the bridge down, but I knew the laws of Hamal would be ferociously strict about the minutiae. The law would no doubt have already prescribed the very punishment he must undergo for exactly this misdemeanor.

So, stopped as we were, I gave the Gerawin holding my legs a twisting kick, at which he fell back, yelling, grabbing for support above that windy height. The next Gerawin fell half through the slats of the bridge, over the edge, grasping it and screeching. The one with the longsword tried to run, but tripped. Then the familiar silver wire-wound hilt snugged into my palm grip and I turned, ready to slash them all—and the damned bridge, too, so ugly was my mood.

The bridge swayed. Gerawin were running. I felt the

172

breeze. The suns were declining now. Also, I felt most decidedly queasy. My legs trembled. My arms somehow brought the sword up with a speed I knew would mean my death in a fight. I shook my head and those old devil Bells of Beng Kishi rang and caroled, shooting silver and green sparks through my eyes. I felt as though a herd of stampeding chunkrah had trodden all over me.

The Gerawin, no doubt completely unprepared for an unconscious man to recover and get into action as fast as I had—and I, a Krozair of Zy, knew just how slow I had really been—nevertheless went methodically about their man-snaring again.

"Come on, you rasts!" I said. My voice sounded like a whistling faerling with an ague. "Fight like warriors!" That was pitiful, of course, but I threw it in as a player throws in his last charge of Deldars across the final drin at Jikaida.

They sneered at me. They were professionals. But, for all that it was perfectly clear they did not wish to cross swords with me. The great longsword—that bar of iron—kept them back.

The iron chains flew again. The loops snagged. I struggled to free myself, hampered by the swaying bridge and the ropes and supports. More chains settled about me. I knew that running, fighting, defiance itself, were over.

With a last yell I stretched up tall, dragging on the chains. I whirled the longsword over my head.

"For Zair!" I shouted, and hurled.

The Gerawin flight leader was quick. He ducked. The longsword, a blinding bar of silver in the lights, for they had wiped it off, spun through the air. It arced high and then fell. Over and over it tumbled, glittering, a silver brand of silver fire falling away and away into the mat of vines far below.

"Zair rot you for a pack of cramphs!" I said. And then the last loop of iron chain sledged into my head and, once again, I plunged into the darkness of the enveloping black cloak of Notor Zan.

During all my sessions in relating my life on Kregen I have attempted to speak the truth. No matter how fantastic what I say appears to be, it is the truth as well as I can express it. For the next few days of my life on that terrible if beautiful world I feel it expedient to gloss. I will cover the events as quickly as may be until I found

173

myself back in Ruathytu, under strong guard, heavily chained but back to strength. The attack of the Wild Men on the Volgendrin of the Bridge had been beaten off with loss; my recapture had been a mere small incident. The Kov of Apulad, bearing down with all the authority of a Kov, had asserted his prior claim to my carcass and had insisted on taking me back to the capital for judgment. After he was through with me, he had told Pallan Horosh, the Pallan might have what was left to send to trial for the deaths of the two Pachaks.

So, here in Ruathytu, I was lodged in those grim, famous, horrific, and extraordinarily diabolical dungeons of the castle of Hanitcha the Harrower, the infamous Hanitchik.

An unduly great part of my life has been spent in prisons of one sort or another.

The Hanitchik was a most unpleasant specimen. Torture was a way of life. The food was atrocious, yet it always came up at regular intervals and was enough to keep body and soul together. The prisoners had the laws of Hamal to thank for that.

Escape, of course, was the primary concern.

Just in case you have forgotten—and I most certainly had never forgotten—it is written in the laws of Hamal that the nearest relative of a murdered person may choose between certain dire tortures which may then be inflicted upon the murderer before he is dragged off to be hanged. I fancied the Kov of Apulad would decide on the most unpleasant tortures the law allowed.

The trial, with which I will not weary you, wound its way to its inevitable conclusion. Stoutly protesting that I was not Chaadur at all, I was indicted by the Kov. Now that he had taken up his new post under the Queen, his weight and prestige were fully sufficient to have me condemned.

Even during the proceedings, which were carried out with a great attention to scrupulous fairness in every detail, even though the whole affair's outcome was cut and dried before it began, thus making a nonsense of the very justification for laws at all, I mulled over Ornal ham Feoste and his new appointment. He had been in charge of a small voller factory in Sumbakir. It had all been very provincial. Now, after the death of his wife Esme, he was here in Ruathytu high in the Queen's favor and even more strongly connected with the vollers.

On Kregen two and two make four—sometimes.

The Nine Faceless Ones who chose the high nobles to oversee the secrets of the vollers must have chosen this Kov Ornol ham Feoste. There seemed no other explanation.

So as the guilty verdict was brought in by the three judges—they did not run to the jury system in Hamal for all the laws—I had found another piece of the jigsaw. It appeared it was going to do me no good at all. It certainly wasn't going to stop what the Kov planned to do to my hide.

Because like any normal human being I did not believe I was going to die just yet and that must mean I would escape in some way, I had refused to offer up the alias of Hamun ham Farthytu as a means of alibiing myself. If Rees and Chido were apprised of my plight they would be there to do all they could, and I fancied their testimony might shake the hard identification of the Kov. This was comforting. One of the turnkeys, an apim with one eye and a crippled left leg, smashed that bubble.

"The Queen's happier'n a vosk in swill," he told me as I took my regulation one bur of exercise in the enclosed yard, roofed with iron bars, the suns invisible and only the streaming mingled opaz light falling across the grim stone walls. "The army o' the north's won the big victory we've all waited for."

I felt the chill. I swallowed.

"Yes," he went on, chewing his cham from one cheek to another. "Havil smiled on us. Those rasts of Pandahem were all smashed up. It was a great victory."

"Where was this?"

"Oh, I dunno. Those foreign places is all the same to me. By Kuerden the Merciless! The stories! The army chased after 'em for three full days. The loot! If'n I had both my eyes and a sound leg I'da bin there, believe me, with my sack stuffed with gold and jewels—ah! It don't bear thinking of."

It certainly didn't bear thinking of. But I had to think. And there was more.

"The Queen—may Havil bless 'er!—is going to be crowned Empress! That'll be a sight! Ruathytu'll go mad. The procession will take all day to pass, an' I'm going to see it, right from the top of the Hanitchik." He chewed. "Well, that's my right, ain't it?"

175

"Yes," I said. "Was it only the Pandaheem? Any other . . . ?"

"Oh, you've heard the tales, too, have you? Yes, they say there was an army out of Vallia. Rasts of Vallians! May Hanitcha Harrow 'em to hell!" He chuckled and spat. "All smashed up. Tumbled back to a place they call Jholaix—they're hiding out there now. All we've gotta do is go in and finish 'em." He spat again. "I've heard of Jholaix, not that I've ever bin able to afford to drink of it, never not once in my whole life."

Thus spoke Nath the Keys, my jailer and an enemy, yet just an ordinary man.

One of the most telling indictments of the gul Chaadur had been that he had pretended to be a Horter.

The official torturing was scheduled for three days away.

I could delay no longer. Rees and Chido, and the others who had known me in Ruathytu as the Amak of Paline Valley, must be called on. Hamun ham Farthytu must be used as an alias. I should not have delayed so long. The remnants of the armies of the countries of Pandahem, and my army of Vallia and Djanduin, were penned up in the extreme northeastern corner of Pandahem, in Jholaix. One final battle would destroy them utterly and put the whole island into the power of Hamal. My place was with my army.

Having reached that decision I called for Nath the Keys and he was there already at the cell door, swinging his lamp and jangling his keys.

"Stop your bawling, Chaadur! Your time has come, there's no sense in kicking against it, lad. You did a foul murder and now you must pay the price." Soldiers with iron chains stood with Nath the Keys.

"But," I said stupidly, "there are three days."

"Naw. Naw, lad. The Kov's in a hurry, like. It's now."

They dragged me out and I fought, so they wrapped the iron chains around me and knocked me out. When I came to I was chained up to the stake in a small court-yard of the Hanitchik with an assembled party of gloating nobles and Horters, with the guards . . . and with the black- and red-robed tormentors.

Kov Ornol ham Feoste was in a jovial mood. He had brought a group of friends. He called out, "I have chosen well for you, Chaadur, murderer!"

They had gagged me so I couldn't yell back. I glared

176

"The chief torturer advanced . . ."

in murderous fury on this miserable Kov, but I could not break the chains.

The fires banked red in their braziers, the hot irons glowing. The tongs, the knives, the scalpels, the screws, all were at hand. The Kov sat back on the front chair, upholstered in green brocade, and he lounged in fine style to enjoy the spectacle. Those with him, sitting on chairs placed in the spots reserved for them, perked up at the prospect of a bur or so of pleasure. I looked at them as the chief torturer advanced, holding a tiny knife. He wore a black hood and his eyes glittered at me from the holes cut in that ominously black material.

I looked at the assembled nobles and Horters of Hamal and I considered once more that the country was evil, that this glittering, decadent city of Ruathytu was evil, and that the greatest evil of all was Queen Thyllis herself. There were one or two men there I had seen during my days in Ruathytu; but not one I had known well enough to imagine he would recognize me as the Amak of Paline Valley. My position was such that I would joy in being recognized as someone—anyone—other than Chaadur, the condemned murdering gul.

My wish was so rapidly fulfilled I wondered if the Everoinye or the Savanti had a hand in it. But, apart from what I suspected they might have been doing lately, the Star Lords and the mortal but superhuman men and women of Aphrasöe left me strictly to my own devices on Kregen. They would let me be tortured and killed if they had no immediate need of my services.

Sitting two places away from Kov Ornol, a man lounged in his chair. I recognized him as my gaze passed along the nobles. He wore a natty costume of blue, gray, and black stitched into a hexagonal pattern very like the hide of a chavonth. He looked a lot like a sleek, treacherous chavonth lounging back, this man I had rescued from the snows of the Mountains of the North at the behest of the Star Lords.

So I stared at him as the little knife in the leprously white hand of the torturer sliced toward my skin for the first cut. I was stripped naked. My body glistened with sweat. The gag choked me. I know my eyes must have held all that old powerful look of the devil as I gazed at Naghan Furtway, he who had once been the Kov of Falinur.

Now my comrade Seg Segutorio was the Kov of Falinur, and this Naghan Furtway a fugitive from Vallia, a man who must be riddled with anger and resentment. Once before he had unmasked and betrayed me, there at The Dragon's Bones.

Would he recognize me again?

Naghan Furtway had once held enormous power as a Kov of Vallia. His passion for Jikaida had been inordinate; I had played him enough times in the Mountains of the North, waiting for him and his nephew Tyr Jenbar to regain their strength and for Genal the Ice to take his icy load down the mountains, to know he played as he lived, hard, ruthlessly, without mercy.

Yet he had raged at the cramphs of Havilfar for selling us defective airboats. Clearly his disgrace and flight had changed his mind. He was here in Ruathytu for no good purpose. He had become a renegade.

The knife pricked my skin, slid, cut, and withdrew with a sparkle of my blood on the tip. This would take a long time.

I watched Naghan Furtway.

The knife cut again, cunningly, painfully.

Naghan Furtway stood up, drawing that chavonth-patterned cape back, resting his hand on the hilt of his rapier. The knife licked out and the pain stung. Soon that pain would coalesce from many tiny pains into an insupportable agony.

Kov Ornol looked up, frowning.

"Sit down, Horter Furtway. There is much to come."

So they knew, here in Hamal, who Furtway was.

"I think not, Kov."

"What in Havil's name do you mean! As Malahak is my witness, Horter Furtway, this cramph of a Chaadur suffers torment to my orders before he dies."

"I think not, Kov. This man's name is not Chaadur."

Kov Ornol spluttered. "That is what he says, the lying rast! You believe his story?"

"No. For I know him, aye, I know him well."

"That is nothing to me. He murdered my wife and has been adjudged guilty. I will have what the law allows—"

"I have the ear of the Queen. I think she will not be pleased if you persist, Kov Ornol."

That was threat enough to make any man think twice.

Between these two, the Kov and the ex-Kov, there was a great gulf. For all his bluster, cruelty, and evil, Kov Ornol ham Feoste was a mere blunderer, an oaf, com-

179

pared with the refinement of cunning and calculation of purpose of Naghan Furtway. The sheer hardness of the man in the chavonth-patterned clothes blunted all Kov Ornol's bluster.

"The Queen must be informed at once." Furtway was looking at me much as a leem stares at a ponsho. "If you persist, Kov Ornol, the Queen will order done to you what you do to this man."

"You cannot speak to me like that! I am a Kov of Hamal! I know—"

"You know nothing, Kov. The situation between Hamal and Vallia is what concerns us here."

"You are a Vallian disgraced and thrown out of your own country!" Ornol blustered on, very plum-colored of face, struggling to rise and confront Naghan Furtway.

"So I know what I am saying."

The tormentor and his little knife withdrew, thankfully. He wasn't going to commit himself until the argument was settled.

Ornol ham Feoste gestured with irritated anger at the torturer. "Get on with it! Take no notice of this fool of a man who thinks he is a Kov still! Cut him!"

"I will tell you, Kov Ornol, since you are bent on running headfirst into mortal danger. The Queen will want to deal with this man herself, personally. She will excuse no one who balks her of that. I tell you, you foolish man, and you will not listen."

Kov Ornol puffed himself up and half drew his thraxter.

If he set to with Furtway the latter's rapier would spit him before he could call on Malahak as a witness.

"Guards!" bawled the Kov of Apulad, this foolish, incensed, half-demented Ornol ham Feoste.

"Then you will have to know and see the truth, and the error you fall into Kov Ornol. And once I tell you, the guards must seal this yard and the Queen must be told. At once! There is great danger here for us all."

"What in a Herrelldrin Hell are you talking about?"

"This man, this murderer you call Chaadur, is a man the Queen will give great riches for. And I am the man—remember that, Kov Ornol, and you who sit here—remember, I am the man who brought this rast to justice." He swung around, the chavonth cape flaring. He pointed at me, evil triumph lending him a spurious but frightening dignity.

180

Chapter Nineteen

The Empress Thyllis takes me for a stroll through Ruathytu

King Doghamrei slashed me across the face and
screeched: "You lie, cramph, you lie!"

Queen Thyllis sat forward on her crystal throne, with
the golden steps, the zhantil pelts, the Chail Sheom
chained in their golden chains, and the manhounds lolling fearsomely below her. She propped her chin on one
white hand and regarded me with those slanting emerald
eyes.

"Bagor ti Hemlad!" she said. "What you say cannot
be believed, for you could not have survived."

I'd felt pretty rough, I can tell you. This cramph Doghamrei had drugged me and had me thrown burning from
a skyship, as I have told you, and I suppose it was natural
that Queen Thyllis should not believe that. She was far too
wily a bird to believe what King Doghamrei said. She
had that onker's card marked. He was the King of
Hirrume, a moderately sized kingdom within the Empire
of Hamal, and he hankered after getting rid of the
Queen's husband, the King who was a mere cipher and a
friend of Rees, and then King Doghamrei planned to
marry the Queen and settle himself in comfortably as
Emperor. I fancied that Thyllis, with her intuitive grasp
of affairs, kept her husband under strict control as a
counter to this idiot Doghamrei, who still had adherents
and men who would cry for him.

So, feeling weak, I lolled against the guards and used
them to prop me upright. The torturer and his knives had

181

done no real damage; my weariness came from many sources of punishment over the past sennights. I'd bellowed to the Queen what Doghamrei had done when I was being played with by the Queen, and she, not really finding it possible to believe what I said, while certainly not believing what Doghamrei said, chose a middle course and beckoned to Naghan Furtway.

Furtway approached the golden steps. The slanting emerald eyes regarded him, and before she spoke the white pointed teeth bit onto a full moist lip.

"So you claim Bagor ti Hemlad is the Prince Majister of Vallia?"

"I know nothing of this Bagor, Majestrix." Furtway spoke up. "But this is Dray Prescot. I know."

"Majestrix!" brayed Ornol ham Feoste, struggling forward. "The cramph is Chaadur, the murderer of my wife!"

The Queen regarded the two of them in turn, and then looked at me. "So the man who is Bagor ti Hemlad, and with whom I have an account still open, is Chaadur and also the Prince Rast of Vallia, hey?"

The situation would have brought that marvelously delightful tinkle of laughter to my Delia's lips. Even I could see the humor of it, and I was pig in the middle. They were debating here in the great hall of the palace, debating on a man who had three names, and all wishing to claim him as theirs. The Hammabi el Lamma contained many a dark secret and many a hideous story; I doubted if the stinking place had witnessed such a farce before. I had acted like a great onker here once, dressed in ridiculous and humiliating clothes. I had been hairy them. My beard now, although nowhere near as long, presented the Queen with strong memories of Bagor ti Hemlad, that was sure.

Across the shining marble lay the slab covering the hole beneath which grew the leprous-white syatra. Men and women who made mistakes and displeased the Queen were popped down there. . . .

All these people knew they plotted on the knife-edge of disaster.

So, as I glared up at the Queen and pondered if I slew her now would that materially assist Vallia, I was aware that my Delia would laugh in amusement at the situation, but would feel absolute horror at the plight of her husband. Thank Zair, she was safe in Valka, in

Esser Rarioch, and her women would be readying the layette. Doctor Nath the Needle and Thelda would be there, and Aunt Katri, also . . .

"Bagor! Do you wish to feed the syatra?"

"No, Queen."

"Are you Chaadur?"

One lie was as good as another.

"No."

"Are you Dray Prescot?"

I stared up at her. Could I deny it? I saw the green glitter of her eyes, the corner of her lip caught between her teeth, the way she leaned to look at me, the betraying movement of the golden bodice. And I saw that she already knew the answer. Other men besides Naghan Furtway must have come to Hamal, fugitives from Vallia. There was his nephew Jenbar for a start. Possibly Nath Larghos, who had been Trylon of the Black Mountains, was here. I'd knocked his eye out and maybe he was dead. Anyway, Inch was now Kov of the Black Mountains. There must be others of the third party who had escaped. They were hatching a plot here, that was certain; but more immediately they could identify me. I was sure they already had. That would be Queen Thyllis' way.

So I stared up at her and pushed myself upright from the guards, plunking my chained fists on my hips. She saw my face. She did not flinch back, but—and I admit now I enjoyed it—her eyebrows drew down as though in sudden pain, and her teeth bit so hard she drew blood from that ripe lip.

"You stupid onker," I said. "Queen Thyllis. Vallia has thrown out these rasts, and now you plot with them. They are failures, and so are you. Your evil Empire of Hamal is doomed. Vallia will crush you like a fly."

I was not too happy with the fustian this time. It had not boomed and rolled out. It did not convince me.

Thyllis was offended, but she was not convinced either.

"So you are the Prince Majister of Vallia!"

"Aye!"

"And you think I shall ransom you? Demand a huge sum from that evil Emperor, so you can sail home to plot against me?"

"You can try to extract ransom from the Emperor, if you wish. You'll waste your time. If you want ransom—"

"Ah, but, Dray Prescot! I shall not ransom you!"

In my heart I knew she would never let me out of her clutches for ransom. I wondered what the Emperor, that dread ruler who was Delia's father, would do if he had this woman, this Qyeen Thyllis, penned in his dungeons in his capital city of Vondium.

She threw a sweetmeat to one of her jiklos; it lifted its maw and caught the fragment out of the air, chomped once, and the piece was gone. It wore gold necklaces, I noticed, but the bands around the creature's neck and the attached chains were of solid steel.

"Shall I feed you to my jiklos?"

I didn't bother to reply.

At my back the great hall was packed with courtiers, soldiers, guards, and the petty clients from the lands owing allegiance to the Empire of Hamal. They made a gorgeous picture of barbaric magnificence. The Queen would not be hurried. She wanted to make the most of her bur of triumph.

"Would you fight in the Jikhorkdun?"

I was tempted to say "Put a sword in my fist and see!" But I ignored her.

Her personal bodyguard, stalwart apims clad in the beautiful mesh link mail manufactured in some of the old countries bordering the Shrouded Sea, stood lined out on either side of the throne. Feathers and golden ornaments made them popinjays, but they could fight well enough, I knew. The Chail Sheom, lovely and yet pathetic in their scraps of sensil, glowed with beauty in chains along the steps. The zhantil-skin pelts reminded me of the magnificent wild animals slain to provide a touch of grandeur to the surroundings of this evil woman.

"Answer me, nulsh! Is it the Jikhorkdun?"

"I do not care," I said at last. "Hamal is finished, whatever you do to me."

"Liar!" she screamed suddenly, and painful blood flooded into her white face. The green eyes blazed. She beat her fist on the arm of her crystal throne. "Liar!"

"You're a fool," I said, and leaned back on the guards to rest my legs.

"We have smashed the armies of Pandahem—aye, and your raggle-taggle bobtail of an army from Vallia! Now we go forward into Jholaix and all Pandahem will be mine! Mine!" She was panting. "As for Vallia! We'll attack Vallia and smash that Lem-forsaken blot from the face of the world!"

184

"If you trust in Lem," I said, "you're more of a fool than I thought."

She almost lost control. But she was a Queen. She had suborned good men to put her on the throne. Rees had fought for her. She forced herself to lean back, to let her hands uncurl from fists to claws. She smiled. "I know what I shall do with you, Dray Prescot, Prince of Cramphs! But first you shall taste the cup of bitter humiliation while I drink from the cup of victory!"

I did not know what she meant then, but two days later—days spent in a hole in the wall below the palace—I found out.

It is in the nature of a man to be himself, despite himself, and it was in the nature of this woman Queen Thyllis to be a bitch. Also, and this seems unarguable, it is in the nature of a victor to be seen to be victorious.

I was dragged out. They did not remove the chains. They cleaned me up and fed me so I felt better. The stone walls of the dungeons dripped with moisture, niter-gleaming. The guards contained many more diffs than there had been before in the Hammabi el Lamma. A little Och came forward with a strip of red cloth. My blue breechclout was taken away and the red cloth was wrapped around me. It was not the old brave scarlet, but it was red. In the circumstances I took no great heart from that. I suspected the reasons for the red, and I did not like them at all.

They gave me a huge breakfast of slursh and red honey, then a Brokelsh, cracking off jokes typical of the witticisms of his race, sawed off a quantity of my hair and beard. They handed me a skin bag of wine—a foul red rubbish from the lees of all the barracks, I suppose—but I drank it off. They gave me a handful of palines. They wanted me sober and able to appreciate what was going on. Then they led me aloft with the iron chains, up the narrow stairs, slimed and gloomy.

By this time I had fathomed out what was going on.

It was, given the circumstances, both obvious and simple.

I will not go into all the doings of that day. It was a day of Hamal's greatness. Queen Thyllis celebrated a huge triumph. She gave public thanks to Havil the Green for the victory of her armies before she finally took the crown and the scepter. At last she sat on the throne, the Empress of Hamal.

Her husband the King went through all the procedures

as a pale shadow hovering near, deferred to by those of lesser ranks, but a cipher, a puppet, a pawn, there only for the legality of the whole proceedings. Thyllis had adapted with great cunning all the high thrones, daises, and platforms on which they rode as well as the boloth palanquins, so that she always sat higher than her husband the King.

The procession was vast, glittering, magnificent, superb. It wound slowly through all the chief thoroughfares and boulevards of Ruathytu. I knew many of them well as we went along. All the vantage points were loaded with sightseers. Every foot of the way was crowded with people shouting and cheering.

"Hamal! Hamal! Thyllis! Thyllis!" And how triumphantly she must have heard their new yell: "Empress! Empress! Havil keep the Empress Thyllis!"

Dust puffed despite the slaves and their swinging watering cans. The suns shone down. The flags flew. The trumpets shrilled. Bands played all the famous marches of Hamal, swinging down boulevard after boulevard, circling the kyros and the Jikhorkdun and the merezos. On and on went the procession, animals caught for the display, chained slaves, the trophies of battle, loot taken from the despoiled palaces of Pandahem. Regiment after regiment marched, and even in my state I could observe that many of the regiments were brand-new, composed of young men from the guls. Probably there were clums there, also, for Hamal had formidable population resources if she admitted the despised clums to the ranks of her army.

Cavalry trotted. I wondered if Rees was there, so I asked my guards, to be told no one had heard of him. They were all new men. . . .

Above us in the sky flew the vollers and the flyers, creating patterns against the opaz glare, a proud symbol of Hamal's might. The noise of cheering buffeted every step of the way.

As for Thyllis, true to form, she had bedecked herself in gorgeous simplicity. A long green gown, loaded with gems, fitted the needs of the occasion with a singular appropriateness. She looked regal—no, rather, she looked imperial!

How superbly she aped those notorious Queens of Pain of Ancient Loh, aped them and surpassed them!

Her howdah aboard a massive boloth which swayed along on its sixteen legs had been so lavishly decorated I wondered how many families of guls might live for how many years on the value of the jewels and gold alone. She sat high. She sat with only a feathered fan behind her head so she might be seen by everyone. The sight of that barbaric magnificence must have thrilled everyone who watched. For the cruel empress of a cruel empire, the Empress Thyllis was supreme and superb.

After all that long procession of booty, slaves, and soldiers had wended for bur after bur through the streets of Ruathytu, Empress Thyllis in her fantastically decorated howdah aboard the equally fantastically decorated boloth followed. Apart from an honor guard of zorca cavalrymen who brought up the rear, she let everything precede her and so lead on in a mounting frenzy of expectation to her own glittering arrival.

A space had been left between the last marching body of men before the boloth. These last were her personal bodyguards in their link mesh, and others marched on either side of the boloth, with zorca-mounted officials. In that space a single calsany trotted along. People guffawed when they saw that beast of burden, the lowliest of the low, trotting along with down-bent head, always ready to accept the beatings with sticks which were the lot of the calsany.

Chained to the tail of the beast, dragged along, went the man who was known to the crowds as the Prince Majister of their hated enemy Vallia.

How they booed as I was dragged past, trying to keep on my feet, being dragged by the chains and the tail of the calsany. Every time the calsany became frightened by the noise and the close-pressing throngs he did what all calsanys do when they are startled.

The cramphs of Hamal had not forgotten a thing.

Lashed to the harness of the animal in an upright position a flagstaff nodded along. Someone had told them, Furtway, probably, and they had stitched up a red flag with a yellow cross. This fluttered from the staff atop the calsany's back as I stumbled along at the rear.

So, I, Dray Prescot, Prince Majister of Vallia, took a proud part in the coronation procession of the Empress of Hamal, and I stumbled along with Old Superb flying over me.

I do not believe I wish to dwell more on that day.

It was absolutely certain that if Rees, Chido, Nath Tolfeyr, Casmas the Deldy, or anyone of that circle of

187

friends and acquaintances I had made in Ruathytu, saw me as I staggered along, the chains clanging and hampering me so that often I fell and was dragged before I could claw up to my feet again, then they would never recognize this man at all. It makes sense. If you see a man you know to be the Prince Majister of Vallia, all filthy and grimed, chained and humiliated, dragged through the streets at the tail end of a calsany, how could you possibly for a moment imagine he was Hamun ham Farthytu, the Amak of Paline Valley? No, there was no risk that I would be mistaken for the Amak.

The day ended at last. Thyllis had spent four burs in the Great Temple of Havil the Green being crowned, and I had spent the time getting my wind back and slopping up a bowl of slursh, without red honey this time, and no palines, either. The guards looked curiously at me. But they must have seen walking dead men many times before, working as they did for the Empress Thyllis. At the end of the day when the twin suns of Antares at last sank I was carted off, still in my chains, and thrust back into my hole.

The gloom of the dungeon matched my thoughts. I had felt no humiliation, no shame, during that parody out there in the streets of Ruathytu. Anger I had felt, of course. Determination to bash a few skulls and escape, yes.

But the Opaz-forsaken chains would not yield. I could not bend or break them. What Thyllis had in store for me next would be physically unpleasant. The psychological unpleasantness she had already handed out would have pleased her, no doubt assuming me to be crushed in spirit. But that kind of naked display of power offends me. Taking no material store in it for myself, it could not inversely harm me. Had Thyllis been in my position on that day she would have been asphyxiated with shame and humiliation.

Dark figures moved into view under the single torch and I bawled down at them.

"Jump to it, you rasts! It's time for supper and I'm famished!"

But it was not my guards who stepped forward into the torch light.

"Dray Prescot?"

I did not answer.

The cloaked figures moved closer. There were half a

188

dozen men in bulky armor beneath their cloaks, with naked thraxters in their hands. They were Katakis. Their bladed tails curved above their heads. Blood shone thickly on four of the blades. There had been four guards on duty in this deep inner cell.

These Katakis I ignored. I stared at the man, powerful, hard, arrogant, who led them.

Strom Rosil na Morcray, the Kataki Chuktar.

I looked with a swift searching stare for his employer, Vad Garnath, for that cramph would know me as Hamun ham Farthytu.

This Kataki Strom would not know my face, for when we had clashed in Smerdislad I had been wearing the Dudinter mask and he had thought me to be Quarnach Algarond, the Vad of the Dudinter District, of Ba-Marish. I knew this man to be violent and dangerous, a lethal tool in the hands of unscrupulous men, a man who would turn on them to his own profit. The Katakis are slave-masters, expert in the manipulation of slaves, as I have said.

He spoke again, harshly, impatiently, flicking a whip against his boots.

"You are the man they call Dray Prescot?"

"If you watched my little promenade today you would not need to ask the question."

He drew in his breath with a hiss.

"I see the wizard was right!" He gestured to his men. "Unchain him."

I rubbed my wrists when I was freed. They were raw.

"There is no time to dillydally. We have bribed and killed our way here. Grak!"

There it was again, that slave-driving word. . . .

So they shepherded me along the runnels and the corridors and we met no one except the four guards they had slain to gain ingress. We came out under the light of the moons at that very same postern where King Doghamrei had sent me off with Ob-Eye to set me alight and dump me overside from a skyship. A voller was waiting. We clambered aboard and the flier leaped aloft.

"You do not ask why we rescue you?"

"No doubt you have your reasons."

Again he drew in his breath with a hiss.

"I was waiting for my supper," I said, just to keep him on the boil. "Do you have anything aboard?"

They rummaged out a wicker basket and I set to on

189

bread, cold vosk, and palines. They did not know what to make of me, and that suited me. I of course could have no idea what their plans were. For sure, the wizard, this certain Phu-si-Yantong of whom I then knew nothing, must consider me vital to his mad schemes of taking over Hamal and through me controlling Vallia. It seemed to me as I ate and thought that he must no doubt consider me the only man in Vallia who could hold the empire together after the old Emperor's death. If I died, he would be faced with the task of controlling many splinters. Through me he could run the entire place. As I say, I did know this of the Wizard of Loh, Phu-si-Yantong, even then: the man was a megalomaniac of the highest quality.

The notion crossed my mind that if he was a megalomaniac for wanting to run Vallia, what did that make me? I had no desire to run the place, however, and I wished Delia's father long life.

"You will be required to do certain favors for your rescue," said the Kataki Strom in his hissing voice. "But for me and my masters you would be unpleasantly dead on the morrow."

I munched vosk, swallowed, and took a fresh bite.

"You act very coolly. When the wizard has dealt with you you will fly a different wing."

"As to that," I answered, "I am my own man."

"No longer!"

He wore a thraxter. His tail was bladed. There were five others similarly armed with him. Their shields ranked around the coaming of the voller. I was not feeling on my top form. Zair knows, I had been through much. But the old Dray Prescot began to struggle and fight his way through all the good intentions I had been trying to impose on myself. I had been kicked around and tortured—only the beginning of that, I grant you—and hung in chains. I was feeling mean. Very mean.

The only gratitude I felt to these Katakis was that I wouldn't slay them unless they forced me.

Over our heads the Maiden with the Many Smiles and She of the Veils shone down lambently. Their gold and pink light fuzzed the edges of the voller and shone on the close-set helmets of the Katakis and their bladed whip-tails.

I said, "You rescued me. For that I give you thanks. But you did not rescue me because you were sorry for my plight. If you have a quarrel with Thyllis I am not your pawn." That should make them think I did not know the fuller plans of the wizard.

"What are you talking about, Prescot?"

"I have given you thanks. Now you had best set the voller down and let me go about my business."

Strom Rosil laughed. His Kataki tail lashed above his head, very deadly in the golden pinkish light.

Ruathytu fled past below. The familiar streets and kyros vanished with the domes and towers into the pinkish haze.

"You are coming with us to receive your instructions?"

"I think not," I said, leaning forward, very smoothly, very fast, and drew his thraxter from the scabbard.

They are man-managers, the Katakis. But they had none of their damned iron chains with them now.

We fought.

The tails of the Katakis are superb weapons, but they have their limitations. Against my thraxter their thraxter-work could not stand, and the straight sword chunked into the throat of the man who threw himself at me in front of his leader. Rosil staggered back. The voller bored on. The next came at me and I ducked his tail, slashed it off so that the bladed tip spun far out into the void. He screamed. I stuck him through the throat, also, for these cramphs wore armor. The next two sparred for a moment and I leaned to avoid their thrust. I took a tail blade on my sword and so slashed across and down. Then, shortening the sword, I drove it in low and deep enough on the second one. That left two of them with Rosil raging to get at me. He snatched the thraxter from the hand of his man and the blades crossed and twinkled in the pink moonlight.

"You ungrateful cramph! Is this how you repay our guile and cunning in freeing you?"

To confuse him further, I said, "Thyllis probably paid you well to lay this trap, kleesh."

He did not like that.

His man flung himself at the controls and the voller lurched and swooped down. Trees flicked past, dusky golden blobs in the shifting light.

"Get behind him, onker!" bellowed Rosil.

He was a fine fighter, and his tail was a marvel. I missed a slash at the tip and had to jump, weave, and parry to avoid his counter. The voller skidded along the ground, a cornfield going past with a loud hissing of broken stems. The last man tried to obey his leader and brought his tail up through his legs in that deadly stabbing thrust. I swirled the blade down, lopped the tail, and swung back to Rosil. He looked around. The voller came to rest. He had four dead men and one holding a bladeless tail, looking stupidly at the blood gushing out of the stump. The Kataki Strom was a cunning and resourceful man. I did not doubt his courage. Evidently the Wizard of Loh, Phu-si-Yantong, had studied the Prince Majister of Vallia most carefully, but he had not discovered that I could be an onker when it came to taking orders. He must have realized I was some kind of fighting man; Strom Rosil knew that, now.

With a baffled yell he sprang over the side of the voller and vanished into the moons-shot darkness. He yelled back:

"Your day will come, Prince. The wizard will cut you down to size!"

His tailless man followed.

I had command of the voller.

I threw the thraxter down into the blood-reeking pit and hauled the bodies out, tossing them overboard. I kept all the weapons, and I chopped all the tail blades off, too.

Then I set the controls and up we went, the silver boxes performing their usual uncanny function, sending us fleeting over the surface of Hamal.

I set the source.

Peacefully, equably, feeling a lot better, I sent the voller speeding north to Pandahem and Vallia.

Chapter Twenty

Armada against Havilfar

"You have done wonders, Majister!" I said, for the hundredth time, feeling the breeze on my cheek and joying in the free onward rush through the air.

"Most of the credit belongs to your sage, San Evold. But for his tireless energy the fleet would not be ready."

"But it is ready," I said, overjoyed. "And now we will show those cramphs of Hamal what real fighting men of Vallia are like."

All about us in the air floated the new sailing navy of the Vallian Air Service. The ships were mere wooden boxes, built in great speed, built solidly and crudely, built to fight. Each ship was upheld by a pair of silver boxes produced in the workshops of Valka. Those boxes held only half the secrets I had sought, for they would only lift a ship into the air; but with the promise of the remaining four minerals dazzlingly before us for the future, these crude ships made a proud sight as they flew from Vondium, the capital of Vallia, to Jholaix, which lies in the northeastern angle of Pandahem.

The new ships flew in long strings, towed one behind the other behind a voller equipped with genuine vaol and paol boxes for forward motion. We flew crosswind. Each of the ships had been equipped with masts and sails; that task had been easy for an ancient seafaring nation like Vallia. The skills of centuries of ship construction had gone into these vessels' masts and sails. Mind you, the hulls were different, for you cannot lift an ordinary wooden ship into the air without it falling to pieces without the water to support it.

Each ship consisted of a simple slab-sided wooden hull,

heavily built to keep its shape when in the air. The masts rose from the deck, three of them, fore, main, and mizzen. The masts were joined at the top by a smaller box-like construction which gave strength to the whole. And from every bulwark and top these sailing ships of the air sprouted catapults and varters.

We flew south over the sea.

Jholaix in northeastern Pandahem lies something like three hundred and forty dwaburs from Vondium in Vallia.

With us came all the flutduins Naghan Kholin Donamair, that majestic fighting Djang, could scrape together. They were housed in various of the ships and would take wing when the action began. There were Crimson Bowmen of Loh. There were regiments of my Valkan Archers. There were fighting men of my freedom-fighters, fierce active men who had won Stromnates and were not likely to forget the glories they had won under Old Superb. There were mercenaries of many and many a race, and notable among them the Chuliks recently hired, and the Pachaks I so much valued for their loyalty. But there were Rapas, Brokelsh, Womoxes, and plenty more, and we were blended into a fighting force the like of which had seldom been seen before in Vallian history, certainly not since the time of the Emperor's great grandfather and the period of the troubles. That ancient history, too, could serve a purpose now.

At my side Seg, the Kov of Falinur, said, "You took a chance. If Tom ti Vulheim cannot hold them until we arrive—"

"He is Tom Tomor ti Vulheim now, the Elten of Avanar. And he will hold long enough for us to reach him."

No one needed to be told the importance of an open bridgehead. If the Hamalians swamped over the last defenses of Pandahem we would have a much tougher job landing. For the flying ships were also packed with men. I had seen what could happen in a sea battle when the decks were crowded with useless soldiers.

Delia's father had attempted diplomacy and had been met with a hostile wall of contempt and hatred from Thyllis, secure in her newly won power. She had taken Pandahem and was Empress of Hamal. The Vallians were next on the list. The Emperor had had little trouble in persuading the Presidio and his nobles of the necessary course. Even Kov Ulverswan of the Singing Forests had admitted he could see no other recourse but an all-out stoppage of the Empress Thyllis—now.

I had seen my Delia. She had chided me. I had chided her. We were both consumed by a love that joyed and feared in the doings of the other lest disaster strike. I had given instructions that were totally unnecessary to Doctor Nath the Needle. Thelda had fussed, and Seg had laughed and drawn her away. Aunt Katri had been coping with the twins. All in all I had spent a hectic time since my return to Valka in the voller so thoughtfully provided by Strom Rosil na Morcray, the Chuktar Kataki.

Work had been going on all day and all night since that first successful experiment with the flying boxes in Esser Rarioch. The fleet had been cobbled together. The task could not have been accomplished without cutting every corner. The hulls were mere wooden boxes, sturdy and reinforced with crossbeams, and the sail plan had been ruthlessly simplified. Many a mast and sail had even been uprooted from a seagoing ship and transferred bodily to the aerial sailing ships.

Two things are worth recounting here, and the first made me look at the Emperor with fresh eyes. He was a much-feared man. His powers, for all the Presidio and the nobles plotted against him, were immense. He had told me that his secret agents in Hamal—and that was the first I'd heard of them, by Zair!—had fought their way through to the cell to find dead guards and no sign of the prince they had come to rescue. Their report had reached Vondium after my arrival. But, as I say, I looked afresh at Delia's father.

The other event was altogether more strange. Strange and shuddery, to me, a plain sailor man of Earth who had become a warrior of Kregen.

Walking in our sweet secret garden among the flowers, I had felt an odd, chilling shiver in the air, most eerie, and had looked up. I was walking alone, for I needed to think about the sailing ships of the air, and I saw the figure of a man standing against the red brick wall with its freight of perfumed flowers. He was indistinct, vague and blurry, as though a mere reflection in a pool of water. As I looked up he disappeared. Disappeared. I started forward at once and the rapier flicked from the scabbard. How could he have reached the gate so rapidly? Besides, the door was locked and only Delia and I held the keys. Perhaps I was overwrought, strained far more than I realized, and the man had been a mere figment of my senses, tired and weary as I was. He had worn a long robe of black and green, with a wide cummerbund of red-gold. The vagueness of the vision—for it could have been nothing else—prevented any clear definition of his face. I merely had the impression of great force and power.

Troubled—I had no wish to lose my faculties at so important a moment in history, when the fate of empires hung balanced—I did not mention this occurrence to anyone.

I had walked back to the long open terrace overlooking the Bay and Valkanium. This terrace supports that smaller, more private terrace higher up on thin white columns entwined with vines. It is a pleasant place for those of the fortress who care to stroll in moments of leisure. I saw San Evold Scavander in deep conversation with the Emperor's personal wizard and, not caring for conversation at that time, turned to go another way up to my rooms.

"Prince!" And Scavander approached, his face betraying a mental struggle. "My Prince—"

"Yes, Evold?"

"San Deb-so-Parang has told me of something . . . something you should hear."

I think I guessed then, but my ugly old face betrayed nothing. "San," I said to the Wizard of Loh, this Deb-so-Parang. I have said he was a pleasant old buffer; although he had failed to warn the Emperor of the plot of the third party, he was a useful man to have around the court.

"Prince . . ." He hesitated.

"Go on."

"Men say many things about the wizards, my Prince. Many are untrue, and many are true. By the Seven Arcades! I have no wish to alarm you at this time." He licked his lips. Then: "I have a duty to the Emperor . . ."

"And he is my father-in-law."

"Quite so." He took a breath. "I have felt an intrusion here in the fortress of Esser Rarioch. It was fleeting. It was, I cannot be mistaken, the visitation of a wizard in lupu."

"Do you know the wizard?"

"No. There seem to be many new wizards these days. The older ones die . . ."

196

"We're all mortal, San."

"I am not mistaken. A wizard was spying here."

"If you feel this visitation again, San, you must tell me."

We talked for a space then. But I knew what had happened. It was frighteningly obvious. That infamous Wizard of Loh, Phu-si-Yantong, had placed himself in lupu, that trancelike state in which the wizards may often see at a distance, and had paid me a visit. What he had seen I did not know. I wondered if a sword might not help to dispell the phantom.

Deb-so-Parang spread his hands. "Many of the wizards practice swordomancy. Some are very cunning with its use. I cannot do this myself, which is annoying."

We talked about swordomancy, often called gladiomancy, and I gathered a further inkling of the powers of the Wizards of Loh, powers that, as I have indicated, may be seriously overvalued but powers which nevertheless remain frighteningly real.

I did not mention Phu-si-Yantong's name to Deb-so-Parang.

I wondered just how skilled a swordomancer Phu-si-Yantong might be.

So, as we sailed on through the bright air toward Jholaix and a battle for empire, I had much to think of beside the strategy and tactics of the coming engagement. As we neared the northern coast of Jholaix, which juts proudly forth from the main island of Pandahem, I thrust concern for Delia, dark thoughts of wizards and swordomancers, from my mind. Now every nerve, every sinew must be bent to the struggle, every thought for the victory we must win.

A swift-winged patrol of flutduins scouted us, quick, agile forms among the clouds. They must have seen our banners. Every ship carried her proud freight of colors. The yellow saltire on the red ground floated from every ship. Many of the vessels flew Old Superb, those vessels from the Valkan yards crewed by Valkans. Many of the other provinces of Vallia were represented, a brilliant plumage of color fluttering in the wind of our passage.

Against the very circumstance of that flutduin patrol I had caused to be flown in the bows of the lead ships the brilliant orange of Djanduin. The Emperor might twist his lips and make funny remarks about my being some

197

sort of king of Djanduin, but he cocked his old eagle face up at those fliers, and I guessed what he was thinking.

Very soon Kytun Kholin Dorn and Tom Tomor flew up to the armada. I greeted them with relief. Tom alighted with a sigh of gratitude; flying monstrous great birds of the air comes strangely to those unaccustomed to that mode of travel.

We talked there on the quarterdeck of that selfsame flier my men had taken in Hyrklana. It was now the Emperor's flagship. He had named it *Jen Drak* for the mythic hero of Vallia. For myself I had chosen to fly in one of the new sailing vessels, and it had been named *Vela*. Before I left the flagship to go aboard my own ship we talked, there on that windy quarterdeck.

"We still resist, Majister," said Tom, standing very straight before his Emperor. "Your arrival is barely in time."

"Aye," put in Kytun, very martial in his trappings, his harness and weapons about him. "Aye, Emperor. We fight for you because the King wishes. But you must take your share now."

I interposed as smoothly as I could. My Djangs are not a mealymouthed bunch when it comes to talking to foreign royalty.

The plans were laid. In truth there was little else we could do but what we did. We put our trust in the Invisible Twins made manifest in the everlasting glory of Opaz, and we flew down to battle.

The Hamalians had seen the imposing armada flying through the air toward them. I confess that as I took a small two-place flier from *Jen Drak* to *Vela* and saw that mass of ships spread out through the air my old heart gave a skip. The ships were stringing out, still under tow, to land their troops for the field battle. Then they rose again, sometimes somewhat jerkily as the tow lines came on, and soared up to take their battle stations.

If Kov Hangol, the Hamalese Pallan of the northern armies, thought we would enter action in long lines under tow, where he could swirl around us and cut us to pieces, he was the idiot Rees had named him. All our sails had been furled. Now, as the Hamalese sky force rose to challenge us, the orders were given.

The tow ropes were cast off. The agile sailors from both below and aloft cast loose the canvas and muscular heaves

198

sheeted it home. The yards braced around. The canvas filled and the sails bulged proudly.

Very few nations of Kregen know anything of balloons and, I fear, many writers on this our Earth know nothing of balloons, either. One so often hears of balloons and airships being equipped with sails and acting like ships on the sea. This is not possible, of course, for no tacking is possible, and balloons and sails will all be swept away downwind. The two silver boxes which held us in the air, although they gave us no directional movement, did serve, as I have said, to grip the fabric of that force which upheld us. In my mid-nineteenth century understanding of the universe I thought of this in terms of the boxes latching onto the ether, so that when in line they acted as the keel of the vessel, dipped into the ether, affording us the necessary grip to tack windward. There was a little leeway made, of course, but these sailing vessels reacted better in the air than their counterparts in the sea below. With the sails sheeted home and the yards braced hard across the decks, the wind pushed us so that we skated along well up into the wind, like an orange pip squeezed against a window.

By turning the silver boxes, that window could be turned to take full advantage of the wind. I felt I could bring the heads of these vessels further into the eye of the wind than ever I had done with the sauciest schooner, certainly four points off.

No, if we had sailed balloons or airships with sails, as so many foolish people pretend to have done, we'd have tumbled away downwind in the stupid tangle that should reward all such idiotic stories.

But, and now the real business would begin, we had nothing like the agility and maneuverability of the vollers. I had impressed the skippers with the absolutely vital necessity of maintaining formation. We must sail as a great armada. We must keep our line, distance, and formation. The ships we had knocked together were large. They carried a lot of men. Their weaponry was enormous. We must sail in lines and shoot down the enemy fliers with catapults and varters. Our small force of Vallian Air Service vollers would do all the dodging and maneuvering that was necessary. We provided the weight and punch.

When my men saw the Hamalese skyships rising they understood the battle that lay ahead. These ships were like the ones which had sunk the Vallian galleon before I had smashed them. They were strong, powerful, well-armed, and armored. We would be at a serious disadvantage. One thing was in our favor: we could shoot the massive Vallian gros-varters. The Hamalians did not possess that superb weapon.

Turko the Shield grunted when he saw that array rising through the level air toward us.

"You remember to keep to this shield, Dray."

"I shall try to remember."

I do not wish to dwell overlong on the battle. It came to be known as the Battle of Jholaix. Down there the vineyards smiled up, row after row of luscious grapes waiting to be made into the wine which was justly famous all over this continental grouping of Paz. Making wine was a far better occupation for a man than killing other men in the air above the vines. By far.

The outcome of this battle would be decided in the air.

The land forces we had set down, in conjunction with those already there, ought to be able to stand off the army of Hamal. Only the gigantic skyships and the agile vollers of Hamal had given them their easy victories. I was as well aware as anyone of the professional expertise of the Hamalese swod, but now he faced fighting men backed by the terrible Lohvian longbow and cavalry mounted on nikvoves. It seemed to me, as we sailed through the thin air, that if the air services could only pull out every stop and really go for the Hamalese skyships we would win. It would not be easy. I looked along the line of ships, noticing with critical appreciation their line and dressing, and I must say I thought of the times I had done this, back on Earth, gone sailing down to action in the rigid lines prescribed by the Sailing Instructions.

How different this was from a swifter fight on the inner sea! Or, come to that, a battle with the swordships up along the Hoboling Islands!

The Hamalese skyships held no strict formation. Confident in their power and no doubt somewhat incredulous of what must appear to them to be a succession of sailing boxes, they bore on.

Our nimble vollers were going ahead. The flutduins were winging forward. Many a man there carried an earthenware pot filled with combustibles which would spell the end for a proud Hamalese voller.

I looked aloft.

Up there the protecting formations of vollers and flutduins prepared to prevent the Hamalians from flinging down their own pots of fire. Grimly, I knew that many a fine flying wooden box from Vallia would burn this day.

No, I will not dwell on the battle.

The skyships attacked in a fine display of panache and daring, and we shot them out of the sky. Ships burned. *Vela* almost burned but the fire-fighting parties managed to extinguish the blaze except for the loss of our mizzen. Seamen now proving themselves to be first-class airmen rigged a jury mast.

Arrows and bolts crisscrossed through the bright air.

Our gros-varters wrought frightful execution. I saw a fine Jiktar smeared into a red and greasy lump on the deck before me. At once the Hikdur leaped forward to take his place. What was left of the body was heaved over the side. The battle went on. The gros-varters more than avenged that Jiktar. I saw a hurtling rock smash clean through the iron grille surrounding the controls of one skyship. It dropped and the next smashed into it. A flyer astride his flutduin, his four arms most useful, swooped in like a dart and dropped a pot of fire. Both ships burned.

We bumped the lead skyship and a roaring torrent of Valkan swordsmen flooded over the bulwarks. Somehow or other they were led by a maniac called Dray Prescot, wielding a longsword built by Naghan the Gnat, a longsword sister to that one lost in the mat of vines of the Volgendrin of the Bridge. The skyship was taken.

The breeze did not fail us. We could not make the speed of the Hamalese vollers and we could not sail against the wind, but before the Hamalese Air Service decided they had had enough we had burned or taken over half of them. The rest fled. The Emperor in *Jen Drak*—a very fine craft built in Hyrklana but less than half the size of the Hamalese skyships—led the pursuit. Our fliers took more Hamalese vollers before the last remnants fled over the horizon rim.

Korf Aighos had fought with his Blue Mountain Boys in the land battle. Balass the Hawk had seen the regiments he had trained fully vindicate our belief in them. With the techniques adapted from the rigorous training of the Jikhorkdun and the drillmasters from Djanduin, those blade comrades of mine from Valka had successfully employed their newfangled shields and the sword we had improved over the thraxter and the clanxer. Under their proud red and white standards of Valka crowned by that loyal bird, the valkavol, they had met the iron men of Hamal face to face and whipped them.

The seven-foot-tall streak of Inch at the head of his Black Mountain Men had been foremost in the battle. With that Saxon ax of his blurring a deadly arc in the forefront, who could doubt the victory? Inch, the Kov of the Black Mountains, fought well that day.

The mercenaries earned their hire, and many of them won the coveted honor of being dubbed paktun. So the armies of Vallia advanced in their might and the field was won.

Seg Segutorio and Tom Tomor ti Vulheim observed the fantamyrrh as they came aboard *Vela*. They were smiling. I held out my hands. There was no need, at that moment, to say anything.

Much in the way of clearing up remained to be done. There were men with me to attend to that now.

The Hamalese sky force had been swept away and the Emperor's tent was set up with the orderly rows of vines and their luscious grapes as background. The old devil sat there in high state to receive his various chiefs. Representatives of the nations of Pandahem came to him. With the news of this victory spreading across the island the Hamalese garrisons had to shut up shop and return home, or face extinction in blood. I saw with great satisfaction this beginning of a new era in relationships between Pandahem and Vallia. There would be misunderstandings in the future, for that is the way of mankind, but the beginnings of a true understanding had been made. This afforded me great comfort, for much of my apprehension for the future centered on the shanks coming over the rim of the world to attack us here in Paz.

As for Pando and Tilda, they arrived with their King Nemo among all the Kings, Kovs, and high nobles of the nations of Pandahem. And then—explain it how you want, for I can't—I could not face them.

With Turko the Shield, my staff, and a small group of my closest friends, I went aboard a small voller and we sailed back with all speed to Valka. I hungered to see Delia.

The Emperor and the representatives of the Presidio could handle the new turn in the affairs of the world of Kregen quite well without me. All I wanted in life existed with my Delia, my Delia of Strombor, my Delia of Vallia. I knew that Queen Thyllis, now Empress, her vaunting ambitions blunted for the moment, would conclude a peace with Vallia. The distances involved made that certain. She might even totter, for a tiny moment only, on her throne. Then she would recover herself and set about creating new forces. That seemed sure. But it was equally sure that much time must pass before these two, Hamal and Vallia, would be at each other's throats again.

Most of my work in Havilfar had been completed. I looked down from the voller as we rose into the air. There were enormous shouts of "Hai Jikai!" as we soared aloft. "Hai Jikai! Prince Majister! Jakai! Hai Jikai!"

For the very first time on Kregen that great call reached me blunted, meaning less than it should. The glittering forest of upraised blades below, the banners, the shouting, all dropped away as we rose, for all the High Jikai I wanted waited for me in Esser Rarioch, my high fortress overlooking Valkanium in Valka.

I was not finished with Havilfar. From my first encounter with the enormous continent, with the Manhounds of Faol, I had been employed on many different schemes; the latest, discovering the secrets of the vollers, had been only one. I fancied a small, swift party might visit the Volgendrin of the Bridge and bear off a sack or two of pashams. Evold Scavander would cough and sneeze and set to work on them. We might not be able to build perfect fliers in Vallia yet, but we had done very well indeed with those we had built. We would succeed in the future, by Zim-Zair, yes!

As we soared back home it seemed to me that what I had done in Havilfar was like weaving an intricate pattern, that the different colors and designs each held its own significance and the totality would create an overall picture. The Star Lords, most certainly had an idea of what that picture was, despite my defiance of them. I had a thousand years of life to look forward to. If that vast continent of Havilfar held no more adventurings, dangers, and sheer zest of living for me, then the future looked dark and dull indeed.

The Great Armada from Vallia had dealt with Hamal for the time being. But Hamal was only a part of Havilfar. That splendid and enormous continent must exert continual pressure on world events in the land masses of Paz, half the world of Kregen. I knew that. But I had finished most of what had consumed me in Havilfar. The outstanding accounts remained and would be settled; I did not forget them. But mostly my mood this moment was a heady one of victory. For now I could lay down that burden begun with the commands of the Star Lords in distant Faol. They had not interfered in my life for a long time now with their old intemperate demands. They would return— I was not fool enough to believe they had finished with me.

But in these my recent dealings with Havilfar I must have been successful. Failure would have flung me back four hundred light-years across space to the world of my birth.

Ahead lay the long-delayed investigation into the Savanti nal Aphrasöe, and my possible return to the Swinging City. Much of my interest in them had waned in the swift rush of events in Kregen after I had been thrown out of Paradise. Was even Aphrasöe so much of a paradise beside my island of Valka, beside Strombor, beside Djanduin?

As for the Eye of the World and Nath and Zolta! Ah! There was a thought to set the pulses thumping!

In our swift passage across the face of Kregen beneath Antares, my old scarlet and yellow flag, Old Superb, fluttered and rustled in the wind.

With my friends about me—hard-won, enduring, precious friends—I stepped from the voller on that high landing platform of Esser Rarioch. The day beamed superbly about us.

I had to speak to Delia about the plans I had for young Drak. She had her own plans for Lela, that I knew. And there was—or were—the new arrival—or arrivals— to cherish. There was as much to be done at home as ever there was in adventuring with a flaring cloak and a glittering longsword beneath the Moons of Kregen, across the broad and dangerous lands of Havilfar.

She ran out to greet me, radiant, gorgeous, that brown hair with those outrageous chestnut tints lighting up in the mingled opaz radiance of the Suns of Scorpio. Her brown eyes met mine with the look of homecoming. She held out her arms to me.

"Delia," I whispered, holding her close. "My Delia, Delia of Delphond, Delia of the Blue Mountains!"

"Dray . . ." She would not let me go. "Oh, Dray, my Krozair!"

A GLOSSARY TO THE HAVILFAR CYCLE OF THE SAGA OF DRAY PRESCOT

References to the six books of the cycle are given as:
MHA: Manhounds of Antares
ARA: Arena of Antares
FLA: Fliers of Antares
BMA: Bladesman of Antares
AVA: Avenger of Antares
AMA: Armada of Antares

> NB: No words are given which appear in the two previous glossaries to the Saga of Dray Prescot: that for the Delian Cycle in Volume #5 PRINCE OF SCORPIO, and for part of the Havilfar Cycle in #7 ARENA OF ANTARES.

A

Admiral Constanto, The: An inn in Valkanium.

Adria, Cleiter: A hyr-kaidur in the Jikhorkdun of Huringa.

Algarond, Quarnach, Vad of the Dudinter District of Ba-Marish, His identity was taken by Prescot to penetrate into the fortress of Smerdislad in Faol to rescue Saffi from the Manhounds. (AVA)

Alley of Cloves: Narrow street in the sacred quarter of Ruathytu in which stands the inn *The Kyr Nath and the Fifi*.

Ama of the Shining Hair: Daughter of a poor man in a Vallian story.

Amak: Rank of nobility below Elten.

Apulad: A kovnate in Hamal.

arbora: A bird whose bright plumage is used for helmet decoration.

Arnor, Island of: Lies on the east coast of Havilfar to the north of the mouth of the River Havilthytus.

Asshurphaz: A Warrior God of Djanduin.

Avanar: An estate in Valka near Vulheim.

Aymlo, Dorval: A Lamnian merchant of Ordsmot rescued by Prescot from the Manhounds of Faol. (MHA)

B

Ba Fela: A free city on the west coast of Havilfar.

Bagor ti Hemlad: Alias used by Prescot in Hamal.

Balass the Hawk: A hyr-kaidur of the Jikhorkdun in Huringa who escaped with Prescot. His home is Xuntal. He helped train up Prescot's new army of sword and shield men; a good comrade.

Balintol: Southern sub-continent of Segesthes.

Balkash: A Stromnate in Falinur in Vallia.

Ba-Marish: A free city on the west coast of Havilfar opposite Ng'groga.

banber: A superior cucumber.

Bandermair, Kharon Wonlin: A Djang bought by Prescot in Ruathytu and freed from slavery. (BMA)

Barflut the Razor Feathered: A flutsman's oath.

Barfurd: An oath of the Hamalian army.

Bartak the Hyrshiv: Twelfth son of Bartak the Ob. Escaped with Prescot from the Manhounds. A brokelsh from Hyrzibar's Finger. (AVA)

binhoy: A deep-hold square-built cargo flier of Hamal.

Blessed Xerenike: A minor religion of Havilfar.

bobs: Nickname for Valkan medals. The official names is: The Strom's Medal for the Valor of a Warrior Heart.

Boulevard of the Goldsmiths: One of the wealthiest boulevards of the sacred quarter in Ruathytu.

Brand, Avec: A gul of Orlush in Hamal who travelled and worked on vollers with Ilter Monicep and Prescot. (FLA)

Brodensmot: A town in Hyrzibar's Finger in southeast Havilfar.

C

Cafresmot: A military headquarters town in Djanduin.

Capela, Encar, Kov of Faol: Master of the Manhounds of Faol.

Capnon, King: King of the Canops defeated in battle. (ARA)

Casmas the Deldy: A banker and loan shark and bookie of Ruathytu.

cayferm: Mysterious gas affording half the power to a voller.

Chaadur: Alias used by Prescot as a gul in Hamal.

Chan of the Wings: A loyal merker of Djanduin who first raised cry of: "Notor Prescot! King of Djanduin!"

chank: Vicious white-shark of the Outer Oceans.

Chavonth Chamber: Informal conference hall in Esser Rarioch.

Chelestima: Sister to Chido ham Thafey.

Chezra-gon-Kranak: An evil deity of the Katakis.

Chimula the Sumptuous: Alias used by a Chulik Kovneva in Smerdislad. (AVA)

clanxer: A common sword of Vallia similar to cutlass.

clef: West.

clum: One of the great mass of very poor people in Ruathytu, free but often no better off than slave.

Conelawlad: A town of Hamal.

Coper, Ortyg Fellin: Once Pallan of the Highways of Djanduin, rescued from a burning inn by Prescot, made regent of Djanduin when Prescot as king left the country. An obdjang and a good comrade.

Corg: Deity sworn on by the seafarers of Vallia.

Court of the Stux of Zodjuin: Outer court in Palace of Djanguraj.

crebent: castellan, bailiff.

Lykon Crimahan, Kov of Forli: A Vallian noble hostile to Prescot.

Crippled Chavonth, The: A low-class inn of Urigal in the Kovnate of Waarom in Hamal.

Cup Song of the Och Kings, The: An Och drinking song.

D

Dancing Rostrum, The: A fashionable dancehall of Ruathytu.

Dawn Lands: Earliest settled portions of Havilfar around the Shrouded Sea. Now a confused quilt of many independent countries.

Deb-so-Parang: The Wizard of Loh at the court of the Emperor of Vallia.

Derson Ob-Eye: Guard in employ of King Doghamrei who set Prescot alight and threw him overboard from a skyship. (BMA)

Djan: The Supreme Being in the Pantheon of Djanduin.

Djan-kadjiryon: The Warrior manifestation of Djan.

Djondalar: A Warrior God of Djanduin.

Doghamrei: King of Hirrume within Empire of Hamal.

Domon, Lara Kholin: A rich and high-spirited young lady of Djanguraj.

Donamair, Naghan Kholin: Djang brought by Prescot to Valka to train a flutduin force.

Dorn, Kytun Kholin: Djang warrior noble who fought for Prescot and loyally supports O. Fellin Coper in military management of Djanduin during Prescot's absences. A good comrade.

Dovad: Town of Hamal situated on River Mak by lake and waterfall.

Drak: Prescot and Delia's eldest son, twin to Lela.

Drak na Vallia: A marching song of great popularity in Vallia. The swods in the ranks call it *Old Drak Himself.*

Dray: Seg and Thelda's eldest son, the Strom of Balkash.

Dudinter: Electrum.

Dwadjang: Name given to the four-armed Djangs.

dwazn: Twenty.

dwaznob: Twenty-one.

dyrolain: Fat and nourishing bean favored by mirvols.

E

Ehren, Captain Lars: Captain of Vallian galleon *Ovvend Barynth.*

Elten: Title of nobility between Rango and Amak.

Endo, Lorgad: Lamnian merchant of Vallia who assisted Prescot. (AVA)

Eomlad: Town of northern Hamal to the east of Skull Bay burned during the revolution that brought Queen Thyllis to power. (BMA)

Esme: Kovneva of Apulad, slain by her slave girl, the Fristle Floy. (FLA)

Eurys: Vadvarate on coast of southeast Hamal opposite Niklana.

Eurys, Vad of: Chido's father. (AVA)

Exand, Jiktar: Commander of the fortress guard of Esser Rarioch. (AMA)

exorc: A dog-sized cat with green leathery skin, hooked-clawed webbed feet, four legs, gaping mouth with four enormous canine teeth. Rudimentary wings deeply scalloped on trailing edge mounted on two thick columns rising just abaft shoulder blades. Barbed whip-tail. Must glide down onto prey and is then flown back to eyrie by mother for fresh attack.

F

Faerling Throne: Name given to throne in Djanguraj.

Fahia, Queen: Fat and pathetically unpleasant queen of Hyrklana. (ARA)

Falkerdrin: A Kovnate of Vallia, with extremely rich lands.

fambly: Term of affectionate abuse without rancour.

Famphreon, Natyzha, the dowager Kovneva of Falkerdrin: Noblewoman of Vallia of very great wealth, controlling her son the Kov, the Pallan of the Armory, with a rod of iron. Bitterly opposed to Prescot and his schemes.

Fanli the Fristle Fifi and her Regiment of Admirers: A risqué song.

Farthytu, Hamun ham, Amak of Paline Valley: A real identity given to Prescot by the old Amak on his deathbed, in honor, and used by Prescot in Hamal.

Farthytu, Naghan ham. The old Amak of Paline Valley, slain with his son Hamun during a raid by the wild men from the west. (BMA)

Feoste, Ornol ham, Kov of Apulad: A noble of Hamal connected with voller manufacture who believes Prescot as Chaadur slew his wife.

Five-handed Eos-Bakchi: A Vallian spirit of luck and good fortune.

flutduin: A powerful and superior saddle flyer of Djanduin.

foburf: Small four-legged mammal of the taiga of S. Havilfar with superb glossy black fur much used for flying furs.

Forli: Kovnate of Vallia often called The Blessed Forli lying on an eastern tributary of the central river.

Foul Fernal: A demon of Havilfar.

G

Gerawin: Short squat diffs with thin bandy legs, from Gilarna the Barren. Armed with long thin flexible swords and tridents. Immensely efficient guards working with army of Hamal.

ghat: east.

Gilarna the Barren: In Hamal, home of the Gerawin.

Gleen the Envious: A minor spirit of deviltry in many of the pantheons of Kregen.

Golden Talu, The: A high-class tavern and restaurant in the sacred quarter of Ruathytu.

grak!: A cruel and ugly word used by slavedrivers as they crack their whips, meaning: 'Hurry!' 'Move!' 'Jump to it!' 'Work 'til you die!'

gul: A poor freeman of Hamal with some rights; often a tradesman.

H

Hall of Notor Zan: All black hall of judgment in Hammabi el Lamma.

ham: Middle name of the most ancient families of Hamal.

Hangol, Kov: Newly-appointed Pallan of the armies of the north of Hamal fighting in Pandahem. (AMA)

Hanitch!: Battle cry of the warriors of Hamal.

Hanitcha the Harrower: An avenging spirit of punishment much respected and sworn by in Havilfar, and whose name is much used in threats.

Harding: A tutor of Aphrasöe.

Harshur, Rees ham, Trylon of the Golden Wind: A noble Numim of Hamal, a remarkable man, brave and generous, a Bladesman with Prescot and a good comrade to Hamun ham Farthytu.

Havil the Green: Supreme deity over much of Havilfar, whose worship is the official religion in Hamal and Hyrklana and elsewhere.

Headless Risslaca, The: A constellation seen from Kregen.

Heart Heights of Valka, The: A marching song of Valka.

Heavenly Mines: Mines of S.W. Hamal producing one of the minerals used in the flying boxes of vollers. A place of horror.

Hemlad: A town of Hamal to the east of Dovad.

hersany: Heavy, ugly, six-legged saddle-animal with thick coat of chalky-white hair, of Pandahem.

Hestan, Garnath ham, Vad of Middle Nalem: A noble of Hamal and deadly enemy of Rees, employs the Katati Strom Rosil and is associated with the Wizard of Loh, Phu-si-Yantong.

Hirrume Warrior: Hamalian skyship belonging to King Doghamrei destroyed by Prescot. (AVA)

Hito the Hunter: Guardian spirit of the treacherous guides of Faol.

Hoko the Amusingly Malicious: A minor spirit of deviltry in many of the pantheons of Kregen.

Horosh, Pallan Hennard: Official in charge of production on the Volgendrin of the Bridge. (AMA)

hulu: One who is a bit of a villain and a bit of an idiot.

Hyr-Jiktar: Colonel in Chief of regiment.

Hyr Khor: A large island off the west coast of Djanduin, north of Uttar Djombey, contains the Kharoi Stones, Prescot is the Kov.

Hyrzibar: A shishi of mythology exclusively serving the minor godlings.

Hyrzibar's Finger: A long promontory of S.E. Havilfar above Quennohch.

I

ich: Suffix to a title indicating the second twin, Icha feminine.

Ifilion: A kingdom on the east coast of Havilfar between the northern and southern mouths of the River Os. Has retained its independence.

Insur ti Fotor: First lieutenant of the galleon *Ovvend Barynth*. (AVA)

Iyam: Nation of North Pandahem lying between Lome and Menaham.

J

Jagdur, Nath Djin: A Dwadjang, once Kov of Hyr Khor, for a brief space King of Djanduin, leemshead, disowned by his tan, slain in the ritual fight in the Sacred Court of the Warrior Gods. (FLA)

Jaws of Nundji: A high pass in the Mountains of Mirth.

jen: Lord; A Vallian term equating with the Hamalian Notor.

Jen Drak: The Emperor of Vallia's flagship in the Battle of Jholaix. (AMA)

Jholaix, Battle of: In which the flying Armada and ground forces from Vallia, with the Pandaheem, defeated the Hamalese army of the north leading to an uneasy peace with Hamal. (AMA)

joat: Powerful and superior saddle animal used by cavalry in Djanduin.

Jynaratha: Island off east coast of Vallia from which Prescot was taken by the Scorpion of the Star Lords back to Earth. (MHA)

K

Kaerlan the Merciful: Beneficent spirit much called upon by the masses in Hamal.

Kaidun, By: A kaidur oath.

Kardo: Son of Melow the Supple, twin to Shara.

Kataki: Diff with thick black hair oiled and curled, low brow, flaring nostrils, gape-jawed mouth with snaggly teeth, wide-spaced eyes narrow and cold. Has a long whip-like tail to which is strapped a steel blade. Slave-masters seldom found as slaves in any part of Kregen, the Katakis are formidable fighting men.

Katri, Aunt: Aunt to Delia, the emperor's sister. Kind and warmhearted.

Kavinstock: A Vadvarate of Vallia.

khand: Guild, caste or brotherhood of profession, trade or calling.

Khe-Hi-Bjanching: A Wizard of Loh.

Khokkak the Meddler: A minor spirit of deviltry in many of the pantheons of Kregen.

kish: steam.

Kodar ti Vakkansmot: Chief of Prescot's corps of trumpeters.

Kolanier, Rogan: Zan-Chuktar commanding Army of the East of Djanduin, deceived by Nath Jagdur and Gorgrens. (FLA)

Kov Logan na Hirrume and the two Fristle fifis: A legendary story of Havilfar.

Krozair Cycle, The: The Third Cycle in the Saga of Dray Prescot.

Krun, By: A Hamalese oath.

Kuerden the Merciless: Malignant spirit much used in vilification by the masses of Hamal.

Kyr Nath and the Fifi, The: An inn in the sacred quarter of Ruathytu with a convenient tree for secret comings and goings much used by Prescot during his days of espionage.

Kyro: Square, plaza, piazza.

L

Lamahan, Naghan: Name used by Prescot as merker on Volgendrin of the Bridge, borrowed from alias of Gordano ham Thafey, Chido's cousin. (AMA)

Lament for Valinur Fallen, The: A famous song of Valka telling of early defeat and final triumph.

Largan the Rule: Palace architect of Vondium.

Latimer: Voller owner and shipping merchant rescued by Prescot from the Manhounds of Faol. (MHA)

Lay of Faerly the Ponsho Farmer's Daughter, The: A merry little ballad concerning a Fristle fifi.

Lela: Daughter of Delia and Prescot, twin to Drak.

Leotes ti Ponthieu: A Bravo fighter of Zenicce, master swordsman, as a Bladesman in Ruathytu defeated by Prescot. (BMA. AVA.)

Lesser Sharangil Archipelago, The: A considerable grouping of moderately-sized islands in The Shrouded Sea.

Lilah, Princess: Princess of Hyrklana rescued by Prescot from the Manhounds of Faol. (MHA)

Livahan, Nath ham, Kov of Thoth Uppwe: Known as Nath the Crafty in Ruathytu. Has an obsessional hatred for diffs. (AMA)

looshas pudding: A succulent dessert much favoured in the army.

Loxo!: The call shouted by link-men to attract customers.

M

Mag: Twin brother to Mog, High Priestess of Migladrin. (MHA) (ARA)

Mahmud, Orlan, nal Yrmcelt: Young horter and courtier of Hyrklana. (ARA)

Mak, River: Rises in the Black Hills of Hamal and empties into the River Havilthytus at Ruathytu. Black waters, whence its name.

Malab's Blood: Deep purple wine of Hamal, not favored by Prescot.

Malahak: Spirit of Hamal called on as witness to actions.

malsidge: Melon-sized, tart fruit with green flesh and brown wrinkled skin, an anti-scorbutic.

Martial Monks of Djanduin: A semi-religious order of men devoted to Djan. Habitually shave their heads.

Mask of Recognition: A blazing golden mask worn by Prescot at the Battle of Tomor Peak. (AMA)

matoc: A non-commissioned officer.

Med Neemusbane: A young Miglan who went with Prescot and Turko the Shield through the syatra-guarded passage into Mungul Sidrath (ARA)

Melow the Supple: A jikla whose twins were eased into the world of Kregen by Prescot, and who is now a part of the household of Esser Rarioch.

Memphees: A poison distilled from the tree Memph, with

additions of the cactus Trechinolc. It saps the strength and can kill.

merezo: Circus or hippodrome for zorca and sleeth racing.

merker: A messenger usually flying a vol or flutclepper.

Merle: Daughter of Trylon Jefan Werden.

Middle Nalem: A Vadvarate of Hamal west of the Black Hills.

Migshaanu: The deity of the religion of Migla, proscribed by the Canops but successfully restored by Prescot. (MHA. ARA)

Mindner. Felder Kholin: Dwadjang, Jiktar of Prescot's flying forces in the struggle for Djanduin. Cousin to Lara Domon.

Mog: Cronelike witch rescued by Prescot from the Manhounds of Faol. Chief Priestess of the Miglish religion of Migshaanu the All-Glorious. Called the Mighty Mog, or Mog the Mighty. (MHA. ARA)

Monicep, Ilter: A gull of Orlush, a smith, nephew to Avec Brand. Travelled with him and Prescot in Hamal and then built vollers in Sumbakir. (FLA)

Morcray: Home of Strom Rosil Yasi, the Kataki Chuktar.

Morro the Muscle: Deity of the Khamorros.

Mother Diocaster: Goddess of easement and fertility and womanhood in the pantheon of Djanduin.

Muruaa: A volcano that erupted and partially buried Orlush in Hamal, where the Star Lords set a task to Prescot's hands. (FLA)

"My wings are yours to command,": Ritual response of the merkers.

N

Naghan the Gnat: A superb armorer rescued with Prescot from the Jikhorkdun of Huringa and now armorer in Esser Rarioch.

Naghan the Wily: Valkan song telling how the rich and ugly silversmith of Vandayha, Naghan the Wily, was trapped into marriage by Hefi, daughter of a bosk herder.

Nalgre the Penitent, Bridge of: Bridge over the Black River in Ruathytu due south of the Kyro of the Horters.

Nath the Arm: Kaidur trainer for the Jikhorkdun in Huringa. (NB: Nath the Arm does not appear to have had the same powers or possibilities of bargaining as a

Roman lanista, and he disappears abruptly from Prescot's story in Hyrklana.) (ARA)

Nath the Guide: A treacherous Guide of Faol. (MHA)

Nath the Keys: Turnkey in the dungeons of the Hanitchik, with one eye and a crippled leg, gruffly pitying Prescot during his imprisonment awaiting torture and hanging for murder. (AMA)

Nath of Thothangir: Rescued by Prescot from the Manhounds of Faol. Prescot believed this name used as an alias. (MHA)

nidge!: A Djang insult.

Niklana: Small island to the north of Hyrklana. An exception to the usual rule that nik as a prefix means half and as a suffix small.

nikvove: Half-size vove without fangs and horns.

Nikvove of Evir: Galleon of Vallia burned by Hamalian skyship. (BMA)

Notor Zan: The Tenth Lord, the Lord of Darkness. Rises when there are no suns or moons in sky of Kregen.

Nulty: Retainer of Paline Valley privy to secret of Hamun ham Farthytu appointed by Prescot as Crebent to Paline Valley. A loyal man.

Numim: A diff of powerful physique and lion-like face with great golden mane and whiskers. The Numim girls are very beautiful.

Nundji: Once a warrior god of Djanduin but because of his evil jailed by the other warrior gods in a leem-hell.

O

obbie: Slang term of swods for an ob-Deldar.

Obdjang: The two-armed gerbil-faced Djang of Djanduin, not a warrior but one of the executive and administration Djangs.

Obfaril: Young lad rescued with Prescot from Jikhorkdun in Huringa. His burning desire to become a kaidur changed to an interest in vollers as part of household of Esser Rarioch. Nicknamed Oby.

Obquam, Strom of Tajkent: A flying man of Havilfar who assisted in the rescue of Delia and Prescot and their friends from the Jikhorkdun of Huringa. Not a volrok. (ARA)

Ogra-gemush: Island kingdom slightly isolated from the Hoboling Islands to their northeast in the Sea of Opaz.

Ombor: Mythical flying monster of immense size and fiery heart, who dying is yet reborn, whose breath scorches cities, whose tears water the oceans, whose hearts beat for all humankind. Gives name to enclave of Strombor in Zenicce.

Onglolo: Constellation of Kregen.

Operhalen: A noble House of Zenicce, colours blue, green and ivory.

ordel: Cattle animal of Kregen, similar to Earthly shorthorn.

Os, River: Very large river of Havilfar rising in the Mountains of the West and flowing eastwards to empty into the Ocean of Clouds by two large mouths opposite northern Hyrklana. Called He of the Commendable Countenance.

Otbrinhan: Chief of Yuccamots who extended hospitality to Prescot and the shipwrecked crew of *Ovvend Barynth*. (AVA)

Ovvend: A Kovnate province of Vallia to the west of Delphond.

Ovvend Barynth: Galleon of Vallia saved from burning by Prescot but subsequently driven ashore and wrecked. (AVA)

Oxkalin the Blind Spirit: Minor godling of chance, appealed to by gamblers for good luck.

P

Pachak: Diff of middle height, with two left arms, a whip-like tail equipped with hand, straw-yellow hair. Very highly-valued as guards and mercenaries, intensely loyal, favoured by Prescot, who believes their berserker rages when fighting are part of their carefully controlled image. Highly skilled fighters.

Paktun's Promenade: A marching song of Kregen.

Palazzo of the Four Winds: Palace in Djanguraj.

Paline: Maid to Rosala of March Urt. Taunted Prescot in his rescue, urging and mocking him with the jikai. (BMA)

Paline and Queng, The: A tavern in Djanguraj whose objang landlord made the best vosk pie in the city. (FLA)

Paline Valley: An estate in northwest Hamal close to the Mountains of the West. Prescot became Amak in curious circumstances.

Panshi: Prescot's chamberlain in Esser Rarioch.

parclear: A sherbet drink.

pasham: A honey-melon-sized fruit smelling like old socks

and tasting like the sweepings of a totrix stable. Processed for use in voller production.

Pastale: A wine of Segesthes, the export monopoly of Operhalen.

Paz: The grouping of continents and islands of Kregen including Loh, Segesthes, Turismond and Havilfar; and Vallia and Pandahem.

Pe-Na, Planath: A Pachak, Prescot's personal standard bearer.

Pereth, Kov: Commander of the armies of the north of Hamal, relieved of command by Queen Thyllis. (AVA. (AMA)

Persinia: Promontory of southern Segesthes between Port Paros and Balintol, north of the Undurkor Islands.

Phu-Si-Yantong: Wizard of Loh.

Piraju: Island of the Risshamal Keys off northeastern Havilfar.

Planath the Wine: Proprietor of *The Loyal of Sidraarga* in Yaman (MHA)

Podia: A Lamnian village on the island of Shanpo in the Lesser Sharangil Archipelago of the Shrouded Sea.

prianum: Shrine, one for each colour, for trophies received in the Jikhorkdun. The priana in Huringa were: Green, the Emerald Neemu; Blue, the Sapphire Graint; Yellow, the Diamond Zhantil, and Red, the Ruby Drang. This last was Prescot's colour.

Pride of Hanitcha: Hamalian skyship destroyed by Prescot. (AVA)

purtle: Cheap pine wood of the taiga of Southern Havilfar.

Q

Quesa: Feather-brained apim girl rescued by Prescot from Manhounds. (MHA. ARA)

Que-si-Rening: A Wizard of Loh,

Quivir: A Stromnate within Prescot's island Kovnate of Zamra.

R

Radak the Syatra: An enormously powerful wrestler from a semi-barbarian tribe living close to the Mountains of the West in Hamal. Bested in a contest with Rees, he subsequently refused to attack Rees's people and took refuge in the estates of the Golden Wind. (BMA)

Rango: Rank of nobility between Strom and Elten. Feminine is Ranga.

Ranjal, Stromich: Twin brother to Strom Rosil na Morcray.

Ranks: The four main military ranks on Kregen are often abbreviated as: Chuktar—Chuk. Jiktar—Jik. Hikdar—Hik. Deldar—Del.

"Rank your Deldars": Usual challenge to open a game of Jikaida.

Rapechak: A Rapa who escaped with Prescot from the Manhounds of Faol and who was believed drowned in the River Magan after escape from Mungul Sidrath. (MHA.ARA)

Rashi: Wife to Rees, Stromni of the Golden Wind.

Rees: Son to Rees, nicknamed Reesnik. Slain by assassins of Vad Garnath (AVA)

Resplendent Bridzilkelsh: A brokelsh spirit used as oath.

Rhapaporgolam the Reaver of Souls, By: A Rapa oath.

Rig: A Warrior God in the pantheon of Djanduin.

Risshamal Keys: Strings of many islands stretching like fingers from the northeast corner of Havilfar.

Riurik, Vangar: The Strom of Quivir, owing allegiance to Prescot.

Roban: Younger son to Rees.

Rogahan: Nicknamed Wersting. A Deldar of varters, a fine shot.

Rogan, King: Husband to Queen Fahia of Hyrklana, a nonentity. (ARA)

Rosala of Match Urt: Beautiful but icy-cold maiden of Hamal appealed to Prescot acting as Hamun for help. Taken from intended marriage with Casmas the Deldy. (BMA)

Rumferling, Naghan Stolin: Chuktar of the army of Djanduin, assassinated by the leemsheads. (FLA)

S

Sacred Court of the Warrior Gods: In the Palazzo of the Four Winds in Djanguraj where Prescot fought the last fight with Nath Jagdur.

Saenda: Hare-brained apim girl rescued by Prescot from Manhounds. (MHA)

Saffi: Golden lion-maid, daughter of Rees. Abducted by Vad Garnath and brought back from Cripples Jikai in Smerdislad by Prescot. (AVA)

218

Savapim: Agents of the Savanti.

sazz: A fruit-flavored sherbert drink.

scarron: Brilliant scarlet jewel of great value.

Scavander, Evold: Wise man of Valka, given courtesy title of San.

Scented Sylvie, The: A riotous tavern of the sacred quarter in Ruathytu.

Schtump!: Abusive way of saying clear off or get out.

Sea of Opaz: Extension of Southern Ocean between Vallia and Pandahem.

Secret Lore of San Drozhimo the Lame, The: A book of wisdom composed a thousand years ago by the sage Drozhimo.

Sensil Quarter: One of the districts of Ruathytu famous for its manufactories turning silk into sensil.

Shanpo: Island of the Lesser Sharangil Archipelago.

Shara: Daughter of Melow the Supple, sister to Kardo.

shif: Contemptuous term for serving girl of slave wench.

Shining Quarter: Situated on a slight eminence inside the Walls of Kazlili in southwestern Ruathytu, occupied by wealthy horters.

Shinnar: An Och village on the island of Shanpo.

Sidraarga: In conjunction with Magoshno, subsidiary deities to Migshaanu of Migladrin, although the connection is unclear.

Singing Forests, The: Kovnate province south of the Mountains of the North in Vallia, rich in valuable timber.

Sinkie: Charming wife to O. Fellin Coper.

Skull Bay: Sickle-shaped bay on north coast of Havilfar.

slursh: A rich form of porridge, superb with red honey.

Smerdislad: The fortress city of the Kov of Faol.

Sogandar the Upright and the Sylvie: A drinking song of Kregen which always causes great merriment among the swods by reason of the refrain which goes: "No idea at all, at all, no idea at all."

Song of Tyr Nath, The: A marching song derived from the myth cycle, *The Quest of Tyr Nath.*

Sorah: A prosperous island of The Shrouded Sea, headquarters of the slave trade carried on by the Katakis in that area.

South Lohvian Sea: Sea between Loh and Havilfar.

stavrer: The size of a wolf with a fierce wolf-head, eight legs and stumpy tail, variously marked and colored, a loyal watchdog.

Stikitche: Assassin.

Street of Sweetmeats: Street of the sacred quarter in Ruathytu off which is the alley containing the tavern *Tempting Forgetfulness*

Street of Threads: Street of tailors in the sacred quarter of Ruathytu opening off the Kyro of the Vadvars.

Stuvan: A middling quality wine.

Sultant, Nalgre, Vad of Kavinstock: An unpleasant noble of Vallia who led the aborted deputation to Hyrklana and gave Prescot trouble.

Sumbakir: A provincial town of south-central Hamal where Prescot worked as a carpenter in the voller yards. (FLA.)

swod: A private soldier, a ranker, one of the P.B.I.

Swords, Bridge of: Connects the soldiers' quarters north of the Havilthytus with the sacred quarter of Ruthytu.

T

Tamish: Nation to the south of the Tamish Channel.

Tamish Channel: Large bay and inlet of the Ocean of Doubt in southwest Havilfar.

tamiyan: Tree with bright yellow blossom.

tan: A Djang's house or clan indicated by middle tan name.

Tancrophor: Country famous and infamous for its pearl fisheries in The Shrouded Sea.

"Tchik": Command given to a fluttrell that turns the big bird into a savage killer.

Thafey, Chido ham: Good-natured idler of Ruathytu's sacred quarter. Holds a courtesy rank of Amak and will become Vad on his father's death. Friend of Rees and Prescot.

thoth: South.

Thraxter and Voller, The: Comfortable inn in the Horter's Quarter of Ruathytu where Prescot first stayed in the city.

Thyllis: Queen of Hamal. Seductive, vicious, violent, evil. Crowned empress during enormous celebrations in which Prescot played a part.

Thyllis the Munificent: A goddess in an ancient myth whose story was much favoured by Queen Thyllis.

Tilly: Golden-furred Fristle fifi rescued with Prescot from Arena of Huringa and now part of the household of Esser Rarioch.

toc: copper coin worth one sixth of an ob. In Hamal the slang name is Havvey—a bitter and mocking reference to Havil the Green.

Tolfeyr, Nath: Bladesman of Ruathytu who befriended Prescot.

Tomor Peak, Battle of: Fought in Tomboram in Pandahem when Prescot and the small army of Vallia and Valka with Djang aerial cavalry defeated the Hamalian flank force of the army of the north. (AMA)

tralk: Six-legged risslaca with wide horny crushing mouth and two enormous armored pincers. Size of a horse and vari-colored.

Trechinolc: A cactus. A constituent of the drug Memphees.

Tridents, Kyro of the: The imposing paved square surrounded by colonnaded shops standing at the foot of the descent from Esser Rarioch.

Triple Tails of Targ the Untouchable, By the: A Kataki oath.

Triumph of the Gods. The: Song cycle celebrating local legend of Djanduin.

Tryfant: A diff not much larger than an Och, foppish, well led will put in a wild enough charge; but disastrous in retreat. Prescot says he has no great feelings for them one way or the other.

tsu-tsu: Tree giving a nourishing nut favoured by Mirvols.

Tulema: Dancing girl from a dopa den rescued by Prescot from Manhounds of Faol. (MHA)

Turko the Shield: A Khamorro, a high kham, escaped with Prescot from Manhounds and aided him in Mungul Sidrath. Has a mocking way with him. Goes always at Prescot's side in battle carrying his huge shield. A good comrade.

Tyr Korgan and the Mermaid: A rollicking song of Kregen.

U

Ulverswan, Nath: Kov of Singing Forests in Vallia. In opposition to Prescot in his schemes to aid Pandaheem against Hamal. (AMA)

Under a Certain Moon: Once upon a time.

Unglue your wings: Havilfarese expression for hurry up and get started.

Urigal: Dusty little town in the kovnate of Waarom in Hamal.

urn: North.

Uttar Djombey: A large island off the west coast of Djanduin, south of Hyr Khor. Kytun Kholin Dorn is the Kov.

V

Vakkansmot: A town of Valka.

Valinur: A ruggedly beautiful area of northern Valka.

valkavol: Small red and white bird of Valka, harmless unless attacked. Then becomes frighteningly ferocious. Symbol used atop Valkan standard poles.

vaol-paol: The Great Circle of Universal Existence. In voller production of silver boxes, the vaol boxes contain the mix of minerals, and the paol boxes contain the cayferm.

Vela: Prescot's sailing flier in the Battle of Jholaix. (AMA)

verss: Finest white linen.

Volgendrin of the Bridge: Flying island of west Hamal. Volgendrin often shortened to vo'drin. (AMA)

Vorgar's Drinnik: Wide parade ground, the Mars Field of Valkanium.

Vyborg: A Kovnate province of Vallia.

W

Warrior Gods of Djanduin: Victorious martial array of the pantheon of Djanduin.

waso: Five.

Wazur: King of Ogra-gemush.

"Wenda!": Let's go!

Werl-am-Nardith: A minor religion of Havilfar.

weyver: A long and wide voller, shallow and without a deck, with a small control cabin amidships. Used as barge. Called Quoffas of the Sky.

Wil of the Bellows: A young Djang armorer working with Prescot.

Wolfgang: A Savapim, from Germany, working for the Savanti and encountered by Prescot in Ruathytu. (AMA)

X

Xanachang: The paradise of the mythology of Xuntal.

Xarmon: Prescot's groom at the Battle of Tomor Peak. (AMA)

Xilicia: An ancient kingdom bordering The Shrouded Sea. One of the countries manufacturing the superior mesh link mail.

Xurrhuk of the Curved Sword: A deity of Xuntal.

Y

Yanthur: Rough country of Havilfar between Gorgrendrin and Migla.

Yasi, Rosil, Strom of Morcray: A Kataki and a Chuktar in the army of Hamal, tool of Vad Garnath's, slavemaster, bitter foe to Prescot.

Yellow Unction: A mellow wine of Kregen.

yrium: A word of profound and complex meaning: force, power conveyed by office or strength of character or given to a person in a way that curses or blesses him with undisputed power over his fellows.

Yuccamot: A sleek, otter-like diff with broad flattened tail. Live in villages along the Risshamal Keys, fishing, friendly, and proud of their webbed feet. Welcomed Prescot when shipwrecked.

Yurncra the Mischievous: A Minor spirit of deviltry in many of the pantheons of Kregen.

Z

Zamra: Island off the east coast of Vallia. Prescot is Kov.

zan: Ten.

Zhantil and Sword, The: A brightly glittering constellation of Kregen.

zhyan: A very large very fine saddle bird of Havilfar. Pure white with scarlet beak and claws, with four wings. Most highly prized: Prescot says one zhyan in money terms is worth ten first-quality fluttrells. Their only drawback is their short temper.

Zodjuin: A Warrior God of Djanduin, perhaps the most favoured by fighting men, who bellow, for example: "By Zodjuin of the Stormclouds!" or "By Zodjuin of the Silver Stux!"

☐ **TRANSIT TO SCORPIO** by Alan Burt Akers. The thrilling saga of Prescot of Antares among the wizards and nomads of Kregen. (#UY1169—$1.25)

☐ **THE SUNS OF SCORPIO** by Alan Burt Akers. Among the colossus-builders and sea raiders of Kregen—the saga of Prescot of Antares II. (#UY1191—$1.25)

☐ **WARRIOR OF SCORPIO** by Alan Burt Akers. Across the forbidden lands and the cities of madmen and fierce beasts—Prescot of Antares III. (#UY1212—$1.25)

☐ **SWORDSHIPS OF SCORPIO** by Alan Burt Akers. Dray Prescot IV. With a pirate queen to rescue Vallia's traditional foes! (#UY1231—$1.25)

☐ **MANHOUNDS OF ANTARES** by Alan Burt Akers. Dray Prescot on the unknown continent of Havilfar begins a new cycle of Kregen adventures. Scorpio VI. (#UY1124—$1.25)

☐ **ARENA OF ANTARES** by Alan Burt Akers. Dray Prescot confronts strange beasts and fierce men on Havilfar. Scorpio VII. (#UY1145—$1.25)

☐ **FLIERS OF ANTARES** by Alan Burt Akers. Prescot in the very heart of his enemies! Scorpio VIII. (#UY1165—$1.25)

☐ **BLADESMAN OF ANTARES** by Alan Burt Akers. King or slave? Savior or betrayer? Prescot confronts his choices in the 9th novel of this bestselling series. (#UY1188—$1.25)

☐ **AVENGER OF ANTARES** by Alan Burt Akers. The 10th novel of Prescot in the continent of his enemies—and a real edge-of-the-seat thriller! (#UY1208—$1.25)

DAW BOOKS are represented by the publishers of Signet and Mentor Books, **THE NEW AMERICAN LIBRARY, INC.**

THE NEW AMERICAN LIBRARY, INC.,
P.O. Box 999, Bergenfield, New Jersey 07621

Please send me the DAW BOOKS I have checked above. I am enclosing $_____(check or money order—no currency or C.O.D.'s). Please include the list price plus 25¢ a copy to cover mailing costs.

Name_____

Address_____

City_____State_____Zip Code_____
Please allow at least 3 weeks for delivery